**DO
NOT
GO
ON**

DO NOT GO ON

BRYAN FURUNESS

Black
Lawrence
Press

www.blacklawrence.com

Executive Editor: Diane Goettel
Cover Design: Andrea Boucher
Book Design: Amy Freels

Published 2019 by Black Lawrence Press.
Printed in the United States.

For Ana

From the written statement of D.W. Boxelder:

Advance Letter

Sometimes people ask me if I'm jaded, or if I've stopped caring about our witnesses, and I can honestly say no. Apathy is not an issue. After thirteen years with WITSEC, I actively hate the witnesses. They're hustlers and leeches, always looking for an angle on me and the Program and the American taxpayer. If you had this job, Madame Inspector, you'd hate these bastards, too.

Then along comes a case like the one in question, and everything feels different. Not only because this case would make or break my career, but because of the family involved. Because of Ana.

You already know the skeletal facts of the case, Madame. Which key players ended up dead or gone. How, as the Director-designate of WITSEC, I was responsible for the witness. And how, even though that witness flaked out of the Program, scuttling the case before it could come to trial, I was still confirmed as the permanent Director.

I can't blame you for ordering an investigation; I know how curious these facts must look out of context. But don't confuse facts with truth. Facts, alone, are lies of omission.

I'm not going to dispute your facts. I will put them in context to reveal the truth of the case. I will not, however, grant your request for an interview.

Before you take a notion that I'm not cooperating fully with your investigation, take a closer look at Department Administrative Order (DAO) 207-10, section 6, and Department Organization Order (DOO) 10-10, section 4, which you so thoroughly referenced in your summons. Note the provision for a target of an investigation to "furnish sworn oral or subscribed statements." This is my statement, so help me God. What's more, if the courier has done his job, this letter has reached you before our Friday appointment, which you may now consider canceled.

I understand you've already heard one version of the story from Deputy Marshal Peter Crews. Allow me to be blunt, Madame: Pete doesn't know shit. In the Program, information is distributed on a need-to-know basis, and a low-level operative like Pete didn't need to know much to do his job, which was to keep the Easterday family safe and on track for the trial. Basically, the job of a sheepdog. Which he failed to do.

Some might suggest that if the Department of Justice was truly interested in holding individuals accountable for blowing cases, Pete would be the one under investigation right now. I'm not naïve enough to make that suggestion. I understand this town, Madame. I understand you're hunting big game. You want the chief's head on your pike. And I suppose I can't blame you for working with Pete to make that happen. After all, that's my signature move: Flip an underling on his boss. Live by the sword, die by the sword, right?

Only I'm not going to fall on this particular sword.

If you've done your homework, Madame, you'll know that I spent a couple years at seminary before defecting to law school. But do you know my favorite Proverb? *Truthful lips endure forever, but a lying tongue lasts only a moment.* That's the advice I give witnesses when I tell them to spill it all, confess everything, even the stories that incriminate them—these are precisely the stories that make a witness credible, judges and juries tell us—and now I'm going to follow my own counsel, trusting it will deliver me through this investigation.

Unlike Pete, I know all, and I'll tell all. In the spirit of full disclosure, all documents related to the case will be delivered to your office on Friday afternoon, along with the rest of my statement. After you read my entire statement, you can decide whether to unseal the criminal Complaint against me and send out the requisite news release. Though I don't think you'll do that.

The investigation is yours, but the apologia is mine. You keep your facts; I'll give you the story. As you'll see, I always keep my word.

District of Columbia, 1996   D.W. Boxelder

PART 1

DEADFALL

Chapter 1
Liar's Poker
Morocco, Indiana | October 1995

Start with Ana, before her father fell out of the tree.

It stormed through the evening, rain lashing the clapboard of the farmhouse. In the yard, the big oak groaned. Wind rattled the doors of the storm cellar, but Ana didn't notice.

She should have been sleeping, or catching up on Econ homework, or doing laundry, but instead she was in the basement, huddled in a nest of dirty clothes, poring over college packets with a flashlight. Heavy stock, high gloss, filled with images of fresh-faced students, sunny stadiums, and clock towers dripping with ivy.

All you had to do was ask, and colleges would send you a fat packet. For free. Express mail. Her habit had started small back in Baltimore. Just a few at first, all close to home: Towson, UMB, and, to toss a bone to her more-Catholic-every-day mother, Mount St. Mary's.

Ana's addiction didn't really bloom until the summer, when she fled with her father to Indiana. Now it was fall and the packets were a soft dune by the laundry tub, and Ana had become a leading expert on the form. Big schools, she'd noticed, featured labs and tailgating. Small colleges, like the one from rural North Carolina in her lap, trafficked in bucolic porn.

Picture yourself against this backdrop of soft-shouldered mountains, this one seemed to say. *Imagine yourself in mossy silence. You'd be Zen as hell. By the way, doesn't our library look like a ski lodge?*

A ringing noise interrupted her daydream. Ana lifted the packet to see the cordless phone in her lap. Why had she bothered to bring it down here? An old habit, held over from the days when she was tethered to the phone, when she had people to talk to, people who wanted to talk to her.

She picked up, but didn't say anything, in case it was her mother, in which case she would—

"Ana? Ana, listen—"

—hang up. She opened the Warren Wilson packet again, but the mountains no longer seemed inviting. They looked like stupid clumps of broccoli and Ana could only imagine herself bored and isolated on that hilljack campus, and she got plenty of that around here, thank you very much. She winged the packet into the darkness by the laundry tub and picked up the old reliable, Pepperdine.

Blue, blue, drenched in blue: the sky, endless waves, a boy with blue eyes and a teal Billabong shirt raising his hand in class. Ana could practically hear the hush of the Pacific. Pepperdine seemed like the farthest point from her shit life. If she was going to have to start over yet again, why not in Malibu?

Overhead, a joist creaked. For a second she thought her father was patrolling the halls, checking and re-checking locks on doors and windows. But no, the house was just moving in the wind. Not even a storm could bring him inside anymore.

Ana pulled on her headphones. She pushed play on a bulky tape player, and a vaguely Spanish baritone filled her ears, blocking out distractions.

Suppress, said a poor man's Ricardo Montalbán. *To put an end to, or to prevent the dissemination of information.*

She'd checked the tape out of the library in Baltimore because the promise on its cover seemed like good SAT prep. "Increase your vocab acumen exponentially!" When she had to leave town, Ana jammed the tape into her pocket before walking away from her home, her mother, her friends, her life she'd built with all her days. But, hey, at least she wouldn't have any library fines.

Convergence, said the voice. *The state of separate elements coming together.*

The phone was ringing again. Ana turned up the volume on the tape player. She'd listened to the tape so many times the words had stopped making sense, though once in a while they made a new kind of sense. Just now, they were background noise, soothing as surf. Her eyelids flickered and she pictured herself on the cliffs of Malibu, enjoying the salt breeze, listening to a courtly Spaniard introduce characters from an old Greek tragedy. It was the tale of Perfidious and Lachrymose. Those two kids might have been happy if not for that old devil, Deleterious.

◆   ◆   ◆

There are things the Program can change, and things that can't be changed.

The Program couldn't do anything, for example, about the fact that Ana was seventeen, a junior in high school. Or that she was tall enough to look most men in the eye, and not too shy to do so. She was narrow but solid, like a Doric column.

The Program has sent a few witnesses in for plastic surgery, but it wasn't warranted in this case. A few easy alterations were enough to make the Easterdays unrecognizable. For Ana, it was a matter of subtraction. They bobbed her hair and stripped out the highlights, and the end result was a drab shade she thought of as *Mouse Poop.*

No tanning beds in Morocco, Indiana, and the only sun she saw came through the plate-glass window of Karen's Kitchen where she waited tables, so by the end of the summer her complexion had faded beyond peaches and cream and was now more like milk flecked with dirt. She felt as plain and worn as an old undershirt. Her disguise, in short, was her natural state.

Then there are things that can be changed, but the Program elects not to change. A piece or two of their old lives for witnesses to cling to.

Ana was always her name.

It wasn't a kindness, letting her keep her first name. Merely a practicality. Hesitate when someone calls your name, and that invites questions. Questions breed suspicion; suspicion leads to exposure.

The real trick of reinvention is to change a person enough to make her new, but not so much she becomes unrecognizable to herself.

◆　◆　◆

Ana awoke in the laundry nest to the sound of her alarm blaring upstairs. The storm was muttering in the distance. Wrapping an old beach towel around her shoulders for warmth, she made her way up to the kitchen, where she peered through a ragged peephole her father had cut in a roller shade. Sunrise was an hour away, but the yard was lit up by the twin halogens of a security light. Through the peephole she could see the shingle tab driveway winding down to the road like a black river of forgetting. The rustbucket Fairlane her father hadn't driven in a month. The thistle and volunteer sunflowers in the yard her father had mowed once, just after moving in, then never again. Out there in this new meadow, at the edge of the light, was the tall red oak.

And something else, too. Something new. Midway between the farmhouse and the oak, standing in the rain-bent grass, was an armoire.

◆　◆　◆

An obituary for her old life: Ana grew up in Fells Point and went to Mount Carmel and worked as a hostess in her father's restaurant in the evenings. She loved jangly bracelets, five or six on each wrist. "What's up, slut?" was the way she greeted her friend Danielle. She considered canned mandarin oranges the perfect food, practiced dance moves in her bedroom mirror, and consistently tied up the phone until her mother surrendered and gave Ana her own line. Ana was personally responsible for the school-wide ban on hairbrushes because she'd popped Bobby Swenson in the lips with the back of a fat wooden brush after he cheated on Danielle.

Like a lot of teenagers, she had the feeling this wasn't her real life; this was some kind of pre-life, a training module. When did she think real life would start? After high school, of course. After she moved out of her parents' house. When she went to college. The old world had to die for a new one to be born.

And it did. Just not the way she thought it would.

Her old life ended the night someone pried open a window in her home and rolled a bomb into her parents' bedroom. Her father was rushed to the ER, where he was inducted into the Witness Protection Program as a nurse picked shrapnel from his face and right arm The marshals wanted to get him out of town before someone came to finish the job, so before the sun rose they drove him and Ana to their home in a cargo van and gave them each a Hefty bag and fifteen minutes to pack.

One marshal stayed in the van with the engine running and a gun in his hand while another marshal escorted Ana to her bedroom, telling her not to pack anything with her old name on it. No pictures, no awards. Nothing that could be traced back to her old life. She kept stuffing yearbooks and ticket stubs and concert tees into the bag and the marshal kept pulling them out, saying, No, no, it's for your own good, oh hell no.

She stopped packing. She sat on her bed and looked at the cordless phone on her nightstand. She wanted to call her mother, but what could she say? Come with us? Sorry for what I said in the ER? Goodbye, maybe forever? Ana thought the marshal would stop her from picking up the phone, but he didn't. This was a surprise until she clicked *talk*. No dial tone.

"You never know who might be listening in," said the marshal. "The wrong guy hears you're leaving town, all of a sudden we got a goddamn scene."

Like this wasn't one already.

Ana pulled a pillow to her chest and began rocking in place. The marshal softened. "Look," he said. "In a couple of weeks, we'll send along your furniture. That's something, isn't it?"

When she buried her face in the pillow, the marshal probably thought she was crying, but she wasn't. Not just then. She was breathing in her home, breathing herself. Then the marshal in the van blew the horn and time ran out on this goddamn scene, the last one in her old world.

◆   ◆   ◆

Like most of their outsized furniture, the armoire wouldn't fit in the cramped rooms of the farmhouse. Her father couldn't bring himself to let it go, though, so he'd stowed it in the outbuilding. After months of sheltering mice from the leaky roof, it was no surprise that the armoire was warped and gray. But why was it standing in the middle of the yard like a cheap magician's prop? Or like something from a bizarre horror story: *But an armoire, once loved, can never truly be cast off. It will find its way back to its owner. And when it gets there…*

Ana stepped onto the swaybacked porch. Fat drops of water trembled from the overhang. "Dad?" she called out to the yard. "This shit is not funny."

Back home, her father had been a tender wiseass, a charm monster. He couldn't pass her hostess stand at the Tip Top Lounge without delivering a wry joke or a cup of coffee, or pulling a stack of singles from the register to play Liar's Poker. Ana never beat him, but sometimes she found a roll of bills stuffed into her coat pocket at the end of her shift anyway.

Pulling the beach towel tight around her shoulders, she stepped into the yard and sucked in her breath when her feet touched the wet grass. "Dad?" she called again, hoping against hope to see him come around the outbuilding with some explanation about a yard sale or a bonfire and ask her why the heck she was traipsing around the yard in her bare feet. Didn't she know she could step on a rusty nail and get tetanus? Risk versus reward, Bug. Then he'd tip his head to the side and say, Though if you got lockjaw, it would be kind of peaceful around here.

That fantasy flickered out like the tail end of a filmstrip. He wasn't that guy anymore. And whatever was happening with this armoire, it wasn't a joke. As she waded through the long grass, the image that came to mind was her father inside the armoire, small and naked and curled up like a bean.

She was reaching for the knob when she saw a smear of dirt on the double doors. A rough circle with two dots. Was it...a face?

A door flew open with a loud crack. The world seemed to tilt, but no, it was just the armoire tipping over. When it hit the ground, Ana saw a ragged black hole smoldering in the side.

"Goddammit!" she screamed at the tree. "You almost shot me!"

A rifle dropped to the ground. A few seconds later, a man followed. Her father, Ben Easterday. He wore a brown dress shirt and tan slacks, the closest thing he had to camo, though he looked mostly like a wet paper bag. He had to be cold, he had to be hungry, but he didn't seem to mind any of that as he walked toward Ana. "I needed to see if I could protect you when he comes," he said, like it was the most reasonable thing in the world. Like he was a little hurt, frankly, by her ingratitude.

Ana pressed the heel of her hand against her eyelid, which wouldn't stop trembling. "Do me a favor," she said. "Protect me less."

"If you left, I wouldn't have to protect you at all."

Five months. That's how long they had been in Morocco. Enough time to settle in, settle down, and reasonably conclude they were hidden and safe. Her father had gone the other direction. It started with patrolling the house at night, checking locks, peering out into the yard. He stashed guns in dark pockets of the house, taped to the back of cabinet doors, under floorboards, inside light fixtures, where they cast weird shadows. A few weeks ago her father announced it was only a matter of time before Zeeshan found him, and when he did, no one could help. That's when he told Ana to leave, save herself, go back home to her mother.

She refused. He moved into the tree.

His logic—if you could call it that—was to draw the gunfire away from her, and to give himself a good watchtower besides.

Honestly, she hadn't expected him to last a single night up there. Her father was the consummate indoorsman. Italian loafers and silk pocket squares, not hiking boots and bandannas. But in the last couple of weeks, he'd managed to construct a makeshift tree stand out of broken-up furniture, arrange coffee cups to catch rainwater, and, most stunningly, endure.

Ana pressed harder against her eyelid. "Dad," she said. "No one knows where we are. No one is coming."

"You don't know Zeeshan," he said. "He does not give up. And when he comes, you do not want to be here."

She could not have this argument again. Not in bare feet on wet grass. Not after a guerilla production of *William Tell*. Not with a nut who lived in a tree, who would surely perish if left alone. "Do you think I want to be here?" she said through clenched teeth. "I would love to leave. I would leave your ass in a hot second if Mom hadn't beat me to it."

He looked at the tree. Ana could see his throat working. Ah, shit.

"Dad—"

He gave a little shake of his head.

This was her real talent, the skill that never showed up on an aptitude test. Her tongue was a slicing black claw. She could say the worst things; she didn't even have to try. More like the opposite: she had to keep her mouth in check every waking minute, like the eyes of Medusa.

"I'm sorry," she said. "I truly am. But if you ask me to leave one more time, I will take your gun and shoot off your goddamn face."

He studied the tree. She couldn't tell if he was thinking or ignoring her. "I mean it," she said. "I'm not fucking around."

He winced. "Language."

Her old father, the gentleman. He was still in there somewhere. "Sorry," she said again. "But you need to understand that I'm not leaving you. I won't."

He nodded and started back to the tree, picking up the barrel of the rifle and dragging the butt through the wet grass.

Ana went inside the farmhouse and found her shoes. By the time she came back out, he was already up in the tree, hidden in the canopy. As she walked down the driveway, he chambered another round. She shuddered and walked faster.

At the road she looked both ways. Except for the gray hem of dawn, there was little to see. No traffic, no sign of intelligent life anywhere.

Goddammit, she was right. No one was coming.

◆ ◆ ◆

Ana was a runner. Not for sport, or health, but as a way to get herself to work by six in the morning. This made her an oddity in a town where four-teen-year-olds drove with farm permits, twelve-year-olds tooled around on motorbikes, and little kids knew how to bum a ride. Even Govert, a regular at Karen's Kitchen who had lost his license after his fourth DUI, did not resort to self-locomotion. He souped up his John Deere, bungee-corded a boom box behind the seat, and continued to menace the streets and lawns of Morocco.

Ana wasn't anti-driving; she just hadn't learned how to do it. Back home she'd enrolled in Driver's Ed, but the first time she got behind the wheel, she put the car into reverse and promptly flattened a mailbox. The cheerleader in the back seat cried out and grabbed her neck like she'd been whiplashed. Ana rolled her eyes to the instructor. "Old blowjob injury," she muttered.

The instructor didn't even smirk. (How was Ana supposed to know the cheerleader was his niece?) As punishment, he made Ana walk up to the house by herself, where a skinny lady with wormy lips leaned against the porch rail, saying, "Bravo. What are you going to do for an encore—plow over my fence?"

Ana asked the lady if she could use her phone to call her father, and the lady fished a cordless out of her housedress and invited Ana to fling it through the bay window. If Ana was lucky, she might knock some figurines off a shelf. Go ahead, treat her whole house like a carnival game.

"What are your prizes?" Ana said before she could stop herself. "I mean, besides a lifetime supply of bitching."

The woman gave her a look of disgust tinged with respect, then handed over the cordless.

Ben showed up twenty minutes later with a joke for Ana—"I guess we can cross Postal Worker off your list of career options, huh?"—and a soft touch for everyone else. He told the Driver's Ed instructor to replace the bumper and send him the bill, yes, even if the bumper was just scuffed, go ahead and get a new one. Leave things better than how you found them, that was his motto. After giving the instructor and the cheerleader a handwritten note for a free dinner at the Tip Top Lounge, Ben went up to the house. He talked to the lady on the porch for a long time, and from the end of the driveway Ana watched the lady's face soften until she was reflecting his smile and absently fiddling with a string of pearls she hadn't been wearing earlier. When he called in a crew to plant a new mailbox, he told them to ring it with zinnias, the lady's favorite flower.

That's who they were back then: Ana was the one who made a mess, and Ben was the one who smoothed it over.

"Don't make me go back to Driver's Ed," she told him as they walked to his car, a white Triumph blushing in the sunset. "I can't face those people."

"Bug, you have to learn to drive."

She caught his elbow. "You can teach me."

He gave her a look like that was the finest idea he'd heard in months. Ana burst into tears.

The next week, Ben walked into his boss's warehouse at the wrong time, and saw something he wasn't supposed to see. Now Ana still hasn't learned to drive, and Ben has forgotten how to make anything better.

◆　◆　◆

Breakfast, Karen's Kitchen. A laminated sign that read OLD LIARS dangled from the ceiling over a long table of regulars.

"You can't have half. Either you get it or you don't. There is no half-order."

"I'm trying to lose a few pounds."

"So get the diet plate."

The diet plate was a stack of pineapple rings mortared with cottage cheese, served atop a wilted leaf of unknown origin. In the history of Karen's Kitchen, no one had ever ordered the diet plate.

"I don't want the diet plate. I want the biscuits and gravy. Just...not so much. Half would be perfect."

"The deal is All-You-Can-Eat, jagoff. What are you trying to order, Half-of-What-You-Can-Eat?"

"He's trying to order Half-of-What-it-Costs."

Ana etched a star into her scratchpad, waiting for these guys to order. She didn't mind their bickering. This show was mostly for her benefit, she knew, and besides, they were great tippers. Plus, she'd gotten higher than usual before her shift, and morning weed made her ruminative. Or was it remunerative. Ruinative? Oh Spanish baritone, where were you when she needed you?

Her body was at the table, but her mind drifted back to the farmhouse. That shit her father had pulled—a new low. Rock bottom? She didn't dare hope, not again. Because what if there was no bottom? What if it was just sink and sink and sink? At what point was it not safe for him to be alone? At what point was it not safe for her to be around him?

The crude face smeared on the doors of the armoire. The crack of the rifle shot. Were they already at that point?

"IU's a good school," said someone at the long table. "Nice town, good basketball team. Cheap tuition."

"You've got a funny definition of cheap."

"Relatively speaking! It's—"

"Relative, my ass," interrupted Vernon, the oldest of the Liars. Over eighty, took no meds, wore no glasses or hearing aids. He credited his robust health to a daily regimen of cod liver oil, lemon juice, and unwashed greens from his garden, which combined to produce massive amounts of bile that incinerated hostile microbes. "Lava is cool compared to the sun," he said, "but it'll still burn your ass up."

Ana doodled an alligator on her pad. Maybe her father wasn't as bad as he seemed. What if he was faking? He did think Zeeshan was coming, but could he be playing up his paranoia to scare her away? Back when they played Liar's Poker, she could never tell when he was bluffing.

"IU's too big." This from Little Mike, a lanky man with an Adam's Apple that stuck out like he'd swallowed a baby hatchet. His name wasn't meant to be ironic, though; he was little compared to Big Mike, who filled up a pair of XXXL overalls at the end of the table. Big Mike was a quiet man, although Ana didn't know if that was his natural temperament or if he was just tired. Unlike everyone else in the diner, Big Mike was at the end of his workday. He was the night watchman at the salvage yard called Truck Parts, which was locally famous for its huge sign that was so chipped and faded that it appeared to read *Truck Farts*.

Little Mike said, "Plus the team's on the fade. Kids don't want to play for Bobby Knight anymore. She should go somewhere small."

"Like where, St. Joe's?"

Ana stopped doodling. Were they talking about her? When did they get on that subject?

"Why not St. Joe's?" said Little Mike. "Small classes, plenty of personalized attention—"

"Yeah, from *you*. You want her to go to St. Joe's because it's a mile away. You just want to keep her pretty face around here another four years."

Comments like that had embarrassed her in the summer, but not anymore. These guys were, to use an SAT word, avuncular. Only the most avuncular motherfucker would call her pretty anymore. Early in the summer she had tried to keep up her appearance, stashing a caboodle behind the counter, but, hey, you try putting on foundation after jogging five miles in ninety percent humidity. Nowadays Ana settled for washing her face in the bathroom sink and pulling her hair into a ratty ponytail. And, okay, putting on a little eyeliner (she wasn't a cavewoman), but that was as far as she went.

Pastor Jim set down his coffee. "Where do you want to go, Ana?"

Well. She looked up, considering. The old florescent tubes gave a yolky cast to the linoleum floor and the dingy white countertop. She liked this job. Her routine was the same every day. Show up fifteen minutes early, share a joint with Karen out by the dumpster, listen to her rhapsodize about the tight buns on Luis, the cook, and how she plans to shuck his jeans like a cornhusk as soon as the chemo stops killing her sex drive. Walk in the back of the diner, where it was warm and bright and filled with the smell of baking bread and the tinny sound of *cumbia* music. Warm up with a cup of coffee, muddy with cream and sugar. Crack open one of Luis's biscuits, crusty-dusty on the outside, soft and clumpy inside, steam coming up like a prayer.

Still: she didn't want to stay in Morocco. You can be grateful for an oasis even as you dream about getting the hell out of the desert. The Liars' question—Where do you want to go?—usually summoned a daydream of herself on a blanket in a grassy quad, or under a green-shaded lamp in a library, or begoggled in a chemistry lab.

But now? Ana couldn't picture any of those things. All she could see was a girl standing at this long table, like she was watching herself through the security camera mounted over the cash register. The girl wore ripped jeans and an old thermal undershirt with a flannel tied around her waist. Rich kids called this look *grunge*; Ana called it *church basement sale*.

She forced a smile. "Ask me tomorrow."

The Liars groaned, except for Little Mike. He raised his mug in a kind of toast. "To be continued," he said.

Her fear exactly.

◆　　◆　　◆

Homeroom, study hall (read: nap), lunch at 10:15, followed by about twelve Scantron tests, and then Ana was on her way back to the farmhouse. Not running this time, but riding the bus. In most towns, riding the cheese-wagon in high school was *verboten*, the antidote to cool, and Morocco was no exception. Logan, this kid at school—okay, her "friend"—had emphasized this point in September when he offered her a ride after school. He said, "You know the bus is, like, rolling exile."

"I know."

"Social suicide with home delivery."

"Okay."

"You don't believe me?"

In this little town, everyone knew Logan as the kid whose brother caught him watching gay porn. If anyone was a local expert in becoming an outcast, it was Logan.

"I believe you," she said.

Being an untouchable sounded fine to Ana. A little distance from nosy questions and prying eyes? Sign her up. Besides, who knew how her father would react to a strange car rolling up their driveway? Thanks but no thanks, Logan, she would ride the queso express.

To her surprise, she enjoyed the bus. Well, *enjoyed* might be a little strong, but she could depend on the ride home from school to be the easiest part of her day. It was the *Pax Anana*. Twenty-six minutes of blessed nothingness. No coffee pots, no Trig or Chem or Econ, no laundry, no dishes. Nothing to do but lay her cheek on a red vinyl seat that smelled vaguely of body odor when it got warm, as it did on this particular autumn day with the sun pouring in the windows, turning the bus into a mobile hothouse of zombified teens.

When Ana got to the farmhouse that afternoon—it wasn't home to her; it would never be home—she was stupefied by warmth and weariness, which was as close to peace as she got anymore. Her mind was quiet as she started up the long driveway, and it was still quiet when she reached the oak. This time she didn't beg her father to come into the house. Didn't bring out a bowl of hot oatmeal to eat at the base of the tree, imagining the steam drifting upward in cartoon tendrils to hook him by the nose and spirit him down to earth. Didn't brandish a butcher's knife, swearing that if he didn't *come down this instant, she would coat this tree in his blood*. Her hands were empty and so was her mind, and that's when a new idea came to her.

If the mountain won't come to Muhammad, then Muhammad must go to the mountain.

◆   ◆   ◆

When Ana hooked her hands on a low bough, Ben tried to say *Don't*, but his voice was rusty from disuse and it came out as a croak. By the time he cleared his throat, she was already clambering up. He considered kicking her away—just a flick of his foot, shoo, shoo—but if she fell from this distance, she could get hurt.

She wiggled in next to him on the platform, needling him with her elbow until he scooched over. All his bones were tender at the points, especially his sit bones. He'd scavenged a cushion from the chaise longue in the outbuilding, but it had been mashed flat after a couple of days. He cleared his throat again roughly. "What do you think you're doing?"

"Taking myself hostage."

"Get down."

"Sure thing," she said. "As soon as my demands are met."

Goddammit, what was wrong with her? The more he pushed her away, the more she clung to him. Why couldn't she forsake him like a normal teenager? "Bug," he said. "This is not a game."

"If you want a peaceful resolution to this situation," she said, "you'll come down. Otherwise I'll stay up here until we both die of starvation."

Ben looked across the yard, toward the fields and roads beyond. No cars, no movement at all. But the next moment—who knew?

Ana's problem was that she believed the Program could protect them. They had never lost a witness who followed the rules, they said, which sounded good until you realized they had a thousand damn rules, and nobody could follow all of them. So what did the claim really mean? That they *had* lost witnesses. And when they did, they investigated just long enough to find a single misstep, and then they pinned the blame on the victim.

Maybe there was a time when the Program had worked, when a person could hide and never be found, but now that notion sounded—oh, what SAT word would Ana use?—quaint. Archaic. The world was smaller and faster and more illuminated every day, and there was no longer any way to disappear. During those long summer nights of patrolling the farmhouse, he had come to understand it was only a matter of time before Zeeshan found him. He couldn't stop that from happening, but he could get his daughter out of harm's way. If she would just listen to reason.

Ana lifted a coffee cup off a nail, inspected the bark-stained water inside. "You gonna finish this?" She drank it down, then wiped her mouth to hide her gagging.

This girl. What would it take to push her away? Moving into a tree should have been enough. Painting a face on an armoire and shooting it while she stood *just a few feet away* should have definitely been enough. But no—not for Ana. She doubled down. And as long as he stayed on this platform, he realized, she would keep batting against him like a moth to a bulb, until he shattered or she got fried.

Ben struggled to his feet, grabbing a high branch to steady himself.

"What are you doing?" said Ana.

"Coming down."

"Coming down," she repeated slowly. "If this is a trick—"

"No trick. You win."

"If you're lying, I'll climb right back up. You know that, right?"

He nudged her with his foot. "I can't get down if you're in the way."

She looked at him a moment longer, then swung down to the ground, issuing warnings and threats all the way. Ben edged out on the low bough, hands looped around the high branch. On the ground, Ana held up her hands. "Just let go," she said. "I'll catch you."

He kept inching out, away from the trunk. Under his feet the bough groaned.

"Dad," she said. "Careful. It's—"

When he heaved down on the low bough with all his weight, all she could do was cry out—not even a scream, just a betrayed caw as she jumped out of the way—but the bough held. He heaved down again and there was a huge crack and the limb split from the trunk with a sound like the ripping of tendons, crashing to the ground in a hail of coffee cups. But not Ben: he was dangling in the air, hanging onto the high branch.

He looked at his daughter sprawled on the ground, and saw that she was unharmed. Maybe now she would see there was nothing she could do for him. Maybe now she would come to her senses and save herself.

And who knows—maybe she would have if he hadn't slipped. As Ben pulled himself up to the high branch, one hand came loose. That's all it took to turn the world sideways. The wind screamed in his ears and the tree bark ate his knuckles and he had just enough time to close his eyes before the earth crashed into his head, and he became lightning.

Chapter 2
Ball Lightning

Peter Crews was his name, but no one called him that. To his wife, he had been Crews, just Crews, and after she left him, no one called him anything but Droop. This was a reference to Droopy Dog, the cartoon hound with a potbelly and sleepy eyes. Pete had the dog's slumped shoulders, the thatch of hair, and though he wasn't fat (especially by Indiana standards), he had a swaybacked way of standing that showcased his little belly.

He drove a banged-up Bronco, which was good in bad conditions, but pretty bad in good conditions, like now, speeding along the open interstate toward the hospital. There was barely a breeze, but when he pushed the Bronco up to seventy, he felt buffeted and had to wrestle the wheel to keep it straight. Pulling off on exit 215, he saw a tree blown over by last night's storm, a man chainsawing it into rounds near the Trail Tree Restaurant. The man lifted his saw in greeting. Pete nodded at him.

To the good people of Morocco, Droop was a former railroad worker, retired early with a settlement for a back injury. In truth, he was a Deputy U.S. Marshal. His badge was in the Bronco's glove box, buried in a nest of oil change receipts.

Nine years ago he'd worn that badge on a lanyard as he worked the short-term side of witness security in Chicago, escorting witnesses to safe houses and standing watch as they prepared for relocation. After his life fell apart, he had to get away from Chicago, so the Program sent him to

Indiana's northern district, which hung down from the top of the state like a sleepy eyelid. Now he worked post-relo. Now he was a glorified babysitter who had to hide his badge.

That was the deal on the long-term side: you couldn't let people know who you were, because it would attract unnecessary attention. It was almost like being a witness yourself. After a while, you grew into your cover story. Some days, Pete felt retired, puttering around the house to fill the hours and avoid the quicksand of the past. Some days he was visited by a phantom pain in his lower back, though he'd never actually had a back injury.

Now, on his way to the hospital, Pete was in danger of living up to his cover story, at least the part about early retirement. He could practically hear his boss's questions already. What the hell was your witness doing in a tree? What kind of shit show are you running, Droop? Too much going on in Indiana for you to handle?

Bureaucrats. You could always count on them to go heavy on pressure and light on understanding, especially the ones like Boxelder who had never worked a single day as a marshal. How that guy got to be the new Director-designate of Witness Security, Pete would never know. One thing was certain, though: before Pete informed him, he had to come up with some answers. *I don't know* wasn't going to cut it.

He whipped into the parking lot of the Jasper County hospital, hoping Ben didn't get chatty on pain meds. The lot was nearly empty, so he ended up in a spot right in front. He turned off the car and looked at the entrance.

Concrete planters, bristling with leggy geraniums. A lady holding onto her IV stand like it was a subway pole, smoking a cigarette as the wind tousled her gown. Behind her, the automatic door slid open and closed, open and closed.

Pete was thinking of his daughter. All those nights at Wyler Children's Hospital, hallways smelling of bleach, cafeteria full of hollow-eyed parents. The drive on I-90, tires hitting the rumble strip and Pete snapping awake. Parking in a lot like this one, getting eaten by automatic doors like those.

He swung a leg out of the Bronco, and waited out a spinny feeling before he stood. God, he hated hospitals.

◆　◆　◆

Once, Pete saw ball lightning. It fell out of the sky to shamble around his deck like divine tumbleweed, bouncing off benches and chairs and a kettle grill, shaggy and aimless, shedding sparks. He stood under his awning with a beer in one hand and a spatula in the other, aware that he should be afraid, but feeling only mesmerized.

He felt the same way as he listened to Ana rant about her father, the goddamn Program, the tree's "lack of structural integrity," and the quality of care her father had received since the ambulance had shown up at the farmhouse. The paramedics were fat and slow, the doctors full of shit—"Does that look like 'resting comfortably' to you, Droop? Would you be comfortable with a tube in your dick?"—and the hospital a Podunk outpost that couldn't be trusted with anything more serious than ringworm.

In the course of her raving, Pete managed to piece together some basic facts. In addition to sustaining multiple fractures, Ben had swelling of the brain. He hadn't blown his cover (thank God) because he'd slipped from unintelligible to unconscious as soon as they pumped him full of Dilaudid. So it could have been worse. Still, this was pretty bad. What the hell had gone wrong?

"So I have to ask," said Pete after Ana trailed off in the middle of a complaint about the pushy nurses. "What was he doing up in a tree?"

"Living there."

"Living there," said Pete, thinking she would explain further, tell him *It's not what it sounds like*, but she just nodded. He said, "How long?"

She chewed on her thumbnail. He resisted the urge to pull her hand away from her mouth. "Two weeks," she said.

He felt something collapse in his stomach. How on earth. Pete went out to the farmhouse just last week, for Christ's sake. How could he have—

Now that he thought about it, it *had* taken Ben a long time to answer the door. He'd claimed he was in the bathroom when the doorbell rang, but had he actually climbed down from the tree and slipped into the house through the storm cellar doors while Pete stood on the porch like a mook?

Entirely possible. And entirely beside the point, because there was a more important question to ask.

"Ana," he said. "Why didn't you let me know?"

She gnawed on her thumbnail.

"I need to know," he said. "Why didn't you call me the instant your father went up in that tree?"

That line sounded ridiculous, straight out of a nursery rhyme, but neither of them smiled. Ana didn't even look over, which irritated Pete. "I could have helped you," he said. "Don't you know that?"

She glanced at her father in the bed. "This is where the Program's help has gotten us," she said. "I didn't think we could take any more of it."

Pete shifted in his seat. That wasn't fair, but now wasn't the time to argue with this girl, not while her father lay unconscious in the bed. "He'll get better," he said lamely.

"What if he doesn't?"

"He will."

"How do you know?"

Pete opened his hands. He didn't have an answer.

"You don't know," she said. Her voice trembled with anger. "You don't know the first fucking thing about what it's like for us here, and you don't know if he's ever going to get better. Do you? Admit it."

She held his eyes, waiting for an answer, but what could he honestly tell her? *The situation is fluid.* That's what the doctors had said about his own daughter, though her troubles hadn't come from a fall. *We'll have to wait and see.*

The truth is that nothing in the world is harder than waiting to see. Waiting is a blank page your mind fills with dark ink. Waiting gives you time to learn terrible things about yourself. Like how you might want an ending even more than you fear one.

Ana's thumbnail was in her teeth again. He reached for her hand, pulled it gently from her mouth. Sometimes honesty was the worst gift. Sometimes a person needed to rest comfortably.

"Everything will be fine," he said, though his words rang hollow, even to his own ears. He pressed on awkwardly. "I'm here now."

Her eyes narrowed. She spoke clearly and slowly, as though he were a child. "Asshole," she said. "No one wants you here."

Chapter 3
Run to Delight

Back when he was twenty-two years old, Ben—then Bennie—did not dream of being a father. When he thought about his future, he saw himself in the shade of a ragged palm, wearing frayed khakis and strumming a guitar. His uncle Rooster told him he was seeing Mexico.

Rooster had never traveled further than Atlantic City, but the fact that he was a transit agent at the Trailways terminal on West Fayette gave him a certain authority in matters of geography. And the fact that Rooster ran a small sports book out of his kiosk gave him authority in matters of numbers, so when he mentioned that a man could live like the Prince of Todos Santos on twenty pesos a day, Bennie took it as gospel.

Kate, his girlfriend, scoffed. She was still in high school. Cynicism came easily to her. "Pipe dreams."

"Wait and see," Bennie said.

Since graduating high school, Bennie had been a runner for Rooster, carrying paper bags between the bus terminal and points in Pigtown, Otterbein, and Ridgely's Delight. He looked like he was delivering lunches, but the bags were bottom-heavy with cash instead of sandwiches, and bets were scrawled on the flaps. The job was allegedly paying his way through school—Bennie was chipping away at a business degree at City Community, a couple classes at a time—but that was mostly a ruse to keep his mother happy. If it were up to Bennie, he would drop out and run for Rooster full-time, earn his way to Mexico more quickly.

"If you drop out," said Rooster when Benny aired this thought, "I will fire you."

"*You* dropped out," Bennie reminded him.

"Now look at me," said Rooster. "Stuck in this fucking box, sucking bus fumes the rest of my miserable life."

"And making a good living doing it," said Bennie, eyeing Rooster's watch, a Patek Philippe.

Rooster pulled his wrist away. "That's a booby prize. This—" he gestured at his kiosk "—is not for you. And this—" he pushed a fresh tray of paper bags at Bennie "—is temporary."

Rooster was only four years older than Bennie, but he didn't let that keep him from dispensing advice. Rooster had been a self-appointed mentor since dropping out of school, when he began showing up at his nephew's apartment around dinnertime nearly every night. He was always welcome, not only because he was family, but because he came with take-out: styrofoam clamshells of clam strips, steaming tins buckling under the weight of lasagna, soggy huts of moo goo gai pan. If Bennie's mother ever wondered where Rooster got his money, she never mentioned it out loud. Occasionally she said, "What do I owe you?" in a distracted way, never expecting an answer, and never getting one.

While the boys sat at the dinette table, she ate standing up, leaning her elbows on the counter. Bennie knew why she did this—her back ached from cleaning houses, and she was dizzy from breathing ammonia all day—but still, he wished she would sit with them. Hunched over her plate on the countertop, she looked like a dog wolfing down kibble.

After dinner, she would always say, *Time to do the dishes*, which was Bennie's cue to sweep everything from the table into the garbage can. Meanwhile, Rooster picked his teeth with a plastic fork and held forth on everything from the proper distribution of weight in a trash sack to the ideal knot for the top. By the time Bennie got back from the dumpster, his mother would have settled down to her sole hobby, her *raison d'être*, her white whale: tracking down Bennie's father.

All the boy ever knew about his father was his profession, which his mother wryly described as "traveling car salesman." Apparently his father would work at a dealership for three or four months, until the child support agency or Bennie's mother caught up to him and paperwork was put in place to garnish his wages—then he would vanish and the hunt would begin again.

Once, when Bennie was around fourteen, he made the mistake of proposing a solution. What if, the next time she found him, she asked him to come home? Wouldn't it be easier to keep an eye on him if he was here?

She looked up from the stack of phone books she had liberated from the library. "I don't want *him*," she said, like it was the stupidest thing she'd ever heard. "I want what I'm owed."

That was the last time Bennie tried to help with her hobby. In the years to come, he would just sweep the table, run the bags for Rooster, stay in school, and dream of a sleepy patch of warm land where no one would talk down to him again.

◆　　◆　　◆

Every Sunday night Rooster gave him his pay in a lunch sack. Most of it went to household expenses—Bennie didn't want to be a burden to his mother, financially or otherwise—but he put aside as much as he could in an old accordion case.

By the time he was twenty-three, he'd saved up enough money for a one-way bus ticket to Mexico City with enough left over to get to Todos Santos and live comfortably for a year (according to Rooster's calculation, anyway), which seemed like enough time to come up with a plan to stay under that tree.

"Be serious," said Kate, but when he told her he'd saved up enough money for her, too, she stopped scoffing. Even though she knew she would never, ever go—she was a senior in high school, for God's sake; she wasn't going to drop out and move a million miles away from her family to *Mex-*

ico—when Bennie opened that accordion case full of cash and looked at her with love and escape in his eyes, she thought it was the most damn romantic thing she had ever seen.

They didn't get to Todos Santos, but that was the night they went a little too far.

◆   ◆   ◆

Nine weeks later, with morning sickness in full storm, Kate decided it was better to confess than to be caught. She knew her parents wouldn't take it well, but she didn't expect them to go full-tilt fairy tale. For starters, they locked her in the house before she began showing. After consulting with the priest, they made plans to ship her off to her aunt in Dayton, where she could deliver the baby and give it up for adoption. Then Kate could return to Baltimore with a cover story about boarding school, which had been okay, though she'd gotten homesick, and that's why she came back.

Past buried. Reputation intact. Baby's identity hidden forever, maybe even from itself.

The plan might have worked if Bennie hadn't kept coming around. Kate's parents shooed him away, but if he wasn't calling on the phone, he was knocking on the door or mooning under her window. They turned up the TV and tried to ignore him, but on the night he shouted a marriage proposal at her window through cupped hands, Kate's father opened the door before the rest of the street figured out their situation. "Hold on," said the old man. "Stay right there."

Bennie thought he was going to fetch Kate, but the old man returned with a rifle leveled at the boy's chest.

Bennie spread his arms like heavy wings. "Do it," he said. "If you keep me from her, you'll be killing me, anyway."

"Idiot," said the old man, his voice soft with disgust. He lowered the gun a few inches—he couldn't bring himself to kill this kid, but he might feel better if he peppered his balls—but his wife stopped him with a hand on his shoulder. "Boys?" she said. "Come into the house."

After installing Bennie on the couch, she pulled her husband aside and told him if they kept going down this road, they were headed for Romeo and Juliet territory. "Your daughter is tearing out her hair upstairs," she said. "We need a new plan."

The old man gathered everybody in the living room, boys on one side, girls on the other. "Here's the deal," he said to Bennie. "You can propose to my daughter if you show that you can take care of a family. Understand?"

Bennie looked at Kate. She nodded, so he nodded, too.

Young love, thought the old man. So stupid. "I'm a fair man," he continued, "so I'm going to give you three months to prove yourself." He gave the boy a warning glance. "I'm talking about bona fide prospects, not no minimum wage delivery boy bullshit."

Bennie thought for a minute. "You work at the railroad, right?"

The old man nodded slowly.

"Are they hiring?"

The old man stopped nodding. Sure, kid. Thanks for derailing my daughter's life. You know what would be great? Working next to you so I could be reminded of this mess every single minute of my life.

"I'll give you this," the old man started. "You've got a real pair of—"

"Three months," said his wife. "If you come through, fine. If you don't, we never see each other again. Deal?"

Bennie nodded. Then he reached for Kate, but the old man made a sound in his throat, so he pulled back his arm. After he left, Kate walked up the stairs quietly, but slammed her bedroom door so hard a single flake of paint fell from the living room ceiling.

"What now?" said the old man.

"Now we wait," said his wife.

For her, that was the crux of the plan. A delay would cool everyone down. After a few weeks, those kids would start thinking about how hard it would be to raise a child; to be tied down while their friends ran around on weekends; to say goodbye to sleep, seemingly forever—and how easy, on the other hand, it would be to get out of this mess. Three months was plenty of time for Bennie to fail, or just fade away.

◆   ◆   ◆

"I'll help you out," said Rooster. He turned in his booth, pulled some levers, and came back to Bennie with a single ticket in hand. "One way to Ensenada. Closest I can get you to Todos. This one's on me. You keep your money, figure out how to live down there."

Bennie didn't move. The ticket fluttered in the breeze.

"Here's a joke," said Rooster. "Guy goes into the outhouse. When he pulls down his pants, some change spills out of his pocket, goes right down the hole. Guy looks down there, sees a couple quarters gleaming in the shit. *No way am I reaching down there for just fifty cents*, he thinks. So he throws in his wallet."

No laugh. Rooster takes this as a bad sign.

"All I'm asking for is a chance to step up around here," said Bennie. "Haven't I earned that chance?"

"Leave," said Rooster. "It'll be better for everyone. The baby will be adopted by a nice, sad lady. Your girlfriend will get back to her life. You won't have to worry about child support. Trust me: Catholics know how to handle this shit."

Bennie scowled at the ground.

"What's the problem?" said Rooster. "You love this girl?"

"I asked her to go to *Mexico* with me, man."

"If you love her, get over this code of honor bullshit, which is all about you. Do what's best for her and the baby." He pushed the ticket at his nephew. "So do you love her?"

Bennie smoothed his mustache. His lip was quivering. "I owe her," he said at last. "Can you help me or not?"

At that moment Rooster realized he had been lying to himself for a long time. The job had never been temporary for Bennie. The two of them had long been headed toward this terminal of a moment, with Bennie asking for more.

Somehow Rooster hadn't seen it coming. Maybe this is a common lie, telling ourselves we're helping someone, even as we're escorting them to ruin. Maybe that's the lie that lets us live with ourselves.

Rooster tore up the ticket. "You want more work, I can give you more work. I can't promise anything more than that—"

Bennie kissed his uncle on the forehead. Rooster didn't push him away, didn't even flinch. He just looked tired, like he'd lost a staggering bet. It wouldn't occur to Bennie until much later that a guy who spent his days in a cramped booth and was beholden to a mobster named Veedy knew something about being trapped. Bennie didn't hear their conversation as Rooster's vicarious bid for freedom. Not until years later, that is, when he tried to get his own daughter to run away and save herself.

"Yeah, yeah," said Rooster. "Don't get so excited. Welcome to real life, you dope."

Chapter 4
The Fix

When the call came in, Zeeshan was at a neighborhood park, sitting atop a warped picnic table, reading a tatty copy of a book called *The Fix: Break Your Addiction in Ten Minutes*. The wind mussed the tops of the linden trees, but the air under the pavilion was muggy and still. More like August than October. Zeeshan had been out here less than a half-hour, and already the paperback cover was beginning to curl. The silk lining of his trousers stuck to his calves. Zeeshan wanted to take off his shoes and socks, but that's not the kind of person he was, nor had been for a long time.

About Zeeshan: he was tall and thin, with hair that was still more pepper than salt. If you'd walked by the park that day, you'd think he was a professor who had slipped away from campus. Not just because of his houndstooth jacket; there was something about his demeanor that made him look like he was submerged in his thoughts, swimming his way back to the world.

The big idea behind the book in his hand was simple: when a craving hit you—for drink, smoke, pills, sex, whatever your addiction—don't tell yourself no. That's too hard. Instead, tell yourself to wait a little bit. Sit with the need. Let it howl. Let it writhe. For ten minutes, think about your choices, and why you're making them.

Zeeshan was gifted at waiting. Patience was his signature virtue. For that reason, *The Fix* felt like the right book for him, even if he didn't technically have an addiction. But the thing was, there were no books for recovering hitmen. No rehab centers, support groups, prescriptions or twelve-step programs. There was only one step—*stop killing people*—and Zeeshan had to take it alone. Or, now, with the help of this book.

Your old patterns are polished with time and practice, wrote the author, a man named Kleinfelter. The photo on the back cover showed a bald man with a white beard and the hard, glassy eyes of a crow. He didn't look bad for a guy who'd haunted the shooting galleries of Cherry Hill for a decade. His junkie exploits were detailed in the first section of the book, ostensibly to give the author some cred on the subjects of addiction and recovery, though all his war stories carried a weird whiff of nostalgia.

In the second section, though, the sepia tone fell away and Kleinfelter sounded like a mix between a pop psychologist and a coach. *The neural pathways of your addiction are as slick as bobsled tracks; it takes conscious effort to blaze new trails. It's hard—unbelievably hard—and you'll fail a lot, but you can do it. That's the hope as well as the curse. If only you couldn't succeed, you could stop trying.*

Zeeshan wasn't looking to reroute all of his pathways. He wasn't going entirely straight. He would still run his leg of the operation, transporting migrants from the Mohawk reservation on the Canadian border down to Baltimore. He'd maintain his contacts in Kashmir, mostly around Gulmarg where he grew up, to keep the pipeline full of new émigrés. He was just done with killing Veedy's enemies. He wasn't going to do that anymore.

Wait ten minutes. You can stave off the beast for that long. As you watch the seconds bleed away, ask yourself a few questions. Why do I do this shit? What do I really want? Will this give me what I really want?

Why did Zee kill? Because he was good at it. Because Veedy asked him to do it, and Veedy was the one who paid him. Because, like so few things in life, it was expedient and final. Because the benefits ramified: eliminate one problem, and you quell a dozen threats. Because it kept the operation running smoothly. In short, killing was good for business.

Those would have been his reasons a few months ago, anyway. But when Veedy was arrested for human trafficking, it made him stop and think. What about the downside of a hit—didn't that ramify, too? Every job opened up new frontiers of liability. Every job was an invitation for future payback, either by the state or an ally of the mark. How many invitations could you send out before someone RSVP'd with a bullet?

He set the book down on his knee. The wind picked up and the empty swings swayed hypnotically, chains creaking. Zeeshan was thinking about leaving the park when the phone rang. The screen said UNKNOWN CALLER. He picked up, but didn't say anything.

"I can hear the wind," said the caller. "Where are you?"

"A park."

"Sounds nice," said Veedy.

Zeeshan was sure it did. A trash barge would probably sound nice to Veedy just then. He'd been held without bond since his arraignment when the judge decided that a man who specialized in the import/export of the human variety might pose something of a flight risk.

"What are you doing in the park?" asked Veedy.

"Meditating," Zeeshan lied.

"I didn't know you were Buddhist."

"You don't have to be Buddhist to meditate."

"Lucky for you," said Veedy. "You'd make a shitty Buddhist. You know, most of those guys wouldn't kill a fly, much less—"

"Speaking of which," said Zeeshan. "I wanted to talk to you about our problem. I'm looking at alternative ways of solving it."

"So I heard," said Veedy. "Hey, tell me about the park."

Zeeshan stiffened. *So he heard?* Who had he been talking to? And what exactly had they told him? Veedy, who was not known for his patience, waited all of two seconds before prodding him. "City park or neighborhood park? Trees or a playground? Draw me a picture."

"This is why you called?"

"Humor me."

Zee cleared his throat. "Playground. Standard set-up. Slide, swings... Those little animals on a spring."

"What about the weather? Give me some context."

Zeeshan shifted on the picnic table. A dead leaf fell through a crack to the concrete with a little *click* and skated away on the wind. "I'm not sure you understood me earlier. The way I used to solve our problems? I'm not doing that anymore."

"The air," said Veedy. "What's it smell like?"

Disruption, wrote Kleinfelter, *is the key to breaking patterns. Stall. Interrogate yourself. Punch yourself in the thigh. Whatever it takes to hijack the routine.*

"Like nothing," said Zeeshan. "Like air."

Silence on the line. Zee could sense the big man's disappointment.

"Freedom is wasted on you," said Veedy. "You should be the one in here. You're just sitting around all day, anyway, doing nothing—"

"Waiting. I need time to—"

"*Waiting*," growled Veedy. "You think you're the tortoise. Truth is, you're the motherfucking hare, asleep in the tall grass."

Zee didn't say anything. You couldn't talk to Veedy when he got like this. You just had to wait for the moment to pass.

"Look, I'm sorry," said Veedy a few seconds later. "This place, it makes me—I haven't had a decent meal or conversation in a long fucking time, you know?"

"I know."

"I know you're not asleep, Zee. Just like I know how important the operation is to you. Maybe even more important than it is to me. Which is how I know, when the moment comes, you will do what is necessary to save the operation—and save my ass in the process."

Zee thought about pressing his point one more time—*But it won't involve killing the witness. Tell me you understand that*—but he kept his mouth shut. At the time he thought it was because he didn't want to take this argument for another lap around the track, but later, after hanging up the phone, he wondered if he'd stayed silent because he didn't want to take that final option off the table, either.

Don't tell yourself no, wrote Kleinfelter. Zeeshan had absorbed that lesson, at least.

Chapter 5
Short Answers

Ana was looking at a brochure for Tufts when a single sheet of paper slipped out of the middle. At first, when she saw the question blazing at the top of the page—*Are we alone?*—she thought it was someone's idea of a joke, or maybe a plea for help (she imagined a soul-sick grad student tasked with stuffing ten thousand packets slipping this paper into the brochure like a message in a bottle) but then she realized it was an essay prompt. Part of the application. And the blank space under the question wasn't a visual echo of the wide, cold universe, but rather a space for her answer.

Ana found the question disturbing.

It had been a week since her father's "accident," as everyone was calling it. The swelling in his brain was going down, but he was still in the hospital with no clear prognosis or release date. In the farmhouse, the phone rang night and day. Ana did not pick up. It might be her mother, and Ana didn't want to tell her what happened, much less put up with all her I-told-you-sos.

"Why don't you unplug the phone?" said Logan when she complained about the incessant ringing at school. Logan knew her mother no longer lived with them, but that was the extent of his knowledge about their situation. "I should totally do that," said Ana. She wanted to get away from her parents, away from the craziness they'd whipped up, and yet she knew she wouldn't actually unplug the phone, wouldn't blow a kiss to her father while backing out of the hospital room, Sayonara, Pop, good luck with the trial, I'm outta here. She totally should, and she totally wouldn't.

Are we alone?
No. Unfortunately.

◆　　◆　　◆

School, lunch. While other kids slouched toward the cafeteria, Ana went against the stream, carrying the sack lunch Karen had slipped into her hands on her way out of the diner. Opening the door to the library, she was greeted by the smell of old glue and bookmust. The ancient librarian looked up from a copy of *MAD* magazine. Her red hair was so thin Ana could see her entire scalp. The old lady nodded, tortoise-like. "Good afternoon, Miss Easterday."

Ana nodded back, hoping she hadn't hesitated too long. She still wasn't used to her new last name. Really, she only heard it from her gym teacher ("Easterday! Get your head in the game!") and her priggish English teacher ("Can you favor us with your attention, Miss Easterday?"). Hearing her first name was almost worse, though, because it was tied to her old life. Every time someone said *Ana*, it plucked that string, making her feel how much she had left behind.

She passed the rolling cart of books and the copier with its hot ink breath, and wound her way back to the supply closet, where she found Logan turning down the roaring white noise on the TV/VCR cart.

"Well, well," he said in his flattest tone. "Look who decided to show up."

Logan had been experimenting with sarcasm. He probably hoped it would become his defining characteristic, dislodging his reputation as the gay porn kid who worked at his family's video store.

Ana told him to shut his stupid mouth, which might have been the kindest thing anyone had said to him all day. "You got here like five seconds ago," she said. "The movie's not even loaded yet."

"I've been waiting here for ten minutes, twat." He leaned in to explain in *sotto voce*. "Waiting is another of those social niceties you know nothing about. Like 'promptness,' or 'consideration for others.'"

On her way to the library, Ana had stopped by the main foyer to call her father on the pay phone. He still couldn't talk, but it reassured her to hear his breath, the TV playing in the background. Sometimes her father tapped the receiver a couple of times with a fingernail. No way her call had taken ten minutes, but that wasn't really Logan's point: pretending to be annoyed was his way of expressing his gratitude that Ana hung around him. It was his nerdy shtick.

"I was giving you time to finish playing with yourself," she said. "See, I am considerate."

"I finished early."

"Oh?"

"I thought of you and my boner died."

She slugged him in his squishy bicep. That was her shtick.

"Ow, you crazy bitch," said Logan, unable to contain his grin.

This was the AV Club. When Ana joined, she doubled the membership from the previous year, when Logan had abandoned the combat zone of the cafeteria for the bunker-ish safety of this repurposed supply closet.

She had not asked to join his club. She came into Morocco with the mentality of a short-timer: no friends, no joining, no roots. Do the time, get her father through the trial, leave for college, forget about this ugly chapter of her life. That was the plan, anyway, before Logan barnacled onto her.

The first week of school, he'd asked Ana to join his club. She said no, but the next day he asked again. She said yes, then stood him up. The next day he asked again. What gave him hope? Maybe the fact that Ana couldn't bring herself to call him names. Or maybe he recognized a fellow castaway.

Ana finally caved when a group of girls waved her over to their lunch table, threatening to befriend her. A friendship with Logan, she reasoned, was naturally exclusive. Dude was a pariah *nonpareil*. Logan: other friends::garlic: vampires.

Plus he was funny, in his nerdy way. And totally sluggable. And the fact that he had access to pretty much every movie on VHS was a bonus.

The movie for this session of AV Club was *Terminator*. Logan slotted in the tape and settled into his bean bag. His bag was old and covered with

Xs of duct tape, a visual history of blowouts. Ana's bag—which Logan claimed the school had bought with money from a grant to "promote film literacy," though Ana suspected he'd purchased it himself—was still new enough to be slippery. When she squinched into it, she could feel each styrofoam pea through the vinyl.

They laid out their lunches by the light of the Interpol warning, which was Ana's daily cue to tell him he had to start eating better, or his heart would go supernova before he was twenty.

"What are you talking about?" He rustled through the stuff he'd looted from the snack racks of the Video Emporium: Milk Duds, Raisinets, gummi worms. "Dairy, fruit, protein. Balanced meal."

"Gummi worms are not protein, Logan."

He inspected the package. "I'm pretty sure they contain ten percent worm."

Ana snatched the gummies and tossed over her sandwich. "It's bologna," she said. "Twenty percent worm."

Logan clutched his hands together, blinking cartoonishly. "How can I ever repay you?"

"By shutting up."

"I pledge you my featly."

"It's *fealty*, you dingus."

"All I ask in return, milady, is for the smallest token of your affection." He laid his hand on her arm like a dog who wanted a handshake. "A barrette, mayhaps."

Ana snorted.

"I would settle for a Kleenex."

She picked up his hand and flung it away. "I hate to tell you this, Logan, but I don't have a dick."

He slumped in his beanbag. "That's not true," he sniffed. "You're *all* dick."

◆   ◆   ◆

The movie came on and they settled in, bean bags squeaking like fresh snow. The supply closet was big, but it was still a closet, so Ana had to crank her head back as she waited to sink into the movie until it ran like a dream.

But today, every time she started to sink, she saw her father. On the ground under the tree, one hand grasping at the sky, legs swimming in pain. Or in the hospital bed, staring at the parking lot through the window, a blank notepad on his lap.

Every day after school she ran to the hospital, and every day she asked the same question of anyone who came through her father's door, from orderlies on up: "Will he get better?" They tended to demur or prevaricate or offer generic hope, except for one doctor who said no.

This brought her up short. "No?"

The doctor had gray, bristly hair and seemed to vibrate with impatience. Glowering at her father's chart, he pulled a pen from his shirt pocket. "When people ask that question," he said, scrawling hard enough to make a rough music against the clipboard, "what they really want to know is: how soon can everything be like it was before? The answer is never." He made one final scratch on the chart, then looked at Ana. His eyes were ice caves. "The sooner you let go of your old expectations, the better. For him and for you."

He left and it was a minute before Ana could breathe again. She checked the chart. The whole bottom was an angry spirograph. Had he just scratched out the last doctor's notes? She ran into the hallway, but couldn't find him. That was three days ago, and she hasn't seen that doctor since.

Lightning on the TV. The Terminator has arrived. Ana glanced at Logan as blue light illuminated his profile, his floppy curls that were not cool at this buzz-cut school, the stipple of acne on his cheek, a dark smudge on his neck.

"Forget to shower this morning?" she said, poking the smudge. He winced, so she looked closer. It was a bruise, too dark for a hickey. "What happened?"

Crossing his arms, he settled deeper into the bag. "Can we just watch?" he said. "I mean, this *is* AV Club."

She sat up. "Who did it?"

"It's just—you wouldn't—oh, for the love of crap, you made me miss a good part." Logan got up and fiddled with the rewind button on the VCR, despite the fact that he had a remote in his hand. When he settled back into his bag, he pulled his collar up high on his neck.

She studied him in the flickering light. Maybe Logan hung around her for the same reasons she hung around him: she repelled other people, and didn't ask too many questions. Maybe that's all he wanted.

"Fine," she muttered, turning back to the screen, where a naked time traveler was putting his fist through some guy's torso. "Fuck you, too, pal."

When the bell rang at the end of lunch, Ana and Logan stayed in their bags without speaking. The next bell rang, and they ignored that one, too. They hid in the dark, waiting for a knock from the librarian that never came, watching the Terminator stalk a boy in an attempt to rewrite the future.

Are we alone?
More than you think. There is no "we."

◆   ◆   ◆

Later that day—after AV Club, after her obligatory trip to the hospital, after the doctor surprised her with some good news—Ana ran back to the farmhouse. She didn't feel like going inside, didn't feel like being alone in the dark rooms that didn't smell like home, so she climbed the oak tree and straddled a branch, watching a combine shuttle back and forth over a cornfield while the sun melted on the horizon.

The combine toppled twelve-foot stalks and left stubble in its wake. After the machine made its last pass, Ana could see clear to town. She felt exposed. For a second, she tasted her father's paranoia. What if he was right? Not about Zeeshan, necessarily, but in his general sense of doom?

Her father would be released soon. The doctor had told her this today like it was a happy occasion, but Ana wasn't so sure. "You're just trying to free up his bed," she said. "Make room for more customers."

The doctor laughed as though she'd made a joke. "He'll get better faster at home than he will here," he said, backing out of the room.

That was the problem, though: he couldn't go home. The longer they stayed in exile, the worse he got.

He could die here, she realized. Maybe not from Zeeshan or any other outside threat, but from some toxic combination of doom and dismay. A self-fulfilling prophecy, no assistance needed.

She wanted to help her father, she really did. But what could she do?

In the field, the combine shut off with a rumble. Its headlights blinked out. The sky was a violet puddle.

Nothing. There was nothing she could do.

Not by herself, anyway.

Ana jumped. When she hit the ground, a sharp pain flashed in her ankle, but she got up and started running anyway. For a few limping steps, the pain pulsed like a bright new heartbeat, but it faded by the time she reached the end of the driveway. She was almost sorry to feel it go. A part of her wanted to feel that hot new pulse all the way to town.

Are we alone?
Only if we choose to be.

From the written statement of D.W. Boxelder:

As promised, here is the fleet of banker's boxes containing documents, artifacts, and ephemera from the Easterday case. Below is my written statement—the first installment, anyway. The other installments are enclosed in the boxes to keep them in context. Happy hunting!

Onto the Easterdays and my first confession: After Ben fell from the tree, two things became clear. First, this family required extra attention. Second, a deputy marshal who failed to notice a witness roosting in a tree might not be up to the task of paying that attention. As I may have mentioned, I had a lot at stake in this case, so I took it upon myself to provide some additional support. Bugs, taps, cams, occasionally some additional personnel around town, along with more direct oversight from me.

Illegal? Technically. Wrong? Only if it's wrong to do everything you can for the protection of a family. Since it's never good for the Director to be caught off guard (there are no pleasant surprises in this business), I was determined not to be caught off guard again.

Except I was. Almost right away. The surprise was not that Ana called her mother. It wasn't even that she called from a gas station in town. (At the farmhouse, all long-distance calls were routed through our switchboard for the same reason witnesses had to change their names: To make sure what was hidden would stay hidden.) In fact, I had prepared for this eventuality by tapping her mother's phone, too. As I listened to Ana blab to her mother about Ben's accident and injuries, I congratulated myself for being a step ahead of the game.

Then she asked her mother for something I did not expect.

I've combed through these banker's boxes, Madame, searching for the overlooked clue that should have led me to expect her request. What did I miss? What could I have done differently to keep this family on track?

Even now, with the relative omniscience of hindsight, I don't know. I had always thought a true surprise was only available to those who weren't paying attention, but this case proved me wrong, again and again.

"I want you to reach out to Veedy," Ana told her mother. "I want you to make a deal to bring us home."

Chapter 6
Marriage

This was how Rooster helped Bennie: by letting go of his other runners and making his nephew pick up the slack. All day long Bennie hustled around the southwest side of Baltimore, picking up bags, dropping off bags, breathing bags, dreaming bags, crapping bags. He thought about buying a car, but that would have eaten up his savings, so he got a ten-speed instead. So what if he felt like an overgrown paperboy? With the bike, he could cover more ground, make more deliveries, and earn more money, rolling into the rising sun to catch the morning shift at the wire rope and rigging factory, whizzing past sunset with a miner's headlamp and a backpack full of bets.

If he wasn't on the bike, he was either wolfing down rice and Manwich, or was passed out in his bed, waking every few hours with leg cramps. He lost some money placing his own bets on the Colts—should have known better—but even so, the accordion case was brimming with cash in a matter of weeks. That wouldn't be good enough for Kate's parents, though. More importantly, it wasn't good enough for Kate. Her parents were right: she deserved better than a delivery boy. But whenever he told Rooster that he was grateful for the Tour de Baltimore and all, but what he really needed was a promotion, his uncle shrugged and said, "You don't like it, go to Mexico." But they both knew that wasn't going to happen.

Every day, the last run was to pay the boss, Veedy. Between 12:30 and 12:45 at night, Bennie would deliver a scuffed suitcase full of cash to a warehouse. If he missed that window of time, he was not to attempt a late delivery. "Not under any circumstances," emphasized Rooster, who seemed relieved to hand over this duty. Bennie would just have to bring two suitcases the next night. Plus a thirty percent late fee. Out of his own pocket, of course.

Night after night Bennie walked into that warehouse on time, placed the suitcase on a lone pallet in the middle of a cavernous room, and then walked out without seeing a soul. But one night, a month before the deadline set by Kate's parents, he sat down on the pallet and waited.

As Bennie checked his watch, Rooster's voice sang in his head. *You've heard of wrong place, wrong time? If you're in the warehouse at the wrong time, it becomes the wrong place.*

Rooster. So full of shit. The warehouse was empty. What could happen at 12:46 that would be so terrible?

Bennie checked his watch again. Sweat prickled his hairline.

At 12:43, a metal door scraped open somewhere deep in the warehouse. Bennie heard the clack of wooden soles. Out of the shadows came a man. Slim, brown, wearing a houndstooth blazer. He had a slight limp, Bennie noticed. "You can still leave," the man said softly. "I wish you would."

Bennie stood. "I need to talk to Veedy."

"He doesn't need to talk to you."

The man's eyes were heavy with reluctance. *I don't want to hurt you, but I will.* Everything inside Bennie was pulling him toward the door, but he made himself stand still. "Will you tell Veedy I'd like to ask him a question?"

The man didn't answer. He looked at his watch again and said, "Twenty seconds, my friend."

Without thinking, Bennie turned and ran out of the warehouse.

He was sure that nothing good would come of that encounter, but when he showed up with his delivery the next night, the pallet was not empty for once. Suitcases were piled high, spilling over the sides and onto the concrete floor, a mudslide of money.

Behind him, the sliding door rattled shut. Bennie turned and saw a wide man, shaped like a pair of parentheses. Ropy arms. Long, thin hair that fell to the collar of his camel hair blazer. Veedy.

"I understand you're looking for advancement," said Veedy. "It just so happens that I'm looking for investment opportunities." He stopped before Bennie, looked him up and down. Bennie felt foolish in his shorts. Worse, the bike chain had left a grease tattoo on his calf, and he could feel the grime of the street all over his face and neck.

"Make your pitch," Veedy prompted him.

Bennie felt wobbly. His pitch?

Veedy waited a second before curling his lip. And just like that, Bennie knew he had blown his shot. He hadn't seen it coming and now it was past him and Veedy was turning for the door. And there, in the shadows, was the limping man again.

"I'm working on something," called Bennie. "Something big. I just don't have all the details yet."

Veedy stopped walking. He looked at the limping man. "What do you think, Zee?"

"His numbers always add up. He's always on time."

"He lacks vision," said Veedy.

"But not motivation. He's got a baby on the way."

Bennie flinched. How did the man know this?

Veedy blew a raspberry. "Fine, I'll give him another shot." He pointed at Bennie. "Back here in one week. With an actual idea. I'm talking about a serious plan with hard numbers, down to the dollar. I run a tight ship. No room for slop."

Bennie nodded as though they had this in common, a shared contempt for slop. Then, as coolly as he was able, he said, "Any other suggestions as I, you know, polish the final details?"

Veedy's lip curled again, but this time it was almost a smile, like he recognized the bluff, but appreciated it all the same. Waving at the pile of suitcases, he said, "Make sure it processes a lot of cash."

◆　　◆　　◆

"Picture this," said Bennie. "A restaurant."

Rooster tried to exit the ticket booth, but Bennie jammed his foot against the door, so he fell back in his seat with a sigh.

"But not just any restaurant," Bennie went on. "*Ev*ery restaurant, all in one. A different room for each type. A coffee shop. A lounge. A formal dining room. A banquet hall! At any hour, something in the restaurant is busy."

Rooster gave his nephew a weary look. "You were supposed to save up for something legit."

"This is legit," protested Bennie. "Semi-legit."

"That's what I told myself when I first went to Veedy. Now I'm beholden to that evil Grimace for life. If I'd just been a little more patient—"

"Tell my baby to be patient."

Rooster fell silent. Who *was* this kid? What had happened to the boy who wanted to strum away his life in Todos Santos? For years, Rooster had been giving him advice, telling him in a hundred different ways to get serious, to grow up, and man, did he regret that now. Because this—wow—was this ever an overcorrection.

But what could Rooster do? Try to talk him out of it one more time? Every bit of resistance only seemed to harden the boy's resolve.

Is that what this was about for Bennie? Showing everyone? Showing them all, including Bennie's father?

Advice was useless now. His nephew was beyond advice, beyond Rooster.

Rooster opened the door of his booth. "Okay," he said, stepping out. "Good luck."

Bennie grabbed his arm. "What about my pitch? You think he'll say yes?"

Rooster stopped. He couldn't bring himself to look at his nephew's face, full of dumb hope. He looked at Bennie's shoes instead. Square-toed loafers—those were new.

"Yeah," said Rooster to the shoes. "Yeah, I'm afraid he will."

◆   ◆   ◆

For a long time, Kate's parents didn't hear from Bennie. Not one letter, not one call.

"He'll be back," insisted Kate whenever they called her in Dayton. She claimed to be having a wretched time in her "personal Tower of London," but every time they called in the evening they could hear the TV murmuring in the background and her spoon clanking around a dessert dish. "You'll see," she said through a mouthful of butter pecan ice cream or lemon meringue pie or apple cobbler. "The day of the deadline, he'll be back."

"In that case," said the old man to his wife, "I should have given him sixty years to make good. He would have been out of our hair forever."

Then came the day of the deadline. Bennie did not show up, but he did call to request an extension of three months, which the old man granted. "I'm sorry," the old man told his daughter, who received the news in silence. Even her spoon stopped clanking.

The old man wasn't sorry, of course. His wife's plan to give the boy plenty of slack was working. With a little luck, they would never hear from him again.

On the other end of the line, his daughter started to cry. The old man held the receiver away from his ear so he could watch the end of *Love Boat*. Rocking in his easy chair, he thought he could detect, under the strains of her mechanical weeping, the echo of *Love Boat* on her end of the line. He didn't say anything about it, though, and neither did she. They just stayed on the line until the end of the episode, him rocking, her crying, watching everything on the screen come together, together.

◆   ◆   ◆

The night before the opening of the Tip Top Lounge, there were three people in the restaurant: Bennie, his head chef, and Veedy. They sat in the back room, the room Bennie intended as a kind of tribute, a room reserved for Veedy and his guests. After tucking into the veal piccata, Veedy sent the chef home. "You know what sounds good?" he said. "Martinis."

Bennie started to get up, but Veedy put a soft hand on his shoulder, so he sank back down and let Veedy go behind the bar to mix the drinks.

The lounge had come together quickly. Within days of his pitch, Bennie had a deed to a former department store on Light Street, and a demolition crew was on site. He guessed that a good deal of money from those suitcases had gotten processed through the pockets of city clerks and foremen, but he didn't ask and Veedy didn't tell. All Bennie really knew was that Veedy had committed himself to the project, and that made Bennie nervous. What was Veedy going to ask in return?

The big man padded back to their table with a tall glass pitcher and a pair of up glasses. "The hunter returns." He poured a cloudy glass, then lifted an eyebrow at Bennie. "Dry and dirty," he said. "I hope you don't mind."

"Of course not," said Bennie, who had never had a martini, but would order them this way for the rest of his life.

"My accountant will be here at six in the morning," said Veedy. "He'll teach you how to work the money into your books. The morning after that—*every* morning after that—a delivery truck will come by with a pallet of dry goods with a suitcase or two in the middle. From then on, the driver will be your only contact. Understand?"

Bennie nodded, smoothing his palms on his thighs. He wasn't used to wool trousers. The silk lining felt wet against his legs.

"Your job is easy," said Veedy, pouring a glass for himself. "All you need to do is look legitimate. I'm going to help that effort by never coming here again. Don't get sloppy, don't be greedy, don't get curious. It's smart to be a little dumb."

Bennie nodded again. Veedy took a nip of the murky gin, then stood and buttoned his double-breasted coat. "You've got everything you want now?"

Bennie stopped nodding. He tried to picture Kate, but just then he couldn't see her face. Were her eyes green or hazel? All he could see was Rooster, leaning his hammy forearms on the lip of the booth, holding out a ticket. *It's not too late.* He was right, even now; Bennie could still push his chair back and say, "Actually, you know what? I'm not the right guy."

Veedy would be surprised, but it would be easy for him to plug in another useful idiot before the opening. Easy for Kate and her parents to follow through with the adoption plans. Easy for Bennie to haul his accordion case down to the bus station, tell Rooster to print up that ticket to Ensenada. They would understand, all of them. They might even be relieved.

Except for Bennie. He could travel to the other side of the world and never escape this decision. He could sit under a palm tree for a hundred years and never forgive himself.

Bennie cleared his throat. "I do."

Veedy raised his glass in a kind of toast. "Don't forget that," he said, and wolfed down his drink.

◆   ◆   ◆

A wet November evening, the second deadline. An Eldorado the color of rich cream pulled up to the old man's row house and honked twice. A young man stepped out of the car and buttoned his overcoat slowly. It took the old man a few seconds to recognize Bennie through the window; this was not the boy who had wallowed on their stoop six months earlier.

The old man chuckled. Well. This wasn't a bad outcome, either.

His wife was not nearly as impressed when she came to the door. "What is this?" she called into the street.

"Prospects," said the young man, walking around the long front of the car.

The old woman twisted a dishrag in her hands. "Bennie, what did you do?"

"Questions weren't part of the deal." He smiled. "And, please, call me Ben."

The old man waved him inside. "We'll hash this out at the table. You can tell us about your prospects, and if everything checks out, we can call Kate on the phone and—"

"No need," said Ben, opening the passenger door. There was their daughter in a billowing empire-waist dress. Getting to her feet was a struggle, even with Ben's help, and her puffy ankles were bulging around the straps of her heels, but she wore a look of chilly triumph. "Mother," she said. "Father."

"Outflanked," whispered the old man. That was the last word he said all evening.

"What did you do?" the old woman said again, and this time the question seemed directed not only at Ben, but at her daughter, herself, God. She told Kate to get in the house; she warned Ben to get away and stay away. Ben waited until she was done, and then invited her to join them for dinner at his restaurant.

His restaurant. His restaurant?

"How?" said the old woman in a cracked voice. "How?"

The car, the suit, the quick rise, his easy confidence: the answer came to her after she refused his offer and the Eldorado was disembarking from the curb. "He's a gangster," she whispered. From her stoop she cried out, loud enough for the neighbors to hear over the V8 bellowing down the street, but not loud enough to stop a damn thing. "You gangster, you gangster!"

PART 2

BAD FAITH

Chapter 7
All or Nothing

Diner, Pigtown. Ceiling tiles toasted from cigarette smoke and flaming plates of *saganaki*. The smell of lemon rice soup couldn't have been stronger if they'd mopped the floors with it.

It was the belly of the afternoon, only a few people around. At the counter, an old guy stared at the *Sun*, wearing a plaid tam that looked like a thumbtack pushed into his head. In the kitchen, the wait staff horsed around, shouting over the crash of the dishwasher. Kate was in a booth near the back, watching the door, absently running her fingers over the rosary beneath the table, reminding herself there was no reason to be afraid.

She was not the mark. She was in public. Ergo, no danger.

So why was her heart pinging around like a lotto ball?

Maybe because the meeting was with Zeeshan. She remembered the look that had come over Ben's face when the marshals mentioned that name. He looked stricken. Blind with terror.

So there was that.

At four o'clock, a man limped in the diner. Thin, almost frail. Tweed blazer. Was that—? No way. Kate was craning to see if anyone else was coming up the walk when the thin man caught her eye. "Kate?"

Her head dropped an inch in disbelief. He must have taken this as confirmation, because he limped toward her booth. The waitress toddled after him with her carafe. It took about eight years for them both to reach the table. Kate straightened the sugars and jellies and butters until she noticed her fingers were trembling, then she put her hands in her lap.

What was wrong with her? She should be relieved. He wasn't exactly intimidating. Plus, her expectations for this meeting were low. Super low. Almost nonexistent. Ana wanted her to broker a deal to allow Ben to come home. Privately, Kate thought this was the longest of shots—Veedy wasn't exactly known for letting bygones be bygones, after all—but she couldn't say no to her daughter. Not when Ana was finally talking to her. Not after her daughter had lost so much. Not when it was Kate's fault.

The good news was that this meeting didn't have to work. She just had to show Ana she was making an effort. That she was not, after all, a monster. Then they would keep in touch until Kate figured out some other way to bring her daughter home.

At last the waitress finished pouring the coffee and left their table with an elephantine sigh. Kate tapped her fingernails on her mug. "Zeeshan," she said. "What kind of name is that?"

It was supposed to be casual, a light conversational opener, but it sounded confrontational. This happened when she got nervous: everything came out snappish.

Luckily, Zeeshan didn't seem to take offense. He smiled at a sugar packet before tearing off the top. "I'm from Kashmir," he said. "It's between India and Pakistan, up in the—"

"Himalayas," she finished. "Under constant territorial dispute. I'm not an idiot."

Easy, Katydid, her old man used to say when she got jumpy. *Put that dog on a leash.* She gave a lame shrug. "I mean, I read *National Geographic.*"

Zeeshan kept his smile. "Most people hear Kashmir, they want me to knit them a sweater."

Was this a ploy? The limp, the blazer, an awkward joke—was it all designed to get her to lower her guard? With his hands wrapped around his mug, steam rising to his face, he looked as harmless as an actor in an International Coffees commercial, but Kate couldn't tell if he was smiling or smirking. Either way, she decided, she wanted that look off his face.

"I have enough sweaters," she said. "What I'd really like is to bring my family home safely. So tell me—can we make that happen?"

Zeeshan set down his cup, looking relieved. "That's what I want, too," he said. "Let's sort out this misunderstanding."

◆　　◆　　◆

Sorting. In the months since her daughter had left, that had been Kate's main occupation. She'd spent countless hours sifting through her life, looking for the turning point that had set them on this awful trajectory. Sometimes she traced it to the night of the bomb. Other times she went all the way back to the day she met Ben. (Who would Kate have been if she'd finished high school? In those days she had stolid dreams of being a pharmacist. But then she wouldn't have had Ana at all. That was the problem with alternate paths: it was an all or nothing deal. You couldn't smuggle the good stuff from your current life with you.) More often, though, she traced the trouble to the days in her early twenties when she started to think about leaving Ben. The problem between them—the main problem, as she saw it—was the lounge.

The lounge hadn't always bothered her. When she was eighteen, the Tip Top Lounge was a pure boon. In a snap, it had transported her from childhood to Real Life, complete with a ring, a house, a daughter. Yes, she knew her husband laundered money for a man named Veedy, but how bad was that, really? It was a paper crime. At worst, tax fraud, and who didn't commit a little of that? Her mother was wrong: Ben wasn't a gangster, he was a businessman and a gentleman. He was never anything but courteous to Kate. Chivalrous, you could say, though he wasn't around the house much. If the deal was all or nothing, in those days it felt like she'd lucked into all.

Back then, Kate was a rote Catholic, going through the motions in a mechanical way. She attended Mass at Transfiguration, the same church where she'd been baptized, even after she and Ben moved across the harbor to Fells Point. She went to confession in the same way her old man had picked up his lunchbox from the kitchen counter with a sigh every morning for forty years. *Everyone has a job. You do what has been given you to do.*

Then two things happened, bang bang. Ana went off to elementary school, leaving Kate alone during the day. That fall, her old man plowed his Cutlass Supreme through the brick wall of a liquor store. By the time the firefighters cut away his door, the old man was cold, dead of a massive coronary.

Maybe it was loneliness. Maybe the jolting reminder of mortality. Whatever the cause, Kate found herself going to Transfiguration nearly every day, confessions pouring out of her. Afterwards, she often wept, deeply, like her soul had been lanced. She told Father Anthony everything, things she had never even told a girlfriend, things that Ben had asked her never to say. She told Father Anthony the whole truth about the Tip Top Lounge.

It took a few months and a little nudging from Father Anthony, but eventually she saw the Tippy in a different, dimmer light. Sure, her husband may not have been hurting anyone directly, but he was financing a criminal organization. Who knew what kind of pain he was facilitating? But by then, they were both stuck. Ben wasn't going to walk away from the lounge, and she couldn't ask for an annulment. Their marriage didn't come close to any of the appalling conditions listed in the Canons; the worst you could call their relationship was neighborly.

For a while, Kate settled for praying for him, for herself, for Ana. She went to Mass every morning, confession twice a week. She became a Eucharistic Minister and spent her days taking communion to the ill, the aged, the infirm. In this way, she laundered her husband's sins.

It wasn't a solution, but it wasn't nothing, either. She might have gone on like this for decades if Ben hadn't gotten arrested one night last spring.

"It was a bluff," he assured Kate when he got home late that evening. The ADA was taking a run at him in a stupid attempt to flip him on Veedy. Ben sat down heavily in a club chair, and wiped at the smudge of fingerprinting ink on his cuff. "Get this," he said, like it was a joke. "They offered me immunity. Offered to put me—us—into Witness Protection."

Half-grinning, he watched for her reaction. Kate didn't know what her face showed him. She couldn't breathe.

They tried to talk, but kept falling down the wells of their own thoughts. Eventually he got up to pour himself a tumbler of rye, and Kate retreated to her sewing room. To busy her hands, she got out the giant box of cloth napkins she'd promised to stuff into rings for a charity dinner.

Witness protection—it would get them away from the lounge. This was the answer to her prayers, right? So why wasn't she telling him to take the deal? Why wasn't she packing right now?

Because of the pitted sidewalk in front of Transfiguration. Because of Marty's Deli, where she ate lunch every Tuesday with Michelle, whom she had known since the day in second grade when they'd scrapped over whose turn it was to jump in double dutch. Because of the tarnished kick plate on the door of her childhood home. Because of onions sizzling in a pan, Jim Croce crooning on WLIF, her mother walking into the front room, wiping her hands on a dish towel, glad to see her. Because she'd already been relocated once, when she had been pregnant, and she wasn't going to let that happen again.

Her life was here, her whole life, and if she went into Witness Protection, it would be over. *That gangster has killed you.* She could almost hear her mother saying that, reaching for her face with knobby fingers. *He has finally killed you.*

After all those years of prayer, it turned out she only yearned for change as long as it couldn't actually happen. It turned out she was ruled by fear and comfort. No way could she go from all to nothing, no way.

But what if Ben went away by himself?

Kate stopped stuffing napkins. She felt a flare of shame at this thought, but when the shame faded the thought was still there. It would be a terrible sin, of course... but wouldn't it be worse to keep him here, especially if he was actually in danger?

And even if he wasn't in physical danger, wouldn't it be worse for their souls to keep going down the same road, with Ben laundering dirty money, and Kate fat as a tick on the proceeds?

Send him away. They could both be free, and safe, with a chance at another life. They came into marriage as friendly strangers; they could leave the same way.

But what about Ana? Losing her father would devastate her...but it would also eliminate the possibility of her going into the family business. Ben had always sworn he would never let that happen, but then, Rooster had made that same promise about Ben, and look how that turned out. The only way to make sure Ana didn't follow in her father's footsteps was to send him away. Ana would be a raging mess, but she was a smart girl, a mature girl, almost an adult, really, and in no time at all she would come to understand the sacrifices they had both made for her.

Kate looked down and saw a napkin sticking cockeyed through a ring. Same with the one next to it, and the next one. Sloppy, sloppy. That's what happens when you're not paying attention. She uprooted the napkins from their rings in quick jerks, separating them all in minutes. It was faster to tear them out than to thread them in. You didn't even have to think about it. In fact, it was easier if you didn't.

◆　　◆　　◆

It was still dark when she went out to the living room and found Ben in the club chair, running his thumb along his jaw. A car came around the corner, headlights sweeping the wall. She laid a hand on his shoulder, and, to her surprise, he pulled her gently onto his lap. For a moment she was afraid he wanted to make love—she couldn't do that, not in light of what she was about to tell him—but he just dropped his head back against the chair and held her.

"I've been thinking," she started.

"Me, too."

"I don't know where to start."

Outside, a car door shut. Kate ducked her head to listen. When she heard footsteps coming up the walk, she tried to stand, but Ben held her. She had enough time to say, "What if it's—" before the door swung open.

Ana. Lipstick smeared, a little unsteady on her feet. "You guys waited up?" Then she seemed to notice they were occupying the same chair. "Actually, don't tell me what you were doing."

"I could say the same to you," murmured Kate, but without much conviction, because she felt odd. Dizzy.

By the time the dizziness passed, Ana was climbing the stairs, and Ben was shifting under her, which either meant that his legs were falling asleep or he wanted to make love after all.

"We should catch some sleep," Kate said, getting to her feet.

"I'm not worried, you know."

The dizziness returned. She put a hand on the back of the chair. "What?"

He tilted the empty tumbler. "They were trying to rattle my cage. It almost worked…" He shook his head like he was clearing a daydream. "I'll sort it out. It'll be fine. We're not going anywhere."

The tumbler sounded like a gavel when he set it down on the side table. "Coming to bed?" he murmured as he got up, because it was good form, though he didn't seem to notice when she didn't answer.

Her dizziness: it was the way you feel when you get new glasses and everything is too sharp. Or when you're waving to a loved one on a pier as your boat pulls away, and they're shrinking and you feel yourself tipping over, so you have to stop waving and look down into the churning water to steady yourself.

◆   ◆   ◆

In the diner, Kate felt off-balance. This meeting wasn't supposed to work. Especially not so easily.

Zeeshan must have noticed her confusion, because he leaned in to explain. "You want to bring your family home. I want to protect our operation. Once we untangle this misunderstanding, we both get what we want."

"Misunderstanding," repeated Kate. It couldn't be this simple. She was missing something, but what was it?

He leaned closer. "If I could just talk to Ben, I'm sure we could put things right."

There it was: he wanted to lure Ben home. Zeeshan's job would be so much easier if his prey came to him.

Kate put both hands around her mug. "I know who you are," she said, trying to control her voice. "I've heard how you put things right."

He shook his head once. His eyes were blue, pale as a cake of lake ice. "That's not who I am anymore."

"Now you're just a humble human trafficker, right?"

He didn't answer right away, and Kate leaned in to press her advantage. "That's right," she said. "Ben told me. I know what you do."

"No," he said, "you don't. That's the misunderstanding."

"Go ahead." The edge of the table was cutting into her breastbone, but she didn't sit back. "Treat me like an idiot and see what happens."

Zeeshan glanced around, probably to see if anyone could hear her.

"You and I both know that if you find Ben, he's dead," she said. "And if you don't find him—if he testifies—you and your boss and your whole fucking operation are finished. Until we both acknowledge those truths, we won't be sorting anything out."

Zeeshan dabbed the corners of his mouth with a napkin. "I'm sorry we weren't able to see eye to eye today," he said in a stiff voice.

Too late, Kate realized she had gone too far. Too late, because he was already sliding his hand inside his jacket. Her stomach dropped. *No*, she thought. That was it, just one word in her mind. Like a child who doesn't want to leave. *No—*

Zeeshan pulled a fat yellow envelope from his jacket and pushed it across the table.

"What's this?" Kate managed to say. "Some kind of bribe?"

"Reparations," he said, sliding out of the booth. "Like I said, we want to put things right. You might see that if you stop assuming the worst." Buttoning his jacket, he bent toward her and spoke quickly. "If Veedy wanted you dead, you would all be dead. That bomb?" He shook his head. "That wasn't us."

She stayed at the table as he limped out the door. It was another couple of minutes before she trusted her legs enough to walk back to her mother's house.

Chapter 8
When I'm Gone

Every day when school let out at 2:05, Logan drove straight to the Video Emporium. It was only a few blocks away, so he could have walked, but ever since a carload of seniors had trailed him down the road, calling out *Faggot hey faggot I got a cock you can suck right here*, and then pegged him with a mealy banana—well, he drove everywhere now.

"You know what I'd do?" Ana had said in the AV clubhouse after he made the mistake of telling her why he didn't care for bananas. "I'd super-glue a dildo to that guy's hood. A big, wobbly one. Then I'd write *Suck Me* in spray paint around it."

Easy for her to say, thought Logan. She was lucky; no one actually picked on her. Situation was totally hypothetical.

She probably would do it, though, given half a chance. He could totally see her jogging down the street with a tube of glue in one hand and a pink monster in the other.

Fighting back wasn't really Logan's style. He was more of a path-of-least-resistance kind of guy. Did that make him weak? Well, let's see. Water took the path of least resistance. So did electricity. And those were *only the most destructive forces in the universe*. So, sure, call him weak as lightning. He guessed he could accept that.

Ohhhhhhhhhhhhhh, howled the imaginary crowd in his head, impressed by his movie-quality comeback. In the center of that hooting crowd was a scowling senior, Chief Banana-slinger, and he was saying *Whatever, man, whatever,* but he had just gotten scorched and he knew it and everyone else knew it, too. As Logan strutted away, the crowd marveled aloud about how wrong they'd been about him, and how they'd never call him Little Hummer Boy again.

Sometimes he tried these comebacks out loud in the car—"Sure, okay. I guess I'm weak as *light*ning"—but never in real life. He wasn't stupid. He knew how it would go.

Other times, spacing out at a stoplight, he'd picture Ana gluing a dildo to a hood, pressing down on the shaft with both hands to make sure it stuck, and that gave him weird crawly feelings.

At 2:15 he opened the Emporium, but since there were rarely any customers before five o'clock, he faced several lonely hours of rewinding, restocking, and rewatching movies on the big TVs that hung from the rafters.

It was his favorite time of day.

He wore headphones while he worked, big earmuff-looking clappers that blocked out the world. He favored soundtracks on his Discman because he could imagine that he was in a movie. Not as, like, an actor. A character. It didn't even have to be a major character! Take *Raiders of the Lost Ark*, which happened to be playing this afternoon on the TV across from the checkout counter. He didn't have to be Indiana Jones, or even Dr. Brody. He could be the custodian at the end of the movie, the guy who wheels the Ark of the Covenant into a warehouse full of identical crates. Everyone else in the world saw that scene and thought, God, what a waste, what a crushing symbol of bureaucracy—but Logan thought, *That looks like a cool job.* He could keep the oddities orderly. Work alone, wear headphones all the time. Not have to put up with anyone calling him Gaylord. Not have to hear them say, Watch out, he'll stare at your wang in the gym shower. Not have to hear them say he had AIDS. That he deserved it.

That he hung around playgrounds, offering to push little boys on the swings so he could grab their asses. That once he fucked a cat, or a knothole, or the tailpipe of an '82 Omega, or an open dictionary because it reminded him of an ass crack.

According to Charlie Donovan, Logan had announced that he was going to commit a crime on his eighteenth birthday so he could go to prison and "get it all the time."

They said Logan could turn you gay, like some kind of sex vampire. *I vant to suck your deek!*

They said not to sit on the toilet after him, that it was basically rubbing asses with him, which, as everyone knew, Gaylords loved to do. Don't drink after him at the water fountain because you could catch his AIDS. Don't get near him outdoors because a mosquito might bite him and then bite you, and then his blood would be inside you.

In the Video Emporium, Logan shook his head like it was an Etch-a-Sketch. *Whatever, man. Whatever.*

On the TV, the giant boulder was rolling after Indy. Harrison Ford was the coolest, no doubt, but just then Logan found himself rooting for the boulder.

Turning to grab another armload of tapes from the return bin, he bumped into his brother. "Jesus," Logan sputtered, pulling off his headphones. "What are you doing here?"

Jared cocked his head and smiled. It was not a kind smile. "Nice to see you, too, dicksnot."

He brushed past Logan to pop open the register and pull out a few bills. "You know, you should appreciate me more," he said. "I know you think you hate me, but just watch. You'll miss me when I'm gone."

Logan would love the chance to find out, but he wasn't holding his breath. Since graduating last year, all Jared could talk about was saving up enough money to go to the Harley Mechanics School in Phoenix.

Talk about your pipe dreams. Jared had never ridden a Harley, much less worked on one. Couldn't even replace the broken tail light on his Fiero. And if his borrowing habits from the till were any indication, his savings were zilch.

Logan could go on, but why bother? He wouldn't say a word of this out loud. That would be the path of *mucho* resistance.

But leave it to Jared to take silence as a challenge. "Don't give me that look," he said.

Logan neutraled his face. Don't give him a reason, he thought.

"You think shit is bad for you now, just wait," said Jared. "People hold back because of me. But once I'm gone, man…" He shook his head at the coming horror, then looked at Logan and seemed to come to a decision. "You need to learn to defend yourself."

Ah, that's right: Jared didn't need a reason. Or, rather, the collateral crap that Jared had to take because he was the Brother of the Gaylord: that was reason enough.

The fact that Jared was the one who had set this whole shit show in motion—nobody made him walk in on Logan and that movie! nobody made him blab about it to the whole school!—never seemed to occur to him.

Or maybe it had, and that only made him angrier.

On the screen, Indy was getting into a floatplane and escaping. Logan would give anything to be Indy right now. Or the floatplane. Or the television.

Jared snapped his fingers. "Never look away from your attacker. Otherwise you won't see him do *this*."

Judo chop to the throat. Despite himself—story of his life—Logan whined, which earned him another chop, along with a warning to stop being a pussy. From there, the attack was as predictable as a formal dance. Headlock, hip throw, and Logan found himself on the floor, looking up at his brother straddling him. Jared's face was strange, halfway between pleading and panic. If a customer had walked in on this scene, he might have thought that Jared was trying to resuscitate his brother. Until Jared wrapped his hands around Logan's throat, anyway. "Why do you have to *be* this way?" he said, bouncing Logan's skull against the floor as punctuation.

Logan's role in this little show was to kick and claw and *ack ack ack* until Jared would at last climb off, looking dazed, saying something like, Not bad. If you fought half that hard against the pussies in this town, etcetera.

But today? Logan didn't feel like playing that part. Today he raised his hands and rested them on his brother's wrists. A black circle rimmed his vision, and that was fine. Someone was saying, Stop it, stop it, stop it. It turned out to be Jared. That was fine, too. In his mind, Logan had already left the Emporium. In his mind, he was sitting at a bar, Marion Ravenwood's bar from *Raiders*, all big and cavernous, with chunky wooden tables and a snapping fire.

Playing dead, said Indy, sidling up next to him at the bar. *Hell of a strategy. Only problem is, pretty soon you won't be playing.*

The bartender came over with a dusty bottle and two shot glasses. When she set them down, Logan saw that it was Ana. What was she doing here? Before he could ask, she moved down the bar, leaving the bottle behind. Indy poured the shots and Logan tossed his drink back without flinching. Setting it down on the bar, he said, *Another.*

Sure thing, said Indy. *Right after you get yourself out of this mess.*

I'm tired. Logan took the bottle and poured himself another shot. *And don't tell me what to do.*

Indy laid a hand on Logan's shoulder. *I'm telling you as a friend.*

Friends, said Logan. *Is that all we are?*

Indy started to say something, but his voice was drowned out by a rumbling noise. Logan looked back in time to see a giant boulder crash through the wall and bear down on the bar. Indy grabbed his hat and took Logan by the elbow, but Logan shook his head. *It's gonna get me sometime*, he said. *Just let it happen.*

On the floor of the Emporium, Logan's heart was knocking around, but it was a mile away. The big black circle was down to a pinhole and he wanted to fly through the middle like Superman. He went to lift his arms—*Up, up, and away*—but they fell to his sides like sandbags.

Jared scrambled to his feet, looking disgusted. "What the hell, man? What is wrong with you?"

Logan almost smiled at his brother. He would have, if feeling wasn't coming back into his lips, his toes, his hands, flooding his system like a toxin.

Chapter 9
Pocket Gun

Ana couldn't sleep.

Which didn't make any sense. Her father was finally home from the hospital, resting comfortably. The situation wasn't perfect—"resting comfortably" was a euphemism for spending most of his time in bed, tranq'd to the gills—but at least she didn't have to worry constantly about him. At least he was indoors, and his guns were not. They rested at the murky bottom of the rain barrel by the outbuilding, where she'd deposited them before he came home.

Add the fact that she was running at least five miles a day and the sun went down at suppertime, and she should have been sleeping like a bear. But every time her eyelids got heavy, her mind would needle her: call Mom, see if she's close to bringing us home. Look in on Dad. Check and see, check and see.

One night around three in the morning, she wandered out to the kitchen. Opened the window over the sink, dug a joint out of the tea box, telling herself: two tokes. Maybe three. Just enough to make me sleepy.

The smoke went down her throat like a firebrand. She held it down as long as she could before blowing a ragged cloud out the window. In some alternate universe, she was still in Baltimore. Her father hadn't been arrested, her own life hadn't gone to shit. It was Friday night in someone's crowded basement, muggy with breath. Someone held out an open palm and said *Don't bogart that joint,* a girl shrieked laughter, a bottle of Southern Comfort made its way, hand by hand, over to Ana…

Meanwhile, in this universe (the real one, the shitty one), Ana studied her reflection in a butter knife. Then she breathed a fog over her face and wiped it off with her shirt.

It turned out that most of the silverware had water spots. Somehow the whole joint got smoked.

Around four, she looked in on her father. Light from the hallway fell across the bed. He had the covers pulled up to his neck. He made a light rasping noise, not quite a snore, that Ana found soothing. It was like he was saying, *I'm alive, I'm alive.*

Not that he would have said anything that sensible if he'd been awake. *Slip sleep,* he might have said, or, if he got anxious or frustrated, *Tatty dorag* or *Sanka room fuckness,* which he had actually muttered a few days earlier when she turned out his light.

The therapist said he was making progress, but Ana didn't see it. It had been three weeks since his fall, and sure, he was (technically) talking, and if he was calm you could (sometimes, kind of) catch his drift, but if he got the slightest bit agitated, it was word salad.

Which was how the therapist sounded when he tried to explain what was happening with her father. "Receptive aphasia," he told Ana, "manifesting in paraphrasia."

"You mean gibberish," said Ana.

The therapist made a pained face. "Not exactly," he said, explaining that Ben usually got the syntax right, but subbed in some wrong words. "Which is how our speech sounds to him, too," the therapist said. "Garbage in, barfish lout."

Ana was pretty sure the therapist was full of shit. His gray ponytail and leather vest that looked like a quilt of bat wings didn't exactly scream "medical professional." He obviously considered himself one, though. Every time Ana called him a therapist, he found a gentle way to remind her that he was a speech-language pathologist, which made Ana look for an excuse to call him a therapist again.

The guy drove up from Indy in his rattling Jeep three times a week to watch her father fill up sketchbooks with doodles of hats and alligators and other random bullshit. When picture time was done, the therapist broke out his guitar and they played sing-a-long. Songs and images were (allegedly) processed through the undamaged hemisphere. Meaning could still come in and out, the therapist claimed; it just had to use a different door.

Maybe. Or maybe the guy was taking government money to jam with the addled. Ana hadn't been aware that her father knew any dino rock, but he crooned along to "Jeremiah Was a Bullfrog," not missing a word, though neither of them could harmonize for shit. Still, it was better than their version of "Take it Easy," which sounded like a coyote fucking a cactus.

But none of this was the real problem. It all bothered her, sure, but not as much as the fact that her father hadn't said her name since the accident.

She was Antsy now. Or Santa. Once, Pants.

In some alternate universe, her father was walking up to her hostess stand in his cashmere blazer, calling her name. *Hm?* she said without looking up from *The Great Gatsby,* only half-listening to whatever he had to say, because nothing was crucial back then. Not for her, anyway.

Meanwhile, in this universe, Ana leaned over her sleeping father and smoothed his choppy hair. His face, she noticed, was filling out. So what if he couldn't say her name? At least he wasn't in a tree. At least someone around here was sleeping.

Ana sat down on the floor next to his bed and propped her back against the wall. This made the pocket gun dig into her spine, so she tugged it from the back of her jeans and laid it in her lap.

Okay, so she hadn't thrown away all his guns. She found this one taped to the pipes under the bathroom sink. When she went to toss it in the rain barrel, the gummy residue on the grip made it stick to her hand long enough for her to reconsider. She was on her own out here. Holding this pocket gun—compact as a paw, with a rough grip that was satisfying to squeeze—steadied her. That's why she had slipped the gun into the back of her jeans instead of dropping it in the rain barrel: it made her feel less afraid, less alone.

At five a.m., an alarm went off. Groaning, she rubbed her eyes and cuffed herself with the gun that was stuck to her palm. *Fuck*, she croaked, and then she saw her father looking at her.

"What," she said. "The safety was on. I'm not a total idiot."

He just kept looking at her.

"So I fell asleep with a gun," she said. "It's not like you have any room to talk."

He dipped his head, and Ana thought he might be conceding the point, but then he held out his hand. *Hand over the gun.*

In some alternate universe, Ana handed the gun over right away, weeping in shame.

In this universe, the shitty one, she held the gun loosely in front of her, but not close enough for him to reach. "Say my name."

He opened his fingers. *Give it to me.*

She leaned in closer. "Come on, Dad. Who am I?"

The struggle was clear in his eyes. She could see him scrolling through possibilities in his mind, all those sounds, none of them attaching themselves to this girl.

In some other universe, she promised she would dump the pocket gun in the rain barrel, but then tucked it back in her jeans as soon as she left his room.

In this universe, she stood up and looked him in the eye. "No," she said. "I'm not giving this to you."

She said this without spite or hesitation or any other marker of rebellion. Because this wasn't rebellion. Because he wasn't in charge anymore.

She kissed her hand, pressed it to her father's stubbly cheek, then slipped the gun into her jeans and went into the kitchen to make him breakfast.

Chapter 10

Beneath the World

For sixteen years, a delivery man had shown up at the Tippy by 4:45 a.m. to drop off a pallet of dry goods with a hidden heart of cash. Every day but Sunday, which Ben kept sacred for sleep and football. For sixteen years, there was not a single delay, much less a missed delivery. Then came the drizzly Tuesday morning in April when Ben found himself alone on his loading dock, watching the hour hand on his Patek Philippe inch past five.

Maybe the guy had gotten caught in traffic. Maybe he was sick, and a substitute delivery guy was rushing to the Tippy right now.

Five-thirty, still no delivery.

Ben had not missed a day of work in sixteen years, but he knew what to do if he ever did. Upon Veedy's insistence, he had set up three different contingency plans to receive the delivery. But what was he supposed to do if a delivery didn't show up? "Let me worry about my end," said Veedy all those years ago, clapping him on the shoulder.

But Ben had to worry about it now. If the delivery was late, fine. Veedy would be pissed—*I run a tight ship*—but that was his problem. If the guy didn't show up at all, though, that was Ben's problem. He knew enough sleight-of-pen to launder up to five thousand a day, but to skip a day and process ten the next? No good. The bank records told a story, and that story had to make sense.

Then it was six o'clock, and Ben was driving to the warehouse, remembering how he'd biked this route as a teenager, a suitcase lashed to his handlebars with bungee cords. Back then Veedy's main line was bookmaking. Back then some of the older guys still called him "Velcro Dan," a nickname that came from the velcro straps on his shoes, which he allegedly favored because he was too pear-shaped to bend over and tie his laces without getting red-faced. Over the years the nickname was shortened to V.D. and sped up to Veedy, and now he probably had a servant to tie his bluchers and no one dared call him that old name. Now, no one knew all the lines of business he was running. "Shouldn't you know?" Kate had asked Ben once. "Don't you want to know? I mean, you're a part of whatever he's doing."

Look at it like a mutual fund, he told her. You invest, your money makes money, you're happy. You don't know what companies are in your portfolio. You don't know how those companies make their money. All you know is that your investment is growing, just as Ben only knew that the morning delivery had steadily increased over the years, so whatever Veedy was doing, he was doing well.

Beyond that, Ben didn't need to know anything else. Until the day he needed to know what had happened to the delivery.

He parked down the block from the warehouse and walked into the permanent twilight of the adult bookstore on the ground floor. Behind the counter, a man with a loose white-guy afro and brown-tinted lenses nodded at him before returning to his copy of *Cherry*. At six in the morning, Jesus.

Ben looked down the aisles, trying not to touch anything or breathe too much of the moist air. Satisfied that no one else was in the store, he went up to the counter. "Did you get your delivery this morning?" he said in a low voice.

A bit of a gamble, but not too much. If this shop wasn't one of Veedy's, the guy would just be slightly confused. *Delivery of what?* And because it was a porn shop, the conversation wouldn't even rate as the weirdest of his shift.

But when the guy's face registered shock, Ben knew he was dealing with one of Veedy's men. "Just nod or shake your head," said Ben. "I need to figure out what's going on."

The man pawed around the counter until he grabbed a string of licorice-flavored condoms—*Blackjack: Lick the Stick*—and rang them up.

"What are you doing?" said Ben.

"Making this look like a transaction." He tipped his head toward the security camera over the door, and his stupid hair waved like anemone. "Pay me, then get your fool ass out of here."

Ben turned to the camera. "Hey," he said. "I've got a little problem. I could use some help."

The guy moaned. "What is wrong with you?"

"I'm trying to get his attention."

"That is the last thing you want, dummy. Besides, he's not watching right now."

"How do you know?"

"He hasn't come into his office yet."

Ben stepped back from the counter, ignoring the guy's warning that Veedy watched the security tapes at night, and when the big man came across this choice footage, oh boy, they were both fucked.

"Shut up," said Ben. "I'm trying to think." Something had gone wrong; the question was *what*.

Maybe Veedy and the delivery guy had gotten wind of some trouble and skipped town. Or maybe they'd been caught in a dragnet that was sweeping Ben's way even now. In either case, Ben should—

Stop. There were a hundred other likely explanations for a delay. Veedy might have gone on vacation. Or shoe shopping. Who knew. No need to freak out. That was the important thing, Ben told himself as he walked toward the door. Veedy and the delivery guy were just taking a day off, which was okay! Everyone deserved a break every sixteen years or so, only Ben couldn't skip a day, not on such short notice. He'd have to remedy this little problem himself, *tout de suite*. That was his specialty, after all, smoothing out wrinkles, making things better. He'd just make a quick trip to the old room where he used to make deliveries. Maybe Zeeshan would be around. Maybe a suitcase or two was sitting on a pallet. If so, great. Problem solved. If not—well, the problem wouldn't be any worse.

Veedy wouldn't find out about his poking around, because Veedy wasn't watching just then, and the idea that he spent his nights reviewing security tape was preposterous.

But you know what? Even if Veedy did watch the tapes, he'd probably end up thanking Ben for taking care of the issue while it was small before a major aberration showed up on the Tippy's books. If there was one thing Veedy prized more than protocol, it was initiative. That's how Ben got the lounge in the first place. A while back, he asked Veedy why he'd said yes to a pitch from a delivery boy with no knowledge of the service industry and even less entrepreneurial experience. Ben was hoping he would say something about strength of idea or character, but Veedy said, "Honestly? I saw a guy with no margin for error. I knew you'd make it work because you absolutely could not afford to fuck it up. This guy, I told myself, he'll fake it till he makes it."

Veedy was right. In those early years, Ben channeled his desperation into thousands of hours of work. Now, as he walked to the back of the warehouse and slid aside the corrugated panel, it felt like he was traveling back in time. Once again, he was bull-rushing a problem. Now, as before, he didn't have the first clue about what he was getting into.

This time, Ben never even stepped into the pallet room. All he did was open the door, and then, a heartbeat later, close it again. He managed to walk out of the warehouse, but broke into a trot as soon as he hit the street.

Sixteen years. All that he'd built—the Tippy, his career—placed in jeopardy, just like that.

Or worse. He might have just put his head in Veedy's jaws.

When he got to his car he heard soft bells calling the faithful to seven o'clock mass. He thought of his wife walking to church, Ana getting a ride to school, and it came to him that he was still underestimating the damage he'd courted. By opening the door to the pallet room, he had put his entire family at risk.

You've heard of wrong place, wrong time? If you're in the warehouse at the wrong time, it becomes the wrong place.

A van. That's what he'd seen. Its sliding door was open, and inside the dim cabin, brown faces. An arm reached out, pointing at him. On the far side of the van, the shadow of a man, limping.

Shouldn't you know what else Veedy is into? Don't you want to know?

Jesus Christ, why couldn't he have minded his own business?

Breathe. Think. This problem could still be contained. Maybe Zeeshan hadn't seen him. Maybe Ben could pretend this had never happened.

"It'll be okay," he said out loud, settling his hands on the wheel and waiting for them to stop shaking. He said it again, willing himself to believe it, faking it to make it so.

◆   ◆   ◆

Later that morning, the police released the delivery guy with an apology. It turned out there wasn't a warrant out for his arrest after all. Damn computers must have their wires crossed! Still, if he hadn't rolled through that stop sign in the first place, the officer wouldn't have had cause to pull him over, and this whole mess could have been—

"I didn't roll," said the delivery guy through his teeth. He was a short man with a thick, red neck. "I never roll."

The officer pushed back his cap, happy to detain him for a longer conversation. Boxelder was still in the interview room with Veedy, and the officer was looking at this like a competition: whoever could buttonhole their guy the longest would win. Win what? A favor of some sort. Rumor had it that Boxelder would run WITSEC once the current boss retired. An IOU from him would be no mean prize.

"Your hood didn't pop up," said the officer. "That's how you can tell a full and complete stop. Hood goes…pop." He offered to provide a demonstration with the cruiser in the back lot, if the guy cared to follow him.

"No, thank you," said the delivery guy in a strangled voice.

"Next time, then," said the officer, opening the door for the guy. "Because I still don't think you get the idea. I still don't think you know how to stop."

Chapter 11

Stranger Comes (Back) to Town

"I can't let you in."

"But you invited me."

"This is a mistake," said Kate. "We should have just talked over the phone."

Zeeshan shook his head. "Phones will betray you."

"This looks bad, you coming here."

Last week, walking out of the diner, Kate had been sure they were at an impasse. She made it all of three blocks before regret seeped into her mind. *That's it?* she thought, disgusted with herself. One disagreement and you give up on seeing your daughter, maybe forever?

Zeeshan was right about one thing: she did assume the worst of everybody. For someone who spent her days performing acts of charity, she was remarkably uncharitable. What would happen if she gave Zeeshan another chance, an actual chance this time? What would happen if she tried to see the situation from his point of view? He wasn't interested in killing her, apparently. So why not try again? These were peace talks, and it wasn't unusual to start off at opposite ends of Camp David. That didn't mean they couldn't struggle their way toward some hard-won accord. Maybe that would happen today, in fact. And maybe Zeeshan would bring along another packet of reparations.

They were at her mother's house. When she'd invited Zeeshan over, it had seemed like a good idea. Home court advantage. With her mother off to Monte Carlo night at the gymnasium, they'd have a little privacy—but now, as Kate scanned the row houses across the street, looking for parted curtains, shadows hovering behind blinds, she realized there was no such thing as privacy. Who knew who was watching? She was already the talk of the street, she knew. You couldn't lose your husband, even under normal circumstances, without inciting rumors. You couldn't move back to your childhood home without gathering gossip. What would the neighbors say about this man on her porch? And what if one of them knew who he was?

"It'll look like we're consorting," she said.

"Exactly. Consorting to straighten out this misunderstanding."

"That's not what consorting means."

"It can mean that."

Kate didn't think so, but Zeeshan had a slight British accent, which made him seem like an authority on the language. Still: "It's not what people around here think it means, and that's what counts."

She should close the door on him. Show the peepers she was not going to welcome the man who wanted to kill her husband into her home. Former husband. Former home. Whatever—the point would be to show everyone she was cutting herself off from all things Veedy. Only then would these people let her be home again.

But Ana. Think of Ana. If there was the smallest chance of untangling an actual misunderstanding—

Zeeshan lifted a foil package. "I made coffeecake."

"This is a mistake," Kate said again, but just then she wasn't sure what the mistake was, exactly—talking with Zeeshan, or listening to the Program when they said her family needed protection from a scrawny gentleman who made sweets.

Kate stepped aside and Zeeshan limped across the threshold. Before closing the door, she swept her eyes across the street, already preparing her defense in case a neighbor asked about her visitor.

◆ ◆ ◆

Here's what the Program didn't tell her when she decided to stay in Baltimore: you can leave your home, or your home can leave you.

Of course, Kate wouldn't have believed that at the time. Not until
her relatives—the cousins and aunts and uncles who had consoled her
with Berger cookies and too-tight hugs and it's-not-your-faults right after
Ben and Ana left—became scarce. At least her old friends hadn't even
pretended to be there for her. They'd kept their distance from the moment
Ben got arrested. Sometimes she could get one of them on the phone, but
only a moment would pass before they "had to run," and although they
had vague plans that prevented them from getting together anytime soon,
they hoped their paths crossed before too long!

Were they afraid she was going to hit them up for money? Or that her
trouble was contagious?

It was Father Anthony who finally gave her an answer. Every time
Kate asked about returning to duty as a Eucharistic Minister—when she
had asked for a little time off, she was thinking days, not *months*—he told
her to take more time, get adjusted to her new life. A few days after her
first meeting with Zeeshan, she cornered Father Anthony after Mass and
demanded to know why everyone was treating her like a leper.

Father Anthony looked toward his office. Kate thought he was about
to break away, so she grabbed the sleeve on his vestment, but he surprised
her by coming right out with it. "Kate, these folks, they heard what happened—some version of it, anyway—and they think…" He shook his head.
"They think you're mixed up with something bad. And they're afraid if
you come around, someone else will come by later, asking them what they
know about you."

"I'm not mixed up with anything anymore," insisted Kate. "I'm
unmixed."

Father Anthony didn't say anything.

"Look, if someone was after me, wouldn't he have gotten me by now?
It's not like I'm in hiding."

"Kate, I hear you—"

"So tell *them*."

He looked pained. Father Anthony was a kind man, but he never let that stand in the way of honesty. Up to now, Kate had always appreciated that about him. "If it were any other ministry," he started, then shook his head again. "I can't make people open their homes to you."

They may not open their homes to her, but she would open her home to Zeeshan. Welcome the stranger. That's what the Bible said. Love your enemy. Besides, if they already thought she was mixed up with Zeeshan and his boss, what did she have to lose?

◆　　◆　　◆

On the back of a manila envelope, Zeeshan drew lines and boxes to represent four city blocks around the warehouse. "Most of it is abandoned. A couple of years ago, there were only a few businesses left—a TV/VCR repair shop, a bean cannery and Veedy's warehouse."

"Warehouse," said Kate. "The one with a porn shop?"

Zeeshan nodded. He took a bite of coffee cake, cupping a hand below his chin to catch the crumbs. Behold the fearsome assassin. "Property values had bottomed out. The remaining owners thought they were stuck, but then one day, a buyer came along and offered a decent price."

"Who?"

"The city."

"Why?"

"That's what I'm trying to figure out." He took a drink of coffee, crinkling his eyes at the heat. "The bean people took the first offer. The TV/VCR man said no, thank you. He'd been in his building for thirty years. Had a shop at the ground level, apartment above, freight elevator in between. Nobody had seen him outside the building in a decade, and rumor was that he was too big to get out the door. The city raised the offer, but he swore they would get it over his dead body." Another sip. "And they did."

"You're not suggesting—"

"Stroke. City had to knock a hole in his wall to haul him out." Zeeshan tapped the map. "Which left Veedy as the last holdout. The city raised its offer one more time, but he wouldn't consider it."

"Why not?"

"Extenuating circumstances," he said, "which I will get to in time." He reached for another nugget of coffeecake and Kate caught his scent, a pipe shop smell of cloves and cardamom. "When they realized they couldn't buy him out, they indicted him as a common nuisance to the community."

That sounded like an accurate description of a porn shop to Kate, not to mention Veedy's shadier dealings. But wait: "What community? By that point, the block was a ghost town."

Zeeshan licked a smudge of blueberry off his thumb. "You should have been his lawyer," he said. "Veedy's man argued free speech. I think he was angling for a Supreme Court case. Veedy was the one who looked into the city's land use statutes and figured out he wasn't within a thousand yards of anything that could be considered a community."

"Bully for him," she said. "But what does any of this have to do with Ben?"

"Maybe nothing. Maybe everything. Your husband was arrested only weeks after the city's case against Veedy fell apart."

Kate tried to put the pieces together in her mind but they wouldn't fit. The common nuisance charges came from the city. The new stuff—trafficking charges against Veedy, Ben in witness protection, all of it connected to the migrants in the van—was federal. "Why would the Feds care about city business?"

Zee shrugged. "One branch of government tries to uproot Veedy and fails. A month later, another branch comes after him. If he ends up going to prison on trafficking charges, they can bring a civil suit against him and seize his assets, including the warehouse they wanted in the first place. Does that sound like a coincidence to you?"

"What it sounds like," said Kate, "is a naughty boy crying about how everyone picks on him. I'm sure you think Ben is just picking on your boss, too. Have you considered the possibility that you're getting what you deserve?"

Zeeshan tucked his chin to his collarbone. His expression was flat, almost absent. Where did he go when he looked this way?

"You know," Kate said, "for a guy who says he wants to explain, you're leaving a lot of stuff out. The people in the van. Veedy's other business concerns. The 'extenuating circumstances.'"

Zeeshan's eyes focused on her again. "If I told you everything, would you believe me?"

Kate shrugged.

"I won't bother telling you then," he said. Then he surprised her by standing and tipping his head toward the door. "I'll show you."

Chapter 12
Perishable

Pete sat in his truck, drinking his coffee. Picking a grain off his tongue. Watching rain speckle the windshield. Giving the girl plenty of time to look out her front window and see him at the bottom of the drive.

He had tried calling her ahead of this visit, but the phone just rang and rang. The last thing he wanted was to ambush anyone. Witnesses could be jumpy. And even if they knew you were coming, all it took was one nosy neighbor to start asking questions—Who's that guy? What's he doing there?—for a cover story to show its seams.

As a general rule, questions were not helpful. Attracting interest? Also not helpful. Keep it boring, that was Pete's motto.

But when the boss tells you to deliver a message in person, you deliver a message in person.

Pete had a bad feeling. He didn't know what he was about to walk into, but he did know that Ana didn't want to see him; she'd made that clear at the hospital. And the thing was, he got it. He really did. It had been over eleven years since Pete sat by his daughter's side in the hospital, but he remembered every visitor, every useless offer, every cliché phrase from every stupid mouth. They meant well, he knew, but each visit felt like an imposition. Or voyeurism. But when he told his wife he wished the visitors would piss off, she drew back. "Who wants to be alone at a time like this?" she said.

Pete, for one. When he was hurt, or afraid, or ashamed, he curled into himself. His daughter had been like him in that way: a brooder, a wound-licker. On a bad day, she would climb into the cabinet in the bathroom and hold onto the drain pipe like it was a carousel bar—so it wasn't a stretch to think his daughter would feel the same way in the hospital, wanting to hide from these visitors.

Not that he had any way of knowing what she wanted. His daughter had gone into a coma a few hours after she was admitted. The whole thing happened so fast. At dinner, she'd pushed her nuggets around her plate, saying she wasn't hungry. She started shivering before bedtime, and Pete and Leah joked about who would take first watch on Vomit Patrol. When blotches appeared on her arms, Pete said, "Do you think we should take her in?"

Leah said, "To the emergency room?"

They were good parents. They prided themselves on not overreacting, and so far they'd raised a tough kid. She'd weathered worse than this, they decided. If she was still sick in the morning, they'd call Dr. Leffler.

They decided. Together.

His wife woke him around eleven. "She's having trouble breathing. Do you think we should . . . ?"

His daughter was wild as he carried her to the car, thrashing and screaming at him to leave her alone, he was choking her. Her skull struck his mouth, cutting him so deeply that the inside of his bottom lip still has a ridge he can trace with his tongue. By the time Pete got her buckled in, he was wet with spit and tears. She screamed all the way to the hospital.

That was the last time he heard her voice. That night she withdrew into the cabinet of herself and never came out. Seven weeks later, she died.

Pete and Leah tried not to blame each other. On the night their daughter got sick, they'd made all their decisions together. They reminded each other of this fact until it seemed like togetherness was the problem. After the funeral Pete wanted to curl up alone with his grief, and by the time that feeling passed, Leah was gone. The city was a tiger pit of bad memories, so he asked for a transfer to Indiana, where no one would inflict a single condolence.

Now he looked at the farmhouse and wished that he smoked. It would give him a reason to stay out here a few minutes longer.

You know, you have pictures, you have 8mm movies, you can see your child as she was, but after a while you can't remember how she *sounded.* Who thinks to record a kid's voice? Who thinks that will be the thing you forget?

"Enough," he told himself out loud. "Enough of that."

The truck door groaned when he opened it. The rain picked up, of course.

What happened to your father, it's not my fault, he should have told Ana back in the hospital. *It's not your fault, either.*

He tossed the last tarry sip of coffee into the grass before starting toward the porch.

But we should blame each other, anyway.

The grass soaked his cuffs. Wind gusted and rain fell into his ear.

If we blame each other, maybe we'll figure out how to forgive one another.

The porch steps groaned under his feet. Too late to tell her any of that now. Ana wouldn't want to hear about forgiveness, especially after what he had to tell her.

◆   ◆   ◆

When Ana opened the door, it was clear she'd just woken up. Not from a catnap, either. Deep lines on her face like it had been grilled, and she was rubbing hard at one eye. It looked infected. Or maybe she was high, which would explain why she was passed out at four in the afternoon. Pete waited for her to invite him in, but she just stood in the doorway, grinding away on that eye. Finally, he said, "Mind if I come in?"

She glanced behind her.

"Don't worry if it's a mess," he said. "I'm sure I've seen worse."

But when she opened the door and stepped back, he was surprised. It was...clean. No clutter at all. Might have been even more spartan than Pete's duplex, which was saying something. All he saw in that front room was a couch and a TV on the floor. And Ben, asleep in an overstuffed chair with his feet propped on an end table.

"Sorry," whispered Pete. "If I'd known he was sleeping—"

"The horse pills he's on? You could run a jackhammer and he wouldn't notice."

A ratty quilt was draped over Ben's legs, another around his shoulders. Pillows stuck out from his hips like shims. His head was wrapped in a brown scarf, and he was snoring lightly. He looked like a shabby king, or maybe just a piece of furniture bundled up for moving.

"He doesn't like his bed?" said Pete.

"Loves it. Wants to stay in it all the time. But he can only lay on his back on account of his hurt shoulder, so…"

"Bedsores?"

She rubbed her eye again, which he took for confirmation.

He didn't want to deliver his boss's message in front of Ben, even if he was unconscious. Especially if he was unconscious. Somehow that made it worse, talking about him like he was a specimen. Pete cleared his throat. "I was wondering—could I get a glass of water?"

This earned him an eye roll, but she moved toward the kitchen. He followed, telling himself to just come out with it. Speak plain and leave quickly.

When she opened the cabinet, he noticed it was pretty sparse. Only a couple of dishes and bowls on the shelves. One bowl, actually. Although that might just be practical. How much dishware do you really need when it's just two of you? Pete had a full set of Corelle in the duplex, but the plates on the bottom of the stack hadn't been used in…well, they'd never been used. Just for show. Letting him believe that his table might one day be full.

She gave him a glass of lukewarm tap water and watched him drink it. Some people had a way of putting you at ease. This girl had the other way. After finishing, he waggled the glass. "Where should I put this?"

She took the glass from him, opened the garbage can, and dropped it in.

Pete said, "Uh—"

She shrugged in a jagged, defiant way. "The dishes, the cleaning—I couldn't keep up."

"So you just...?" He pointed at the garbage can. She nodded. He opened the refrigerator. No milk. No moldy takeout. Not even a solitary pickle in a jar. Just cold light on naked shelves.

"What do you eat?" he asked.

She leaned back against the counter and crossed her arms.

"Ana?" He gentled his voice. "Are you eating?"

"That's your question?"

"Well, are you?"

She turned to the side, as if addressing someone next to her. "He could say, 'How are things going?' He could say, 'Sorry everything's so fucked up.' But no. Fatty wants to know, 'What's the food situation around here?'"

"That's not why I came by."

"Then state your business, asshole."

Pete took a breath. What he was about to do might be the worst thing he'd ever done. Certainly the ugliest. "I'm supposed to deliver this message to your father, but I know he's having trouble, uh, communicating. I'm hoping he can understand you, though." He dipped his head. "Can he?"

She shrugged.

God, she wasn't going to make this easy, was she? "Look," said Pete. "I need you to remind him of our deal. He agreed to testify, we agreed to protect him."

She nodded slowly. *Yeah, and?*

"So he's got to testify. In May."

Ana stopped nodding. "What if he can't?"

"If he can't hold up his end of the bargain, then we can't, either."

"Hold on," said Ana. "You're not talking about kicking him out of the Program, are you?"

"I hope it doesn't come to that."

"But you *would*. That's what you're saying, right? After dragging us out here, you would abandon us and..." Her eyes tracked across the wall as she followed this line of thought. "He'd be exposed. Outed. You're talking about a fucking death sentence."

That was essentially Pete's reaction when Boxelder gave him this message. Pete argued that the witness needed more time and support, not pressure. If Ben couldn't recover in time, why not just move back the trial?

Boxelder flatly refused. The trial was in May for a whole constellation of reasons that were beyond Pete's pay grade, he said. And while he appreciated Pete's concern for this witness, Boxelder had the entire Program to think about. You let one guy weasel out of testifying, and all of a sudden you've got an outbreak of laryngitis among your witnesses. Overnight, you become nothing more than a retirement plan for organized criminals. No, what this witness needed was a reminder of his deal. And a stiff dose of motivation. And Pete would deliver it, or he would get a reminder of his own.

"I'm sorry," Pete told Ana. "I really—"

"You should go." She looked down at the linoleum, still hugging herself. "I have homework or something."

He went. He drove around the back roads with a troubled mind until he found himself pulling into the IGA. He grabbed a cart and started filling it up. He thought: something easy. Spaghetti and sauce. Tuna and mayo. Hungry-Man meals. He thought: non-perishables. Soup, Boyardees, peanut butter, pickles, saltines. He thought: healthy. Creamed corn, green beans, those long silver cans of asparagus, mixed fruit in light syrup.

The cashier asked if he was stocking up a bunker. He said, "More or less."

By the time he got back to the farmhouse, it was dark. He was hoping Ana might help him carry in the bags, and in turn he could help her put away the groceries. Maybe tell her the message wasn't coming from him, and that he would do everything in his power to help her and her father—but she didn't answer the door, so he hauled the bags up to the porch himself.

Then he found himself back in the Bronco, looking at the house and wondering what to do. Knock one more time? Leave a note? What if the bags sat out overnight and a raccoon tore into them?

That's when Ana appeared on the porch, looking like a stick figure in her father's undershirt, bare legs poking out. He was about to raise his hand in a sturdy goodbye when she picked up a bag and struck out barefoot across the yard in the path of the security light.

"You gotta be kidding me," said Pete.

As she struggled to open the trash barrel by the outbuilding, her shirt rode up in back. For a second he was embarrassed for her, but after she dumped the bag into the barrel, she flipped up her shirttail and the security light shone on her bare ass. When she sneered over her shoulder, there could be no doubt: he was being mooned.

"Jesus Christ," growled Pete. He twisted the key in the ignition and backed out in a hurry, thinking, what a waste. What a shame. Of all the crazy useless destructive shit.

Thinking: if I'm not here, maybe she'll stop putting on a show and take the rest of the bags inside.

Knowing: that's not the kind of girl she was.

Chapter 13
The Extenuating Circumstance

Picture Kashmir, Zeeshan told Kate. Villages like nests in the foothills of the Himalayas. Snowmelt lakes as dark as slate.

Nearly fifty years ago, the British left the territory, but not before carving up their colony like a drunken Solomon into the new countries of India and Pakistan. The lines of partition weren't clear around the Himalayas, though, and both new countries laid claim to the territory. "But it didn't matter," said Zeeshan. "We would never consider ourselves Indian or Pakistani, just as we never considered ourselves British. Only Kashmiri."

They were in his car, driving to the warehouse. The darkness between streetlights grew longer and longer. Kate had felt in control—she was getting what she wanted, after all—right up until she got into his smoke-gray Mercedes and realized that no one knew where she was going. If she didn't come home tonight, her mother wouldn't have the first clue where to look. Essentially, Kate was a hostage on stand-by.

But Zeeshan was still explaining, so maybe he wasn't taking her captive. Or maybe he was trying to keep her calm and distracted so she didn't mess up his car.

Decades of fighting between India and Pakistan had made Kashmir a difficult place to live, he told her. One side or the other was always occupying villages and slaughtering livestock to feed their troops. By the time Zeeshan left his village for America, Kashmir was depressed in every sense.

They passed under the Baltimore–Washington parkway. Cars drummed overhead, and then the Mercedes was drifting up West Ostend past ghost factories and blind row houses. Kate tried to swallow, but her throat was gummed up. "The people in the van," she said. "They're from Kashmir."

"And Jammu. Neighboring territory."

For a moment she kept her mouth shut. Then she figured, screw it, if he was going to hurt her, he'd already decided to do it, no point in being scared or hesitant. "So the prosecutors are right," she said. "You're a human trafficker."

"No more than Oskar Schindler. Or Sojourner Truth."

"I'm pretty sure Schindler didn't pimp out his charges as soon as they made it to America."

His face darkened. A muscle flickered in his jaw. "Is that what they are saying?"

"That's what they're saying."

"The ya:tri are my brothers and sisters. I would never—" He closed his eyes briefly, and when he opened them again, he was once again the guy who had offered her coffee cake. "In the villages, troops are always coming through. It is a hard place to grow up. Especially hard to be a girl." He caught her eye, making sure she understood him. "The whole point of our operation is to take them away from danger. I'm not going to let that happen to them here."

Away from danger. Kate had heard that promise from another man who dealt in exodus. And just look how that relo was working out for her family.

Zeeshan parked under a busted streetlight. He opened her door, a gesture that seemed gentlemanly until he put his hand on her elbow, moving her forward with a light touch. She looked around, trying to memorize her surroundings in case—what? In case she had to describe it to police afterward? In case there was an afterward?

Half the block was rubble. The bean cannery looked like it was waiting for permission to collapse into itself. The only sign of life was a murky light in a far window: the porn shop at the end of the world.

As she walked, her head felt like it was floating a foot above her shoulders. Down there was Zeeshan, slipping a hand into his jacket pocket. Over there was something scurrying into the storm drain. And there, at last, was the warehouse.

They came through a roll-up door into a cavernous space filled with dust and the droppings of an entire ecosystem. Kate steeled herself as Zeeshan guided her toward a corrugated wall.

The warehouse was empty. No van, nobody else in sight.

There was nothing to show her.

Please was a slow bubble rising in her throat, but it never made it to her mouth. About ten steps from the wall, Zeeshan's grip tightened on her arm, bringing her to a stop. "Wait here," he said.

From his jacket pocket, he pulled out a dull lump. In that moment, Kate wanted only to walk out of here. She didn't care what it would take to live, what it would cost her or anybody else, she would give it now and deal with regret later—and in that moment, she finally understood Ben. Why he'd joined the Program. Why he hadn't wavered, even when she told him she wouldn't be coming with him. He thought it was the only way to stay alive.

Zeeshan walked to the wall and placed the lump against the corrugated steel. Something on the other side of the wall went *chnk*.

He used the magnet to drag aside a sheet of corrugated steel, revealing a freight elevator. "This is why Veedy wouldn't sell," he said. "This is the extenuating circumstance. The building itself."

From the written statement of D.W. Boxelder:

Less than a week after he stumbled upon the van in the warehouse, Ben was arrested on charges of money laundering. His trip to Central Booking, per my request, was a rough one. The frisk was aggressive, the cuffs were tight, and instead of driving him downtown in a cruiser, the arresting officers tossed him in the back of a paddy wagon. The seats were torn out and the windows covered with cardboard, but at least he was alone. At first, anyway. For the next six hours, the officers drove around the city, arresting homeless men for bullshit infractions. It was a hot day, but the officers kept the windows closed and the stink built up like a fog bank in the back of the wagon.

One guy screamed the entire time. Another guy pinched everyone within reach. And one dude sat silently, beatifically, producing the worst smells Ben had ever experienced. When the wagon finally parked at Central Booking, the screaming guy tried to kick open the back doors and shit himself in the process. It didn't make the van smell any worse.

(How do I know all of this? A legitimate question, Madame Inspector. Consider my considerable resources, the ubiquity of modern surveillance, my facility with witnesses. Consider, too, what I do for a living: Create characters, redirect lives, and anticipate complications, all in service of allowing a truth to come out. My fundamental duty is *to know.* Call it bullshit if you want, but this kind of omniscience is practically a job requirement.)

Inside, Ben was strip-searched and the admitting officer confiscated his Montblanc. "Can't have you stabbing anybody," he said, admiring the pen in a way that told Ben he would never see it again. The first set of fingerprints came out smeared—"Oopsie," said the officer with a smirk—so they took a second set. These looked even worse, but they faxed them downtown anyway.

When it was Ben's turn to use the phone, he called the lawyer that Veedy had told him to use if he ever ran into a problem. "Don't say a word until I get there," said the lawyer. "I mean to anyone."

"Got it."

"Apparently not, because I still hear you talking."

Ben said nothing.

"That's more like it," said the lawyer, and hung up. An officer led Ben to a holding cell, and you can imagine his joy at finding his friends from the paddy wagon waiting there for him.

When he was called to the interview room, Ben could not have moved out of the pen faster, though the pinching guy provided some extra incentive. The lawyer was waiting on him. On a closed-circuit television I watched him tell Ben not to worry about the security cam by the door; their conversation was protected by attorney-client privilege. (I love technicalities, Madame. They make people so careless.) There was a bit of a hold-up in processing Ben's fingerprints—apparently they were hard to read—so it might be a while before downtown could look up his criminal record and allow him to be released. The good news was that the arrest seemed like a bluff. As long as Ben kept his mouth shut, he'd probably be fine. Best case? Walk away clean. Worst case—and this was the absolute worst case, if the cops somehow figured out everything—Ben would spend a couple of years at a white-collar prison upstate, a racket club with razor wire.

Which was precisely the A.D.A.'s threat when he and I walked into the room. "We know who you are," the A.D.A. began. "We know what you do, and who you work for." If Ben came clean, he said, he could guarantee immunity, protection, a fresh start.

I nodded along, but didn't interrupt, because the A.D.A. had yet to reveal the other end of the deal, the stick at the end of the carrot. If Ben didn't turn state's witness, he said, he was looking at prison. "You'll miss your daughter's last years at home," he said, looking at Ben over the top of his glasses. "What kind of father would that make you?"

The A.D.A.'s play was ham-handed, headlong, toothless. For my purposes, it was fine.

Ben barely glanced at his lawyer before saying, "No comment."

The A.D.A., a friend from Columbia Law, tried a few other hacky moves on Ben, but they were no more effective than his initial gambit, and eventually the A.D.A. threw up his hands and abandoned the interview room.

And then there were three: Ben, his lawyer, and me.

The lawyer turned to me. He looked like a latter-day Teddy Roosevelt: Burly and begutted, with little granny glasses that made him look slightly cross-eyed. A huffy little fireplug. He said, "What are you?"

"Director-designate of Witness Security."

He gave me a tight smile. "Surely," he said, "you didn't think your services would be needed here."

"I was at dinner with my friend," I said, waving toward the door to indicate the departed A.D.A., "and he told me about your client. I wanted to meet him."

Ben's eyebrows lifted. He was, if I'm not mistaken, flattered.

"You met him," said the lawyer flatly. "Why are you still here?"

I covered up a yawn. "My buddy and I are going out for drinks after he finishes his paperwork. Right now, I don't have anywhere else to be."

"Well, I do," said the lawyer, grabbing Ben by the arm. "So does he."

"Your client is free to go back to the holding pen any time he wants," I said. "Or he can stay in here. Provided he's supervised."

What followed was a hushed argument between Ben and his lawyer. Teddy Bear wanted him to go back to the pen, of course, and Ben said that was easy for him to say when his rosy ass wasn't getting goosed. Until his fingerprints were deciphered, Ben would stay in here with the decent chair and the near-total lack of crazy people, thank you very much. I assured them both that the business portion of the meeting was over. "It's fine," I told his lawyer. "We're just a couple of guys, talking."

Talking. That's all we were doing. The talk was easy and pleasant enough (at least between me and Ben; Teddy Bear sat there with his briefcase on his lap like a grump) but the conversation didn't really take off until football came up. Turned out, we both grew up watching the Colts. The *real* Colts, the Baltimore Colts. "I don't recommend this," said the lawyer, strangling the handle of his briefcase. "Any of this."

"You can go," said Ben. "Look, the instant this guy brings up any business, I'll shut it down." He glanced at me. "Nothing personal."

"We strongly advise against it," said the lawyer with a meaningful look.

I understood that Veedy was the silent partner in the royal *we*, but did Ben? I think not, given how lightly Ben brushed him off, saying he could take care of himself. Teddy made a big show of leaving, giving Ben plenty of time to reconsider, but my new friend was already reminiscing about Johnny U throwing down the seam to a loping John Mackey. Oh, and the game where the third-string quarterback came in with the plays written in pen on his forearm, and beat the Rams to lead the Colts to the playoffs? Brilliant. Then there were the villains: Joe Fucking Namath, the crybaby John Elway, and the bastard Robert Irsay, who stole the team from the city under the cover of night in 1984. "Motherfucker," said Ben as softly as a benediction. I echoed the sentiment. By this time the lawyer was gone.

Sometime later, an officer knocked and poked his head in the door. "Good news," he said to Ben. "Your sheet came back. Hey, did you know you have no criminal record? That's the cleanest sheet I've ever seen. Probably not for long, though, huh? Ha ha. Anyway, you're free to go."

I shook hands with Ben and told him how much I'd enjoyed his company.

"Likewise," said Ben, "though of course you know this won't change my answer."

"Oh," I said, "I think it will."

He stopped shaking my hand, but I didn't let him go. I said, "Everyone in Central Booking saw me come in here with you. Your lawyer knows you requested to talk with me alone. That information has probably found its way to Veedy by now. What will he think we talked about?"

Ben's voice was stiff. "We talked about football."

"The second in command at WITSEC took more than *two hours* out of his busy schedule to talk football with a suspect?" I wrinkled my nose. "Doesn't sound very believable when you say it out loud, does it?"

Ben didn't answer.

"In a matter of hours," I went on, "Veedy will see you as a threat. Tell me you understand what that means."

Ben looked sick. I was sure I had him. But he surprised me by slipping away his hand and tugging on his French cuffs, until the silver links peeked out from his blazer. "You have my answer," he said stiffly. "I won't reconsider."

I can't lie, Madame: This was disappointing. I thought he was smart enough to see how this would play out, but I guess that kind of foreknowledge was beyond him. Or maybe he simply wouldn't allow himself to look that far ahead, at least not until he got to Morocco, at which point his daughter would call it paranoia.

In any case, I had to cut him loose. He trusted Veedy more than he trusted my prediction. I can't help but wonder, though, if Ben regretted his choice the next week. When he heard his bedroom window slide open. When he rolled over to see a rough ball wobble across the floor. I wonder if he recalled my prediction in that moment. If he had a pulse of regret right before the ball exploded into a bright new universe.

Chapter 14
Ya:tri

Underground, the hidden room of the warehouse seemed like nothing more than the lowest level of a parking garage—concrete ribs overhead, mysterious wet spots, low yellow light, stale air, desolation—but in the middle of the floor was a cargo van. As Zeeshan started toward it, he told Kate to stay back by the freight elevator.

The van was boxy and windowless, like the one that had taken Ben and Ana away from Baltimore. Kate hated this kind of van.

When Zeeshan opened the sliding door, bodies stirred inside the van. How many were in there? Seven, eight? Could be more: the seats had been removed, people were just piled on the floor. And, Jesus, they were teenagers! A few might be older than Ana, but none looked over twenty. Kids. They might not think of themselves that way—Kate certainly hadn't when she was a mother at eighteen, and Ana probably didn't think of herself as a kid after everything she'd been through—but that's what they were.

A couple of kids poked their heads out of the doorway, looking sleepy and tangle-haired, but not freaked out. Then Zeeshan gestured behind him, and they disappeared into the shadows of the cabin, quick as fish, except for one. A tall girl. She straightened up and glared at Kate. Full of piss and venom, Kate could tell. In that instant, the rest of Kate's fear dissipated and she felt motherly, fierce.

Zee leaned in the doorway, speaking in a fast, clipped tone, failing to notice Kate until she was at his side. "Hey," she said softly into the cabin. "Hello."

They all went still. Zee gave her an irritated look. "I didn't call for you."

"Good thing I don't need to be told what to do." She turned back to the passengers, pressed against the far wall. "Do any of you speak English?"

Silence. That was a problem. She couldn't exactly ask Zeeshan to translate, seeing as how the whole point of this trip was to figure out if she could trust his version of events. How was she supposed to know if—

"Leave us alone."

It was the tall girl, the one who had glared at her. Her face was drawn, her lips cracked. Kate turned to Zee. "Do they have water?"

"The more they drink, the more they have to go, which is … problematic on this leg of the trip. Later, I'm told, there will be plenty of water."

He directed this last part to the passengers as much as to Kate, who was digging through her handbag, pushing aside her pocketbook, tubes of lipstick, a curl of receipts, until she found a squat can of ginger ale. Some nights her stomach burned with worry and anger, and only ginger ale would help. She offered it to the tall girl. "This is warm, but you're welcome to have it."

The girl didn't move. Zeeshan told Kate to put it away. "You're complicating things," he said, and then the girl grabbed the can and snapped it open without a word of thanks, proving, to Kate's mind, that some teenage qualities are universal. The girl passed the can around the van, and they all took noisy sips.

"What's your name?" Kate asked the tall girl.

The can came back to the girl, and she tipped it over her mouth, shaking out the last drops.

"Where are you going?" said Kate.

The girl licked her lips. A few of the others glanced at Kate, but said nothing. Finally, Zeeshan answered for her. "Moscow. She's got a job lined up in a restaurant—"

"Moscow?" said Kate, picturing shipping containers, rough passage across the Bering Strait on the heels of a grueling trip across America in the back of a cargo van. If this girl was going to Russia, why the hell did they route her through Baltimore?

"Moscow, *Idaho*," said the girl, narrowing her eyes in derision.

You little snot, thought Kate, but she kept the irritation out of her voice as she asked her, "What will you be doing there?"

"Four years."

Kate cocked her head. The girl imitated her, enjoying the chance to treat her like an idiot. Zee took Kate's elbow again. "Time to go."

She tried to pull away, but he tightened his grip. Not enough to hurt her, but enough to show that he could. "We can't be here when the next driver shows up."

Kate started to protest, but was distracted by the tall girl. "Miss," she was saying, "Miss," and Kate turned back to the van, thinking this is it, now she'll tell me what I want to know, but the girl was only waggling the empty can in the air. "Got any more?"

◆   ◆   ◆

On the way back to the rowhouse, the road was empty and dark, but Kate hardly noticed. She thought about the kids in the van. Were they hungry? What happened when they had to use the bathroom? Zee hadn't asked them if they needed anything, but that might not be a sign of cruelty as much as typical male obliviousness.

Ben was the same way. If he wasn't hungry, it didn't occur to him that anyone else might want to eat. When Ana was a toddler, he would occasionally take her to the park for the afternoon. As much as Kate appreciated a few hours of quiet (though she never got to rest; it was just a chance to catch up on housework), she dreaded the inevitable slumping return, Ana's face streaked with tears, Ben all mystified and hurt, wondering why his daughter was repaying his kindness with a huge tantrum.

Gee, Ben, when was the last time you fed her? Changed her? Gave her some juice?

Back then, Kate knew what Ana needed. If Ana came running toward her parents, Kate knelt and opened her arms, secure in the knowledge that her daughter was coming to her. But something shifted in junior high. Ana started going to the Tippy directly after school, doing her homework at the bar, marking her page in *Lord of the Flies* with a cherry stem. In eighth grade she started working as a hostess, and Kate no longer had to pick her up at dinnertime, which Ana and Ben presented like it was some great favor. Kate pretended it was fine, because to do otherwise would have appeared small, selfish.

Parenting doesn't seem like a competition until you are losing.

Once in a while, Ben and Ana invited her to the Tippy, told her she was welcome to hang out in the evenings, but that would have been pathetic. What was she supposed to do, watch them like a spectator? Roll up her sleeves and wash dishes? *She didn't want to be there.* So Kate spent her evenings at the church or in the homes of shut-ins, and Ana spent her evenings at the Tippy. They saw each other at the breakfast table if they were lucky, but most days were not lucky. Thinking about it now—all that time apart, all the missed opportunities—made Kate ache, but did Ana feel the same way? Did Ana think about her at all?

"Is it worth it?" she asked Zeeshan as he pulled up to the curb by her mother's house. "Tearing these kids away from their families? Selling them into slavery?"

"Not slavery."

"Not far off."

On the way out of the warehouse, he had explained the business model of the operation: a business owner in the states paid for travel expenses (along with a small fee, of course), and in exchange the owner got a reliable employee for four years. Well, "employee" might not be the right term, because there was no pay outside of room and board. Indentured servant, debt bondage: these were the right terms, Zeeshan insisted, not prostitution. And he would know, because this was the arrangement that had brought him to America in '86. Back then, though, there was no network of employers. Just one sponsor, and Zeeshan owed him. What could Zee do to pay off his debt to Veedy? He had been a shepherd. He could protect his flock, which sometimes entailed killing predators.

A shepherd, thought Kate. What a perfect fit for the kind of trafficking operation Zeeshan was describing. Veedy must have conducted a thorough search before landing on Zee. It wasn't a coincidence they'd ended up together; it was an arranged marriage.

"No one has ever asked to go back home," said Zee.

"Could be they feel stuck. Could be they're scared."

He glanced at her. "Of me, you mean."

"Of you, of getting caught. Having to get back in that van. Going back home to find that everyone's a stranger." Kate's throat tightened. "Could be anything."

"You're thinking about what it would be like to work in a restaurant twelve hours a day, seven days a week, month after month. Living in a tiny apartment above the store, never getting out. I'm sure that seems terrible compared to your life. But the ya:tri, they don't see it that way. They see safety, stability, even some privacy. After four years, they're free in America. They get their papers and they can go anywhere, be anyone. That's why they don't ask to go back."

Kate shook her head, tired and frustrated. "If your operation is so good, why didn't you just tell Ben about it? It would have saved a lot of trouble."

"Plausible deniability," said Zeeshan. "Each person under Veedy knows only what he needs to know in order to do his job. If he gets arrested, his trouble is small. It protects him."

"Sounds to me like it protects Veedy."

"The system worked until your husband broke the rules."

"Which you did tonight, too."

"You needed to see that the Feds are lying about the operation, and that I'm telling the truth." He looked at her directly. "Do you believe me now?"

Kate didn't answer. She was thinking. "The Feds," she said at last. "Why haven't they come after you?"

Zeeshan sighed. "Good question," he said. "Add it to the list."

◆   ◆   ◆

Kate invited Zee in for a cup of tea. She had a decision to make—could she trust him or not?—and she didn't want to put it off any longer. Not much longer, anyway. After turning on the stove, she excused herself and went to the bathroom, wanting a moment to think. In the mirror, her eyes sagged. Deep lines framed her mouth. The row of naked bulbs over the mirror wouldn't cast anyone in a flattering light, but still, she looked like she'd aged five years since Ana left.

Zee's story made sense, she had to admit. And the risks he had taken to make his case to her—well, it was convincing.

Of course, he had every motive to be convincing, and no small amount of practice in persuading desperate people to break from their families and trust him. Convincing wasn't the same as true; it was just making someone want to believe.

Kate reached up to her temple and plucked out a gray hair. Curly, thick as wire. The rest of her hair was dark blonde, limp as vellum. If she hadn't felt the pluck, she would have thought the hair belonged to somebody else.

What was happening to her? What was she becoming?

She had no answers. Everything was plausible. Everything was deniable.

Focus on the question, the one question under all the others: which story do you believe? The one where Zeeshan was a pimp? Or the one where he was a savior, and a reconciler of misunderstandings?

Kate looked in the mirror. She knew how to find out.

When she came back into the kitchen, Zeeshan hung up the phone. "Don't worry," he said with a tired smile. "It was local."

"The bomb," she started. "The one that sent Ben to the emergency room." She took a ragged breath. "I know that wasn't you."

He gave her a curious look. "What do you mean, you *know*?"

Kate went on before she could reconsider. "I wanted him to go into the Program, to move and get a fresh start, but he didn't want to go. He wasn't going to turn on Veedy. You should know that; he wasn't going to turn. He needed—" She took another breath "—a push."

"A push."

"I wasn't the only person who thought so, either. Rooster agreed with me."

"Rooster? The guy in the bus station?"

"Ben's uncle. He made the arrangements. But it was my idea. The bomb came from me."

Zeeshan blinked. He was watching her very carefully.

"So don't blame Ben for this mess," she said. "Don't blame Rooster, either—I told him to do it. If you need blood to make this right, it's mine. If you're looking to make an example of someone, it's me."

Zeeshan didn't move. The room swayed like they were at sea. Kate wondered if this would be the last scene she ever saw, her mother's kitchen, the apple peeler clamped to the counter, the Bunn coffeemaker, the hand towels draped over every handle like the flags of tired nations. If it happened here, she hoped Zeeshan wouldn't leave behind the embarrassment of a body. Let her mother think she had run away, made her own relocation.

"If you managed to send him away," Zeeshan said at last, "you can bring him back."

She could. With a single call to Ana, she could bring them both home. It's what the girl wanted, she was just waiting for the all-clear.

Kate said, "You'd do anything to protect your operation, wouldn't you?"

Zee shrugged in a way that suggested he was helpless before fate, not undecided.

"If Ben stayed on course, if he testified, you'd find a way to kill him, wouldn't you?"

"No one wants that."

That wasn't a no. But it told her what she needed to know. She couldn't be sure what would happen if she went along with Zeeshan, but she knew what would happen if she didn't. Trusting him would give them a chance to work things out. When it came down to it, that's all anyone wanted, wasn't it? Another chance? One phone call could give them all another chance.

Zeeshan let himself out, leaving behind the fat envelope with the line drawing of a blighted neighborhood. With its Xs and boxes, it looked like some kind of game, though Kate couldn't have guessed the rules, or who was winning.

Chapter 15
Lies, All Lies

Sunday afternoon, sky like a black eye. Downtown shuttered. Ana, fresh off her lunch shift at Karen's, on a payphone at the Sunoco, listening to her mother tell her exactly what she had been waiting to hear.

It's safe, her mother said. *You can both come home.*

For weeks she had been fantasizing about this call. About how she would feel a wild leap in her chest before sprinting to the farmhouse, leaving the phone swinging on the cord, pulling her father out to the Fairlane, forget the bags, leave the furniture to rot in the outbuilding, *sayonara*, Morocco, see you suckers in hell.

But now? Now that she was getting this call for real? No wild leap. No dangling phone. The cold receiver was still mashed to her ear. The wind smelled like tin.

"Ana? Hello?"

Her mother had done her homework. After meeting the ya:tri, she'd checked the records at the courthouse. The city had indeed bought up the property around Veedy's warehouse. The common nuisance suit was a swing and a miss, just as Zeeshan had claimed. It all checked out. So why wasn't Ana running to the farmhouse right now?

"Ana? This is what you wanted, right?"

Maybe that was the problem. What's more suspicious than getting exactly what you want? A year ago, she wouldn't have felt that way, but now she couldn't bring herself to trust it.

"What if it's a trap?" said Ana. "How do you know he won't try another bomb?"

A beat of silence. "That wasn't him," said her mother. "He said it wasn't anyone associated with Veedy, in fact."

That claim made so little sense she couldn't even answer. Who else would want to come after her father?

Across the street from the gas station, a door banged open. Ana looked up to see Govert, one of the Old Liars, stalk out of the White Owl with a roadie six-pack in his hand. He cracked open a can, saddled his John Deere, and pulled away from the curb without bothering to check behind him. Fortunately, the only car on the street had stopped a half-block away and was waiting for him to clear the scene. Everyone in Morocco knew to give Govert wide berth when he barreled out of the Owl.

"I don't know," said Ana.

"What don't you know?"

"I don't know what I don't know."

At the stoplight, Govert veered across the intersection and ramped over the curb onto the courthouse lawn, where he stopped long enough to drop his mower deck. Occasionally, he liked to mow messages onto public grounds. It was like skywriting, only upside down.

The cops usually picked him up before he could finish, but one summer night (according to the other Liars) he had finished a message at the police station, of all places. The sheriff, impressed by his nerve and more than a little curious to see what message Govert had for him, came out to watch the artist at work. When Govert finished, the lawn read LIES ALLIES.

The sheriff asked if he'd meant to write LIES, ALL LIES, but Govert refused to admit error. "Then who are the allies?" the sheriff wanted to know.

Govert cracked a beer and pointed a surprisingly steady finger at the sheriff. "That's the million dollar question, brother."

The sheriff confiscated the rest of his twelve-pack, gave him a cup of coffee, and made him mow the rest of the property before sending him home.

Ana's mother said, "We might not know everything, but we know enough."

"Enough?"

"If Zeeshan wanted us dead, we'd be dead." She paused. "And if you don't come home, he's going to want your father dead."

The sky rumbled, long and low. Govert stopped to lift his mower deck, then dropped it again a few feet away. He was a printer, not a cursive man. A fat raindrop hit the Sunoco roof and Ana shuddered. "Okay," she said.

"Okay you'll come home?"

"Okay I'll think about it. I have to go. Rain's starting."

In the end, only one part of Ana's daydream about this call came to pass. She loped away from the gas station, leaving the phone kicking at the end of its rope. She didn't go to the farmhouse, though, not straightaway. Before she made it to the end of the block, rain was jumping all over the street, and Ana ducked into one of the few businesses open on a Sunday afternoon, the Video Emporium.

Logan was adjusting the volume on a hanging TV. At the sound of the door chime, he looked over his shoulder. As soon as he saw her, he said, "What's wrong?"

"Nothing," she said, but Logan just raised an eyebrow, so she said, "It's just... the fucking rain, you know? They said it wasn't supposed to—"

She stopped talking when a tall, ugly kid walked out of the back room and dumped an armload of tapes on the counter. He was older than them, maybe nineteen or twenty, though he still had the acne and gangliness of a teenager. "These all need to be rewound," he told Logan.

"I rewound that batch already."

"Re-rewind them. I found one in there that started in the middle."

"Maybe that was really the beginning," said Ana, relieved to change the subject. "Sometimes directors throw you into the middle of things."

The gangly kid turned to her. He looked like he wanted to sneer, but was holding it in check with incredible effort. "Need help finding something, Miss?"

In a tired voice, Logan made introductions. "Ana, this is my brother, Jared. Jared, this is—"

"Your fag hag," finished Jared with relief. Now he could stop holding back his scorn. He pushed back his curly mop of brown hair, exposing his shaved sides, the international sign of an asshole. Ana bet he drove a black pickup, too. With a *No Fear* sticker on the back window. She bet he had a whole drawer of *Big Johnson* T-shirts. Jared said, "You gonna rent anything today, *homo hagius*, or are you just here to dispense common knowledge about directorial techniques?"

The rain drummed hard on the flat roof. Water fell from the eaves in twisting ropes. Anger rose in Ana like a black tide.

Don't, she told herself.

She turned to Logan, ignoring his brother. "Anyway," she said, "do you think you could run me home? It doesn't look like the rain is going to let up—"

Jared leaned in. "Uh, Miss? I'm afraid this employee is on duty."

"It'll take ten minutes, man," she said. "You've got zero customers."

"Including yourself, apparently," said Jared. "Which makes you a loiterer."

Ana looked at Logan like *Can you help me out here?* but he wouldn't meet her eyes. Jared went on. "Take this as your official notice to stop loitering at this place of business, or the manager"—he tapped the plastic badge sagging from his T-shirt—"will be forced to call the police."

"Bullshit," said Ana. "You're not going to call the police."

"He will," said Logan to the pile of tapes.

On cue, Jared leaned over the counter and picked up the phone.

"Okay," said Ana, lifting her hands in surrender. Backing toward the exit, she pointed at each of them in turn. "Dick," she said to Jared. "Pussy," she said to Logan. "Fuck you both."

Jared waved goodbye, grinning in delight.

That should have been the end of this little episode, but it wasn't. Running through the rain, she saw a riding mower nudged up against the sycamore on the courthouse lawn, Govert slumped over the wheel. She kept running until she got to the end of the street, but then she slowed—Goddammit, Govert—and wheeled around.

When she stepped over the curb, she saw the pattern he'd cut into the lawn, but she couldn't make out what it said.

In just a moment she would shake him awake. Make sure he was okay. Ask him for a ride home. Govert would tug a garbage sack out of his makeshift saddlebag and offer it to her as a poncho. She would consider tearing a hole in the bag for her face, but then she would just pull the whole bag over her head, lay against Govert's wide, warm back, and close her eyes in the blackness.

But first she wanted to see his message. Why not? She was already maxed out on wetness and misery, and Govert (probably) wouldn't be harmed by another minute or two of unconsciousness. She grabbed the lowest bough on the tree and scrambled up the bark.

She didn't have to climb far. CROOKS was carved in huge, neat letters. He must have been really angry, because he'd scalped the grass down to the roots. It would turn brown and die and stay that way until the spring. In case his target wasn't clear, he'd mowed a big arrow pointing at the courthouse. Actually, at that moment, it was pointing to the tree that held Ana.

Who are the crooks? Who are the allies?

Those are the million dollar questions, brother.

From the written statement of D.W. Boxelder:

The night we inducted Ben into the Program, we were all together in the ER: Ben, Kate, Ana, Sherwood, and me. By that point, Sherwood had already announced his retirement from WITSEC, but he was still hanging onto the directorship while we waited on my confirmation hearings, which had gotten hung up in the gears of bureaucracy. Most days he still came into the office to sign off on relo packages I had put together, fiddle around with his memoir, and call subcontractors to check on the construction of his retirement home on the shore. He hadn't handled an induction for months, but for some reason he wanted to run this one.

"Once," began Sherwood, "there was a Chinese bandit named Lao Fu."

Ana stood in the corner, eyes glazed, gnawing on her thumbnail.

"Lao was not only the most feared bandit in the land," said Sherwood, "he was also the ugliest. Mustache like catfish barbs. Eyebrows puffed up with scar tissue. One earlobe gone, *wsshht*, clean off."

Kate sat on the side of the hospital bed, holding Ben's hand as a nurse picked glass shards out of his arm with tweezers. The bomb had been packed with fine-gauge glass—smashed light bulbs, the forensic guys later guessed—and the blast had atomized the shards. Instead of being flayed to death, he'd basically been sandblasted. Painful, terrifying, but not lethal. We chalked it up to luck and shoddy munitions work.

"Lao was a gifted bandit, smart and fearless, and soon his face appeared on posters all over the forests of Xishuangbanna. Although he thought his likeness was uglier than necessary, he was pleased to see himself called the Bandit King, and to see the bounty go up with each new round of posters. Word got back to him that the Bandit King figured in bedtime stories as a bogeyman, snatching children who wouldn't eat their dinner or stay in bed.

"So things were going well for old Lao, and he probably would have had a long run of wealth and infamy before dying at the hands of a greedy henchman, but he made a mistake." Sherwood laced his fingers over his cardigan. "He fell in love."

Please shut up, I wanted to say. All I saw at that moment was a doddering old man holding back the very Program he'd created because he was reluctant to let go. And of course I wanted his job. Which I now have, at least until the end of your investigation, Madame.

"It happened on a routine robbery," said Sherwood. "His bandits stopped a carriage in the forest, then disarmed and disrobed all the men.

"In rode Lao Fu on his black horse like a storm. When he flung open the carriage door, he expected to see passengers cowering or trying to scramble out the other side. Instead, there was only one passenger, the angriest woman he'd ever seen in his life. Before he could say anything, she reached out and tore off a corner of his mustache."

No one laughed. Not even a smile. The nurse kept plucking shards and dropping them into a pan. Kate got up to pace the room.

Sherwood couldn't have been surprised by their (lack of) reaction. He'd done enough inductions to know that new witnesses—torn from their lives, *de facto* dead to everyone who knew them—were in shock. The fact that he aimed for a chuckle seemed at once childish and strangely brave. Thirty years on the job hadn't made him cynical. Not only did he still hope for the best—from his punch lines to the future of his witnesses—he actually seemed to expect it. Which was both admirable and embarrassing.

"Usually, Lao would have killed anyone who dared touch him, but after running off her men and stealing her goods and horses, he let her go, untouched. That act of senseless mercy, along with the soggy feeling in his chest, told him the bad news: He was infatuated.

"But what could he do? If he approached her in polite society, she'd recognize him, an instant death sentence. So after a night of chewing on the remaining half of his mustache, Lao came up with a plan. In the morning he gathered four of his bandits and told them to kidnap the best mask-maker in the land.

"The man arrived in camp, shaking so hard he could barely stand, vowing to make the most handsome mask ever crafted, but Lao stopped him. 'Make it plain,' he said. 'Make it normal.'"

Sherwood paused to let this sink in. Acting normal is the prime directive for a witness, and the hardest to follow. They're used to being anything but normal. Wealthy, powerful, above the law. All eyes on them when they walk into a room, etc. For a witness, blending in takes more than a different name; it requires a different personality. Not that this family was absorbing this lesson. They were all sunk in their own heads.

At the time, I confess, I thought this made the story a waste of time. But when I think back on this scene, I see the old man as a friendly Charon, ferrying his shell-shocked passengers away from their old lives. It didn't matter if the passengers paid attention to the story. He was giving them a few moments of transition so the next step didn't feel like a *non sequitur.* And if they did happen to catch a few words, it would give them something to clutch onto as they were drowning: Story as life preserver.

"The mask-maker created the best work of his life, so artful it looked natural. When Lao put it on, no one could even tell it was a mask.

"Well, you might guess the next part," said Sherwood. No one tried. He went on. "Lao put on the mask and spent his days courting the woman. The bandits grew jealous. They called Lao soft and grumbled about their shrinking bounty now that the Bandit King spent more time wooing than pillaging. When Lao realized that a mutiny was a matter of time, he stopped going to the forest, wore the mask night and day, and made his final leap into civil society by asking the woman to marry him.

"She said yes, and that should have been the end of the story. All he had to do for his happy ending was keep his mouth shut. Easy enough, right?"

Sherwood paused again, obviously hoping someone would say *Wrong.* I could have helped him with that, but I didn't. When he leaned back in his seat with a sigh, it seemed like he'd lost track or heart, and I was about to move on to the official part of the induction when Ana looked up at Sherwood.

Just a glance, but Sherwood and I both saw it. Ana might have been in shock, but she'd been listening. I suppose that's when I started to like this girl, when I saw that, like me, like Sherwood, she was always paying attention.

"As the wedding approached," said Sherwood, stepping up the pace, "Lao grew restless. His secret was like the tell-tale heart—you know that one?—and it was driving him mad with guilt. He loved this woman, and he didn't want to trick her into marrying him.

"So the night before the wedding he took her hand and said, 'I am not who you think I am.'

"Before she could say anything—and before he could lose his nerve— Lao peeled off the mask, which had worn so thin over time that it was little more than a warm layer of skin.

"'I don't understand,' the woman said, and Lao felt foolish, desperate, lost. Just then he didn't understand, either. Why was he risking everything? Why hadn't he kept his mouth shut?

"The woman said, 'Why would you wear a mask that looks the same as your face?'

"Lao rushed to the mirror. The scars, the ratty mustache, the old ugly face of the Bandit King: Gone. What he saw was his new face, *his* face, him."

Silence. I waited for Sherwood to keep going, to roll out a ponderous explanation of the story's lessons like he always did, but when I looked over, he had slumped back in his chair.

That's when I knew he wouldn't have much of a retirement. When his wife found him sprawled on the floor of their new home on the shore, dead of a stroke, I wasn't surprised. I may not have known how he would pass, but I saw the ending on his face that night, and I believe he saw it coming, too. At the end of that story, he took off his mask and let me see him as he truly was: Finished.

I suppose that's why I asked him to name this family. It didn't have to be done that night, and besides, he'd handed over that part of the job to me long ago, but I gave it back for one night. As much as I rolled my eyes at him, as much as I wanted to shove him out the door and get on with my confirmation hearing, I did love him, Madame. This was the man who'd plucked my application out of a leaf pile of résumés, the man who saw my talents for surveillance and prediction (the root and bud on the Tree of Paying Attention), the man who re-made me in his own image, the man who had advised the President to nominate me as his successor.

I asked Sherwood to name this family because I wanted to see the old re-creator at work one last time.

"Easterday," he said, his grizzled head tilted back against the seat. Ben and Kate were too mired in misery to notice their own christening, but Ana watched Sherwood hold up two fingers and swipe a rough cross in the air. I could never tell what degree of irony was involved in this gesture, but I suspect the old man was playing it straight. That was Sherwood to the end: Playing it straight, expecting things to work out, believing in people far more than they deserved, present company included.

"Go," he said, "and sin no more."

This should have been the end of this scene, but it wasn't. The nurse rolled away from Ben's bed, dropping her tweezers into the steel pan with a sigh. I checked my watch and called an audible. I could do the rest of the official induction later. Right now, for their own protection, we had to get this family into hiding.

Kate protested, but I told her that when Veedy found out the bomb hadn't been successful, he would send someone else to finish the job. "Zeeshan might be looking for him right now," I said.

Ben's face pulled tight. Kate looked at the floor. "I can't," she said softly, but we all missed her meaning. A lot of people say that when it's time to go. Some keep saying it as they pack their stuff into a garbage bag, as they stagger into a blackout van, repeating it like a mantra all the way through their hard first year—but Kate meant it.

"I'm sorry," she said to me for some reason. Then she looked at her husband. "I know this is the worst time to do this, but I can't—"

She shook her head, unable to finish, but this time her meaning was clear. Clear to me, anyway. Did Ben understand that his wife was not coming with him? Mostly he looked troubled that she was weeping, though he did nod once, blankly. Was he in shock? Was he, possibly, forgiving her?

Or did I detect a trace of relief in his eyes?

Ana started toward her father, but her mother caught her arm. "Don't go," said Kate.

I felt like crawling out of my own skin. I shouldn't be seeing this moment; even I knew that. This was like watching a stranger die or give birth. I had no right, but did I leave the room? I did not. I stayed. I watched.

"You don't have to go," Kate said to her daughter. "Stay with me." She was trembling, but Ana was steady as she turned and took her mother by the shoulders. Ana leaned in as though she were going to kiss her mother on the forehead—I swear that's what I thought was about to happen, or I would have stepped in right then—but when Kate squirmed, I realized that Ana was digging her nails into her mother's shoulders.

"*Judas,*" hissed Ana.

I reached for her then, but Ana spat on her mother before I could haul her and Ben into the hallway, where a posse of marshals escorted us out the back way to the van idling outside the morgue.

Ana came with Ben; Kate did not. We had made our choices, all of us; now it was time to live with them.

Chapter 16
My Love is Vengeance

"You should be more confident," Ana told Logan. They were sitting on the couch in her living room. A stained burrito wrapper lay open on the floor like the ugliest flower. Since Jared kicked her out of the video store, Logan had been coming by the farmhouse daily with goodies from the Emporium—licorice rope, Jiffy Pop, a two-liter of Dew—presenting them like offerings. Which, fine, okay, especially at first, but a little apology goes a long way, and a whole lot is just annoying.

Tonight, for instance, when he'd stared at the doormat and waggled a frozen burrito at her, she felt the urge to slam the door in his face—but she didn't want to lose his stupid company, even for a single night. In the week since her mother asked her to come home, she'd been stuck in a Hamlet loop—*To leave or not to leave?*—wearing down her nerves. At least when Logan was here, she could turn her corrosive attention on him.

"If you were more confident," she said, "you'd have so many friends. Even a boyfriend, maybe. Confidence is the number one thing of attractiveness."

He shrugged, conceding the point along with the possibility of ever having confidence.

"Take this movie," she said, pointing to the TV. *The Breakfast Club* was playing with the sound down so as not to interrupt her father's therapy. Strains of "Behind Blue Eyes" came through his bedroom door. He and the therapist kept going over the falsetto bit, but neither of them could hit the high note. She said, "Who's the most attractive guy on the cast?"

Logan chewed his thumbnail, considering. "The rebel," he said. "Judd What's-His-Face."

"Wrong. And *ew.* The correct answer is Emilio Estevez. Why? Confidence."

Logan looked at her like she was nuts. "That's all an act. Underneath, he's just as broken and messed up as the rest of them, maybe more—"

"Dude," said Ana. "What's the first rule of AV Club?"

"No spoilers. But, come on, we're talking about *The Breakfast Club* here. Everyone's seen *The Breakfast Club.*" He blinked. "Right?"

"Not everyone owns a video store, Logan."

He held up his hands in mock-surrender. "I was not aware that your previous dwelling was a moon cave. Enjoy the movie, my feral friend. Welcome to the Eighties."

Ana flipped him off, though she liked his dorky sarcasm more than she liked the Snuffleupagus shtick with the peace offerings. Logan pretended to snatch her gesture out of the air as though she'd blown him a kiss. Then he pretended to eat it. Then he acted like it was giving him terrific stomach pains, and Ana knew what was coming next. "Logan, no," she said in her sternest voice, trying to hold back her laughter. "This is not the right kind of confidence."

She was too late. He'd already started the body-rocking spasms that marked his impression of the birth scene from *Alien.* Ana gave him a look that said *I am not amused,* but Logan writhed and groaned MY GUTS OH JESUS GOD MY GUUUUUTS and made squelchy noises with his lips and then—she couldn't help herself—a snort flew out of Ana like her own alien baby, which of course encouraged him to buck and howl and pantomime gut-spray that much more.

After he finished, sweaty and pleased with himself, he went back to watching the movie, but Ana couldn't concentrate. Every time Emilio Estevez appeared on the screen, she thought: *it's all an act.*

Lying down on the couch, she wondered what was so bad about acting, why that was supposed to be an insult. At Karen's Kitchen, she'd heard

Pastor Jim say that faith could start with ritual: you said the prayers, you attended church, you went through the motions until you actually started to believe in what you were doing. Then there was that old guy's story about the Chinese bandit with the mask. And don't forget college, where you tried out the role you wanted to play in the future. But did you go to college to find yourself, or forge yourself? It seemed like an important distinction, but she didn't know how to make it and her eyelids were getting heavy...

One moment Ana was thinking about bandits and prayer and the next she was having the oddest dream. At first all she saw was darkness, but she heard murmuring and felt the warmth of hands padding over her body. Glancing down, she found herself crowd-surfing a pod of monks, all of them wearing masks and droning a secret chant. Their hands were soft and it wasn't unpleasant to be passed over them, hands moving along her sides, stealing up her ribcage and over her breasts—

She opened her eyes. Logan drew back from her face, and his hands stopped moving under her shirt. He had time to say, "What," before Ana kicked him off.

She pulled up her feet, hugged her knees to her chest. "What the hell?" The TV was blank. Her father's room was silent. "What the hell, man? I was *asleep*."

Logan seemed confused. His eyes ran back and forth, like he was rewinding the night. He said, "Are you sure?"

She whipped a throw pillow at him. It clipped his face before disappearing down the dark hallway. She hoped the zipper got him in the eye.

Holding his face, he said, "I thought... I mean, people close their eyes when they're.... Plus you were making these little noises?"

"I was *not* making any fucking noises."

Dropping his hand, he blinked at her. "How would you know if you were asleep?"

"How can you be gay if you molest girls?"

He lowered his eyes to the burrito wrapper and slowly turned the color of the dried sauce. Ana wanted to cut off his hands. She wanted to say forget about it. She wanted to ask what was an act and what was real.

"Ana," he said, giving her the sorry eyes.

"Don't even."

Logan should have left, but he didn't. "It's just that, earlier? When you were telling me to be more confident? I thought that was, like, a message."

Ana closed her eyes. She was silent for a long moment. Then she let her tongue loose.

"You fucking fake faggot," she said in a low voice. "I bet you haven't sucked a single dick, have you?"

She kept going, pouring her darkness over him, anointing him with hate, and Logan stood there and took it. She found new ugliness to hang on him, and when he still didn't leave, she heard herself pray that the next time his brother wrapped a hand around his throat, he would finish the job.

◆   ◆   ◆

In Washington, Boxelder turned off the feed. This was too much; he didn't know how Logan could take it. With the monitors off, his office was dark and quiet for the first time in weeks. The silence was bottomless, and after a while he felt like he was falling into an abyss. He looked at his phone. He didn't have anyone to call, but he brought the phone over to the couch anyway, and held it to his chest when he lay down, feeling the dial tone in his ribcage. He wished his mind had a button like the monitors. He wished sleep was a decision. He wished his decisions were entirely his own.

Shadows from the street swam across his walls, and for once, Boxelder tried not to imagine what cast them.

Chapter 17
Campus Tour

Under a cold and cloudless sky, Ana and Droop followed a preppy kid who trudged backward along sidewalks rimed with salt. Tuning out the kid's bored monologue about B-school rankings, Ana listened to the creek running through the meadow, trickling under a lacey shawl of ice. Ahead on the path was a footbridge straight out of a storybook. At the far end of the meadow, a library loomed like a gothic fortress. The look of the campus was—Ana searched for the right phrase—*medieval erotic.*

Not that any of the college students streaming around her tour group noticed or cared. Swathed in sunglasses and headphones, they walked in clouds of cigarette smoke. They were all incognito.

At the end of the tour, the guide asked if anyone had questions. "Students? Moms? Dads?" Ana and Droop looked away from each other.

When she had asked him to take her on this campus visit, he seemed surprised. Surprised, but not entirely displeased. "Last time I saw you," he said in a sauntering tone, "you made it abundantly clear you wanted absolutely nothing to do with—"

"Don't wet your pants, Droop. I'm asking you for a ride, not to go steady."

On the way to Bloomington, Ana had slouched in her seat and glared out the window. At first, this was just to keep up appearances. If she started showing him basic human kindness, he might grow suspicious. He might wonder, *Why the sea change in attitude?* Better to treat him like a barely-tolerated chauffeur, like any parent on a campus visit. Lull him with silence, and later she could take him off guard with her questions.

It wasn't hard for Ana to act shitty and distracted, and after a few miles of tearing at her thumbnails with her teeth, it wasn't an act at all. She couldn't stop thinking about Logan. Fucking Logan. Why did he have to be a creep? A creep and a liar! A lying hetero molester!

That last word shocked her. But that's what it was, right? *Molestation.* God, how gross. What he did, it wasn't rape, but it was the real deal, uninvited and unwelcome. And who knows what would have happened if she hadn't woken up when she did? She shuddered to think. Literally shuddered with disgust for the stupid roles he had cast them both in. Molester and victim. *Thanks for making me a statistic, douchelord.*

After a while, her disgust ebbed, but a few minutes later came a fresh swell of revulsion. That's how it went, wave after wave, all the way down to Bloomington.

The weird thing was, she didn't mind being around Droop while this was happening. Something about him was calming. He was quiet in a way that let you know it was okay to be quiet, too. And he smelled nice. Not *nice*-nice, but like a man should smell. Like coffee and motor oil and bar soap and just a whiff of dog. She'd never noticed before that he wheezed, a little hiss at the end of each breath. Super quiet, but once you heard it, you couldn't stop hearing it, and usually that was the kind of thing that drove Ana crazy, but just then she found it oddly soothing. Like the last sizzle of a wave on a beach. And whenever he approached an intersection and wasn't sure which way to turn, he had a way of going *hmmm* and saying, "Let's see, let's see," to himself, which was stupid and nice at the same time, and just what Ana needed right then.

Not that she was going to let him know. Every time he talked to himself, she expelled a long breath from her nose like she was barely keeping her temper in check.

It wasn't quiet in the car after all, she realized. They might not be having a conversation, but the whole ride down was a chorus of hiss and hum.

◆   ◆   ◆

After lunch, Ana and Droop installed themselves in leather chairs in a big room at the Union. They held paper cups of coffee and watched firelight play on the glossy coat of a baby grand. Droop looked drowsy. His guard would never be lower. Ambush him now, Ana told herself, and he wouldn't know what hit him.

She took a breath, looked at him, then blew on her coffee. Another minute or two wouldn't matter.

Students used the room as a shortcut across campus, tracking mud across the tile without slowing to wipe the steam from their sunglasses. One guy stepped out of the stream of traffic and lay down on a rug. He covered his face with a paperback and appeared to fall asleep immediately. Ana felt like joining him. That rug looked plush.

"Promise me that won't be you in a couple of years," said Droop. "Find a couch, at least."

Last chance for an ambush, she thought. She was already feeling dangerously sympathetic to the doofus.

"I know the case against Veedy is bullshit," she said. "You guys are trying to make him look like a sex trafficker so you can get his property."

He'll deny it, of course, her mother had said over the phone. She'd been against this plan to confront him, wanting Ana to blow town without alerting the marshal's service. If this whole deal was a shady land grab, they shouldn't trust anyone attached to the case.

What Ana didn't trust was her mother's gut feeling based on the word of a hit man. She trusted Droop. Specifically, she trusted he would be a bad liar. That he'd give himself away with a too-long, too-innocent stare. Or a shoddy explanation. Some crack she could pry open to rake out more information, anything to help her make this impossible decision, to stay or go back home.

Droop finished his coffee, then made a show of scanning the room for a trash can. "You're lucky no one was close enough to hear that," he said in a low voice.

"Tell me why you guys want Veedy's warehouse."

On the rug, the sleeping kid twitched, then slipped one hand inside his waistband.

"No manners." Droop grimaced. "God, you are going to be that guy."

This conversation wasn't going the way Ana had imagined it. At this point, Droop was supposed to be angry or panicking while she prodded him with questions to keep him off-balance. Why wasn't this working? "I swear to God," she started, "if you don't tell me what I want to know—"

"Oh, Ana." He looked into his cup and seemed disappointed it was empty. "Honestly? I don't know a blessed thing about your case."

"Bullshit."

"Think about it," he said with the weary patience you use to explain something for the fifteenth time to an annoying toddler. "My job is to keep you and your dad safe until the trial. Do I need to know every last detail of your case to do that job? I do not."

"You could find out."

He settled deeper into his chair, looking more tired than he had before the coffee. "Think," he said again. "Anyone who knows any dirt is a potential leak and a potential target. The Program protects me from that kind of intel, and I, for one, appreciate it."

Ana picked her lip. The whole trip, the whole day had been about this moment, and it was slipping through her hands. If Droop truly didn't know anything, she was at a dead end. "You know *some*thing," she insisted.

"You think my boss gave me a fat dossier and a long monologue? You and that Logan kid watch too many movies."

Ana stopped picking her lip. "Your boss."

He winced. Just barely, but she caught it. She caught it, and now she had him. Droop must not have realized it yet, because he tried to steer her away from the subject. "Let's talk about *your* job," he said.

"You might not know these answers, but your boss would, right?"

"Your job is to keep your head down. To be quiet. If you call attention to yourself or to your father—"

"What's his phone number?"

Droop's face got splotchy. The SAT word *efflorescence* came to Ana's mind. The word *florid*. He said, "The Program protects me, and I protect the Program. The firewall works both ways. What do you think my boss would say if I brought the fire to him?"

"One call, Droop. Ten minutes."

"Sure. I didn't need this job, anyway. I hear Wal-Mart is hiring."

On the floor, the sleeping guy snorted and sat up abruptly. The book fell off his face. After blinking at the fire, he got up and wandered off, leaving his copy of *Slaughterhouse Five* open on the rug like a broken bird.

"Okay," said Ana. "I understand your position."

"Good."

"I'll make some other calls, then."

Droop cleared his throat. "Other calls?"

"Dad's old friends. Uncle Rooster. Someone will have answers. And if not, those guys are good at finding things out."

Droop looked into his empty coffee cup for a long time before saying, "I have heard some godawful ideas in my life, but that one—"

"And if that doesn't work," continued Ana, "I'll get in touch with Veedy. Get his side of the story."

Droop made a helpless gesture toward the fire. *Can you believe this shit?* "Everyone else who comes to campus gets a tour of Assembly Hall," he said to the fire. "Not me. I get this."

Ana didn't look away from him. "I'm going to call someone," she said. "My first choice is still your boss."

Droop rose with a grunt, straightened his coat. He walked over to the paperback and went down on one knee to retrieve it. When he came back, he said, "You will not, under any circumstances, mention how you got this number." He raised an eyebrow. "Clear?"

Ana grinned. "Crystal."

He scrawled a number on the back flap and gave her the book, telling her to read it, she might learn something from it, like how Vonnegut was full of compassion for his fellow humans, unlike some people he could name.

From the written statement of D.W. Boxelder:

Was I angry at Droop for getting outwitted by a teenager? For giving me up so quickly? Not really. (Though let us sincerely hope he never falls into the hands of a real gangster. He'd flip on his own mother in a minute.) The natural urge is to confess. Truth wants out. I can't tell you how many times I've seen relief bloom on a witness's face when he stops resisting and denying and pettifogging and just...releases the truth. It's not unlike an exorcism, or a long-restrained fart. *Spirit, come out!*

After Ana got my phone number, the question became: How long before she called? And where would she make the call? Not from home — she wouldn't want her father overhearing her side of the conversation. She suspected he understood a lot more than anyone thought. Not the payphone at the Sunoco, either. She couldn't chance being overheard by anyone she knew.

I pictured her at a desk in Trig, puzzling over these questions, picking skin flakes off her lip the way she does when she's lost in thought. Mr. Lang probably snapped at her to focus, not realizing her head was already full of calculations.

As it turned out, she ditched school at lunch and ran to I-65. A few weeks earlier, she would have browbeaten Logan into giving her a ride in his beat Escort, but she hadn't talked to him since the night of the incident. He slipped note after apology note through the gills of her locker until she wrote him back to say that if he left one more note, he would find it taped to the glass wall of the Principal's office for all to enjoy.

The notes stopped, but he made pining faces at her in the hall, and she struggled with the urge to punch him in the throat, and neither said a word to the other.

(Am I taking a bit of artistic license here? Are some of these details made up? Not as much as you might think, Madame Inspector. Consider how well you know your own daughter. Lovely Carrie. You know how, in certain situations, you can tell exactly what she's thinking, what she's about to do? Of course you can. You made her. You've watched her. You *know* her.

Sherwood may have inducted this family, but I created their papers, their backstories, their characters. I watched over Ana. And despite what Droop says, I protected her, especially at the end. So, yes, I might be mudding in some cracks in the story, but the cracks are small and the mud is strong.)

Anyway, that's how Ana found herself on the side of the interstate, sticking out her thumb at northbound traffic. After twenty minutes of trudging backward while attempting to strike an attitude halfway between helpless and threatening, she flagged down a Tracker. The driver was bundled up like a toddler on a snow day, right down to the scarf wrapped halfway up his face. The reason became apparent as the Tracker accelerated onto the highway and the wind shrieked through a gash in the vinyl roof.

"Thanks," shouted Ana. Then she looked at the driver more closely. "Hey, do I know you?"

The man shrugged without looking over.

"Seriously," she said. "You look familiar."

He tugged down his scarf long enough to say, "I got that kind of face." Ana was about to ask his name when she glimpsed a tarp in the back of the Tracker. Did that tarp have…lumps?

The tarp had lumps.

She faced straight ahead, pretending she hadn't noticed, but it was too late. The guy looked at her, muttered something that got lost in the wind, and whipped the Tracker to the side of the road. He got out, popped open the tailgate, and pulled a hacksaw out from under the tarp.

Only me, she thought as she reached behind her back and squeezed the grip of the pocket gun. No one else could move halfway across a continent to escape danger only to hop in the car of a psycho killer. Only. Me.

But when the man failed to materialize at her door with the saw and a leer, she looked out her window to see him bounding down the snow-streaked hillside toward a deer that looked like it had eaten a live grenade. Ribcage splayed open like cabinet doors, entrails burned into the snow. The man knelt down and sawed at the deer's leg.

Reaching into the back, Ana lifted the tarp to see bloody hunks, covered with fur. *Oh, thank God*, she thought, tucking the gun back into her jeans.

When the guy got back to the Tracker with a pair of deer drumsticks, he said he'd appreciate it if she didn't tell anyone about what he'd done. Technically it was illegal, but he wasn't hurting anyone; he was just out here salvaging.

"Scavenging," Ana corrected him.

"What's the difference?"

She couldn't remember, so she told him his secret was safe with her.

(We all want to confess, Madame. At the same time, we want our secrets. We want sunshine and we want a cave. No one understands this more than a witness. In the Program, you can confess *and* you can hide. You can trade in your old secrets for new ones.)

◆ ◆ ◆

When Ana's call came in, my secretary picked up the phone, said, "Hold, please," and gave me a look. "Fernando" was the hold music because it is always the hold music. While Anni-Frid Lyngstad warbled away, I traced the call. Payphone in DeMotte. Fifteen miles north of Morocco, a straight shot on the interstate. The weather report called for wet misery. I pictured a sky of dirty, twisted bedsheets. Little spits of rain pocking the snow. Wind smelling like freezer burn. At the crumbling edge of a gas station parking lot, Ana huddled in the half-booth. Raindrops clung to her wool jacket like tiny light bulbs. She was nervous, and who could blame her? Not me. I was nervous, too. My career was at stake here. Veedy was cooling in jail and his trial was scheduled for May. As long as he was convicted, my path to confirmation as Director would be clear.

On the other hand, if the case went off the rails, I might as well withdraw my nomination "for personal reasons."

From my desk, I nodded at my secretary.

"Miss Easterday," said Trish, "Mr. Boxelder has indicated that you should speak to your deputy marshal about any concerns or questions."

Her delivery was smooth. Didn't sound rehearsed at all. I leaned back in my chair to give her a thumbs-up. She narrowed her eyes at me. Trish was pissed that I'd handed her a script for this call. She'd deflected about a million other calls I hadn't cared to take, she let me know, and she could handle this one on her own just as easily. I told her I had no doubt she could, but as a favor to me, just this once, would she please follow this script?

"I *did* speak to Pete," said Ana. "He told me that my questions were— how did he put it?—above his pay grade. So I looked up this number."

Her delivery wasn't bad, either. She was developing as a liar. I flashed two fingers at Trish. *Scenario Two.* Ana might be gifted at improv, but we had experience and preparation on our side.

In a crisp voice, Trish said, "Does your marshal know you're making this call?"

"He doesn't need to know."

"How about the fact that you've been calling your mother outside of the switchboard? Have you kept that a secret from him, too?"

Silence on the line. Was Ana reeling or calculating? I waved at Trish to finish her off. Trish said, "Whatever the issue, work it out with your marshal. Use the switchboard for *all* long distance calls. And never call this number again. Mr. Boxelder will see you on the day of the trial, but you are not to contact him before that time."

That should have been it. All Trish had to do was hang up the phone. Instead, she decided to veer off-script. "Do you understand?" she said.

Ana didn't answer. I flapped a magazine at Trish to get her attention. *Hang up,* I mouthed.

Trish said, "I said, *do you understand*?"

Here's something I learned in my seminary days of evangelizing and later confirmed inducting witnesses: Every pact has a window of opportunity, a moment when you can cinch the deal.

Once you know what you're doing, you can feel that window open. You can feel it shut, too.

I pantomimed hanging up the phone. I pantomimed hard. Trish looked right through me. Ana's window shut.

"Let me tell you something," said Ana. "I'm staying on the line until I talk to Boxelder. If you hang up on me, I will come to you. I will find him."

Trish bent over her script, flipping through pages to find the contingency plan that dealt with this little doozy. She couldn't find it, though, because it didn't exist. When I put the plan together, I failed to account for the possibility that my trusty admin might go rogue.

On the phone, Ana was saying that she was going to get answers one way or another, and it was up to Trish whether that was over the phone or in her boss's office—

I walked over and punched the hold button on Trish's phone. Trish looked up like she might bite me. I pulled back my hands. "New plan," I said.

◆   ◆   ◆

To Ana, this must have seemed like a good sign, being put back on hold. She had thrown the lady off her game; right now she was probably conferring with Boxelder in a hushed panic; it was a matter of time before he pounded the desk and said, *All right, goddammit, put her on line one.*

(She wasn't far off. That's what Trish wanted—"Isn't this more trouble than just talking to her?"—but the last thing Ana needed was encouragement. This kind of shit could not be rewarded.)

"Fernando" started over. Ana had never heard this song before today, but already she hated it. Needles of ice mixed with the rain seeping into her coat. Cold came up from the asphalt like a weed, threading into her calves. All the heat in her body retreated to her ear that was pressed against the plastic receiver.

The music cut out. Ana heard a lady's voice and her heart lifted—but it was just the automatic ladyvoice asking for more quarters.

She pushed coins into the machine, dropping two on the salted ground because she couldn't feel her fingers. She looked at the gas station. Twenty yards away, a box of heat and light and processed foods. There be hot coffee. There be sweaty rollers of sausages. If she could duck inside for five minutes—hot chocolate, nacho platter, poncho—she'd be good to stand out here for another hour, if need be.

But she knew how holding worked. If she stepped away, even for a second, her absence would summon the secretary, who would say *Hello?* exactly twice before hanging up. (Telephony abhors a vacuum, Madame.)

So Ana held. The skies did not. The sleet picked up, running icy fingers through her scalp. A trickle ran down her back like a snowmelt stream. She sniffed hard, spat. Her sinuses felt scraped out. With a dead finger, she stubbed zero several times, hoping to signal her presence to the stupid secretary who'd probably forgotten about her, probably packed up and went home to her hot tub in front of a blazing fireplace. "I'm still here," she said to goddamn Abba. "Can you hear me? Is anyone there?"

(Always, Ana. Someone, somewhere, somehow yes.)

Her lips were old rubber. They made her sound dumb or drunk. Goddammit, she was going to catch pneumonia. She could see how all of this was going to end for her: With gurgling lungs and a babbling father, the two of them side by side in sickbeds, and oh, look! Here comes Logan to molest their helpless bodies, and hey, thanks for leaving the door open, pal, because here comes Zeeshan to shoot them all in their stupid heads.

Forget going home. Forget college. Forget any notion of the future. She would die in motherfucking Morocco and be buried under her made-up name and no one who loved her would ever know she was dead. She'd just be gone.

Though how was that different from her current situation?

Ana was sunk so deep in her own head that Trish had to say her name twice.

"More quarters?" Ana slurred.

"Listen," said Trish. "Your deputy marshal is at your house."

"Droop? Droop is coming over?"

"He's already there. With your father, who is safe, no thanks to you." Trish shot me a look as she delivered this line. She thought it was overkill, pushing the buttons of daughter guilt, but I had insisted. This little insurrection had to be put down swiftly and surely. "Go home," said Trish. "They're waiting on you."

Ana rallied. "You hang up on me, and I'll come for you. Not tonight, but—"

"I'm not going to hang up on you. But I'm not going to transfer you to Mr. Boxelder, either. I'm going to sit with you on the line until you realize your only move is to go home."

Ana looked at the quarters on the ground, blurry with slush. She looked at the bright station, and sleet poured in her ear. Then she shuddered and spoke through locked teeth. "You tell him to call me," she said. "Either he calls me, or I come to him. You got that, secretary? Write it down. *Tell him to call Ana Easterday.*"

She hammered the phone down on its cradle. A jingling noise was still coming from deep inside the machine as she ran toward the interstate on legs she could no longer feel.

◆   ◆   ◆

I tried to tell Trish good job, but she wasn't having it. "Sure," she said, rummaging through her purse with more vigor than seemed necessary. "Threats are usually a good sign, right?"

She was looking at it wrong. See, Madame, every witness has a moment when they grow into their new identity. When faking it becomes making it. Yes, Ana threatened us, but look: She did it as Ana Easterday.

I tried to explain that to Trish, but she drew a cigarette from a pack in her purse and pointed it at me. "Careful," she said. "Don't start believing your own bullshit."

But that's just it: Belief is everything. The bullshit we believe is who we are.

I didn't say that to Trish, though. We'd had enough of each other for one day, so I gave her the afternoon off, and I took it upon myself to look up the phone number for the Chevy dealership in Morocco.

Chapter 18
Sirens

The woman on Kate's stoop was mousy-looking, with a brown bob and a round cookie tin in her hands. Everything about her, from the oatmeal sweater set to the scuffed Mary Janes, said "troop leader" or "PTA Mom." Probably she was organizing some toothless committee, or collecting signatures for a prudish petition. Looking through the peephole, Kate felt a stir of irritation, followed by a deeper urge—she hadn't talked with anyone but her mother in days, and now her mother was away at San Damiano on a silent retreat, and lo, here was a woman who was roughly Kate's age—so she opened the door.

"Mrs. DeAngelo?" the woman said in an official tone.

Shit. This couldn't be good.

The woman took her hand from under the cookie tin and showed Kate a badge. "Can we talk inside, Ma'am?"

◆　　◆　　◆

Ma'am. As if Kate was older than this woman. Which, no way. Kate did not radiate stodgy mom vibes. Kate's hair was not tinseled with gray. When this woman bent forward to take the cup of coffee that Kate had passive-aggressively reheated—Fresh brew? I don't think so—her belly pooched over the comfort band of her slacks. Now she was sweeping her hand across the tabletop, gathering crumbs into a pile as she introduced herself. "Marshal's service," she said. "Lynne Earley."

Kate half-expected her to say *Just kidding*! and pop open the tin to share her snickerdoodles. Was this lady actually a mother, or was that just a facade to help her get inside homes? Which was the cover—marshal or mom?

"Part time?" Kate asked.

Lynne gave her a dry look. "I won't take much of your time, Ma'am. I just came to deliver a message."

Kate braced herself. Messages were never positive. No one ever dropped by in an official capacity to say *We admire the way you're holding up* or *Your daughter is fine and sends her warmest regards.*

Lynne opened the tin, which was decorated with a picture of cherubic boys ice-skating around a jaunty snowman. As it turned out, this tin held no cookies, no butterscotch drops, no rum balls. Just photos, black and white. Lynne snapped them on the tabletop, one by one.

Zeeshan, limping up the steps of this very row house.

Zee, waiting at the door, glancing over his shoulder.

An interior shot, striped with blinds, of Zee and Kate sitting at this kitchen table.

Kate stood abruptly. For no reason she went to the coffeemaker, touched its cold handle. "This is an invasion of privacy," she said.

Lynne nodded curtly, at once acknowledging and dispatching Kate's claim. "We also know you've been talking to your daughter off switchboard. Mrs. DeAngelo, these are serious violations of protocol."

Kate came back and picked up a photo, the one with her and Zeeshan at the kitchen table. If you didn't know better, you'd think it was a shot of two old friends. Zeeshan's leg crossed at the knee, his sock wrinkled; Kate idly stirring her coffee. *Consorting can be a good thing*, he'd said. Not according to the Marshal's service, Zeeshan.

"You can't spy on regular people," she said. "This isn't legal."

Another dry look from Lynne. Her phaser was set on *wither*. Kate felt sorry for this woman's children, probably catching this look seven, eight times a day.

"Zeeshan Mattu," Lynne said, "is the subject of an ongoing investigation. Your family is under protective custody. You have crossed two bad wires here, Kate, and I am trying to help you uncross them." She cocked her head. "But I have to confess, I find it curious that your first instinct is to nitpick at technicalities. I thought your top concern would be the safety of your family."

"It is," protested Kate. "It's just—"

Lynne bent toward her, re-pooching. "Kate, you mean well. I believe that. That's why I'm talking with you instead of bringing you in." She took a sip of her coffee. Her eyes crinkled at the staleness, and Kate felt a twinge for being so petty. "This kind of thing happens to people in the Program all the time. They want so badly to get back to their old lives that they convince themselves everything is okay now. Or that there never was a problem in the first place. But you need to know this kind of lie always—*always*—ends badly."

Kate looked at the photos. Did Zeeshan know about this inclination? Maybe that was his play all along, to lead her down this well-worn path.

Lynne pressed her thumb into a stray crumb, and dropped it into her little pile. "Right now," she said, "your family is isolated. But you're building a bridge between two worlds. And if you connect them—" She shook her head "—your husband and daughter will be found, and they will suffer."

Kate sat back. Lynne was right, it was clear as a photo to her now, the risks she was taking, the danger she was courting. Kate would have to be a fool or a siren to keep beckoning her daughter—and yet, even then, what she wanted more than anything was to ask Ana, one more time, to come back to her.

All her life as a mother, Kate had wanted what was best for her daughter. That was the story she'd told herself, anyway. But now she saw the deeper truth. Kate didn't want what was best for Ana; Kate wanted *Ana*.

Nothing is greedier than love. The realization made Kate dizzy.

"Your heart was in the right place," said Lynne. "But you need to stay away from Zeeshan. We know what we're doing, and as long as you play by the rules, no one will get hurt." She ducked toward Kate with a little smile of encouragement and budding trust, a smile that would put a quiet yes on anyone's lips, a smile that no one with a heart would ever want to flatten with disappointment. "Okay?" said Lynne.

What could Kate say? What could she do? All at once the answer came to her: nothing.

She wouldn't ask her daughter to come home again, but she wouldn't tell her to stay away, either. She would leave the decision up to Ana. A child isn't blinded by love in the same way as a parent. If Zee was lying, her girl would see it. If he was telling the truth, she would know.

This is what you were supposed to do as a parent of a teen, wasn't it? You did all you could, and then you let go. You stopped singing them home, you let them find their own course. Right?

Kate closed her eyes and nodded.

Lynne sat back and patted her knees once, pleased.

All was forgiven, all was well. Zeeshan wouldn't be pleased, but there was nothing Kate could do about that, nothing in the world.

Chapter 19
The Last Nest

Monday morning, Karen's Kitchen, and the Old Liars were quiet. Not entirely quiet—those mooks couldn't be silent if their lives depended on it—but the jibes and grumbles passed over the table like lonesome tufts of cottonwood.

"Quiet in here," Ana said when she came around with the coffee pots. "Too quiet," she added in a jokey cowboy voice.

Pastor Jim gave her a thin smile. Little Mike looked into his mug. Govert cleared his throat a long time, like a truck engine that wouldn't catch.

"Jesus, you guys," said Ana. "Who died?"

Vernon crabbed over to the front door, locked it, and flipped the sign to CLOSED. Ana heard a rattling noise behind her and turned to see the cook, Luis, scroll down the metal curtain on the order-up window, sealing himself and Karen inside the kitchen.

Ana stepped back from the table, holding out the coffee pots. "If this is one of your jokes, it is not funny. It is the death of funny."

Little Mike stood and tipped his head toward the walk-in freezer. "Come with us," he said. "This won't take long."

"You're right," she said. "In fact, it won't take any time at all, because I'm not going anywhere, so you might as well unflip that goddamn sign, *Vernon,* and—"

Big Mike pushed back his chair. He rose, and his shadow covered her. Christ, he was big. Easy to forget when he was usually hunched over a table. "Let's do this the easy way," he whispered, seemingly to himself as much as to her. "Please."

Ana looked at his craggy face, his pleading eyes. If she said no, he was going to have to do something he didn't want to do.

She set the pots down. Big Mike sighed in relief, then swept his arm toward the walk-in. "After you," he said.

◆   ◆   ◆

They all fit in the walk-in, but barely. Big Mike sat on a box of ground beef patties and held Vernon on his knee like a marionette, which neither of them were happy about. Pastor Jim stood by the door, watching the handle. Was he standing guard or avoiding her eyes?

"Let's start with a simple question," said Little Mike. "What's my name?"

"Shithead."

"Ana. Please. What is my name?"

"I don't know what game you're playing, Mike—"

"Right. It's Mike. And my last name?"

Ana paused. Everyone in the freezer seemed to lean forward in anticipation. This was some Twilight Zone shit right here. She knew these guys, knew all their names. Little Mike's was right on the dealership sign: *Hopkins' Chevrolet.* So what the hell was going on? Why was he talking to her like she was a kindergartner?

"Hopkins," she said with caution.

"Can you guess why that's my last name?"

"Your daddy probably had something to do with it."

Little Mike shook his head. "My name is Hopkins because Sherwood liked the blues. That's why a bunch of white guys in a corn town are named Witherspoon...Dixon...Morganfield..." He pointed around the freezer as he called out the names and when his finger landed on Big Mike, he said,

"But the Director forgot that he'd already named one guy after Lightning Hopkins, so I have to go by *Little* Mike."

The freezer swayed—and then Pastor Jim was steadying Ana by her shoulders. "You guys," she managed to say. "You're all…?"

From a raft of sausages, Govert lifted an imaginary drink. "Welcome to the club."

◆　　◆　　◆

The Program began stashing witnesses in Morocco in the '70s (see exhibit A: Vernon). The town was perfect: quiet, isolated, but close enough to O'Hare to spirit a witness into any courtroom in the country in a matter of hours. Clustering witnesses seemed like an efficient use of resources—a single deputy marshal could tend to several at once—so Sherwood created several of these nests around the country.

At first, when witnesses sniffed each other out in these small towns, Sherwood wasn't worried. An incorrigible optimist, he thought they might support each other in the hard work of making a new life. They supported each other, all right. Mostly in backsliding, setting up conduits for crime, and occasionally assisting one another off the mortal coil. Sherwood had no choice but to break up the nests, scattering witnesses all over the map. By '87, all the nests were gone—except the first one, the one in Morocco.

The town was the Program's Brigadoon, untouched by time or trouble, safe in its mist from the corruption of the world. Boxelder sent the Easterdays there in the hope that the culture of the town would keep them safe and steady. At the same time, he saw the risk of Ben screwing up the fragile equilibrium of the nest, so he had the Old Liars hold off on outing themselves. The plan was for them to exert a gentle, secret influence.

The plan had not worked. Subtlety was wasted on the Easterdays. Direct measures were needed. "We don't make messes," Little Mike told Ana now. "No one in this freezer has ever blown his cover, or gotten in any trouble bigger than a D.U.I.—" Govert raised his hand "—and that just made him fit in better around here."

"Then you people show up," Vernon said, "making a ruckus. Causing a fuss."

Big Mike put his arm across Vernon's chest and shushed him. Little Mike went on. "At first, we thought you were just having a hard time settling in," he said. "Droop told us he could handle it. But you *haven't* settled in. You *haven't* adjusted." He took a deep breath, trying to control his anger. "And now," he said, "you're threatening Boxelder?"

Ana blinked. Boy, you think you know someone. Then it turns out you don't, but somehow they know all about you. They know every last thing you've been up to. Holding up a finger, she said, "I just—give me a minute. Let me think."

Little Mike didn't even give her a second. "You think you're being sneaky," he said, "but all you're doing is calling attention to yourself. To your father. To *us*."

For a moment it was quiet in the walk-in. Twelve years of selling Silverados and Impalas had taught Little Mike when to press and when to let his words sink in. It took Ana a moment—she wasn't dim, but the last few minutes had given her a lot to process—but at last she shook her head in resignation.

"Guys," she said, "I had no idea…I don't know what to say."

Little Mike softened. "Tell us you'll cool it. Listen to Droop. Play along with the system."

"Guys," she said again. Her voice sounded far away to her own ears. "I'm sorry."

Pastor Jim looked up. He pressed his lips together, though Ana didn't know why, and there was no time to ask because Big Mike said, "Good enough for me," and Govert said he was starving and now the door of the walk-in was open and the Liars were jostling out to their table.

"Hurry your ass up. Poor Luis can't hold off Karen's advances much longer."

"*Señora, please. Put your wig back on!*"

Watching these guys transform back into themselves might have been the strangest part of this fucked-up morning. Like flipping a switch. Like nothing had happened in the freezer.

Ana didn't have that switch. She tried to smile when she went around with the coffee, but her lips had a short circuit. She ended up telling Karen that she didn't feel so hot and just wanted to go home.

She wasn't ill, but it was the truest thing she'd said in months.

Chapter 20
Forbidden Chamber

The town library was a former bank branch everyone called the Bookbank. The drive-thru was no longer functional, though sometimes a senile biddy would manage to wedge a paperback into the vacuum tube, and Wanda would have to coax it out with a pair of tongs.

That's the problem with a repurposed building: you can strip it down to the studs and tear out all the non-weight bearing walls, but it's going to retain some structural quirks. With a little imagination, though, inconvenience can be converted into charm. In the Bookbank, the teller counter worked perfectly well as a checkout station. On busy Saturdays, the old brass stanchions with their moth-eaten velvet ropes shaped the patrons into an orderly line. Extracting the iron vault would have run more than five thousand dollars, so instead Wanda installed comfy chairs and christened it the Forbidden Chamber of Banned Books. She stocked it with titles like *Lolita* and *Tropic of Cancer* and kept the vault door slightly open, as though the library might seal it up at any moment, entombing the scandalous titles along with any patron unlucky enough to be caught inside—though in truth the lock and pipe had been stripped out by a locksmith. Good thing, too, because boys were forever shoving their brothers into the vault and trying to slam the door shut, especially in the summer when the Bookbank was a kid-loud glade.

No kids were in the library the winter night that Pete walked in, nodding hello to Wanda. "What's up, Pistol Pete?" said that witchy little Beth, the other librarian on duty. Pete nodded again without looking at her, cruising past the block of monitors in the center of the floor, heading for the single computer tucked into the stacks. The location wasn't ideal—his back would be to the whole library; anyone could sneak up and peek at the screen—but his ears were good and his shoulders were broad enough to block the monitor. He hoped.

Technically he could have used his home computer, but the other day he had found a listening device in his phone. That dickhead Boxelder must have ordered that up in the crackdown after Ana's call.

Pete had expected to catch some suspicion for that call, but he figured there was enough reasonable doubt to give him cover. After all, Boxelder was a public official. Technically, Ana could have looked up his number somehow, right?

But when Box called him on the phone, it wasn't to ask questions or even sling accusations. He skipped those steps and suspended Pete for two weeks without pay. No investigation; Boxelder just knew it was him. How?

The world was full of snitches, some human, some electronic, more every day. All the more reason not to do this search from home.

Besides, going to the library got him out of the house, which never seemed emptier than during the long dark spell of February. In all the world, there were two or three things worse than February in Indiana. Maybe four. No more than that, though.

Deep in the stacks, the computer dialed and dialed. It sounded like a goat getting cornholed. Pete checked over his shoulder. Beth was probably speculating to Wanda about what he was doing back here. *When men go to that computer, they're not exactly looking up scripture.*

Beth was the shock-jock of the bookish set. One of those women who squirm in delight when they're told, *You're so bad.* Sometimes Pete felt like telling her a few things that would shock her provincial ass—but of course he couldn't.

It was the cornerstone of his job: keep your secrets. And if you ever have to wonder if something is a secret, assume it is. Err on the side of shut up.

Could be worse, though. It was worse for the witnesses. This last week of unpaid leave had given him a new appreciation for their hardship. To have your work taken from you. To be trapped by the same identity that was protecting you. To have a story shape you until you became its character—in Pete's case, a disabled retiree.

Bad as it felt to play that role, it felt worse to step out of it. Every few months Pete would drive fifty miles to the bars in the nearest city with the flickering hope of meeting a woman and telling her some truth about himself.

It never worked. The nearest city was a college town, West Lafayette, and the bars were full of girls who put him in mind of his daughter, who would have been nearly their age. When he looked at these girls, Pete was torn by competing desires to buy them a beer or a hot meal. Strip them naked or bundle them up in a fluffy coat. On the rare occasion one would get drunk enough to talk to him, his ambivalence would fizzle and all he wanted was for her to promise not to go home with any of the assholes in the joint, himself included.

On the screen in the library, pictures came into focus, pixel by pixel. Girls, most of them around the same age as the college girls, though they didn't look nearly that young. The text on this site for mail-order brides—no, wait: *International Matchmakers*—was the language of romance, but Pete wasn't fooled and neither were these girls. Their eyes were serious; they were looking for a way out. For an abundant table, the absence of fear, opportunity for their future children. A life in Morocco with a disabled retiree would be a step up for them, which was not something many women around here could say.

He could rationalize this search all day long—arranged marriages have a long and successful tradition; it would give two people a shot at happiness, etc.—but if he was really comfortable with it, he wouldn't have hidden in the stacks. What would he say if someone caught him, accused him of exploitation, *de facto* prostitution, basic creepiness? *International Matchmakers* wasn't the same as the trafficking ring Veedy was accused of running, but it was kin. What could Pete say except that he wouldn't consider it if he had any other options?

He'd tried blind dates, pen pals, dating services, prayer—and then there was the time he went on a singles cruise. During an idiotic speed-dating event on the second day, he heard himself tell some big-haired woman about his daughter. Heard himself cough and then—the horror—choke up. He rushed to the men's room, where he stared at his blotchy face in the mirror and thought: what the hell is wrong with you? Thirty seconds after meeting this woman, you bring up your dead daughter? No wonder you're alone.

While the other passengers turned the discotheque into a floating Gomorrah, Pete spent the next four days in a deck chair, getting sunburned and slowly bombed on Mai Tais. You weren't ready, he told himself. You rushed things, that's all. Try again next year. Maybe.

He came back to Indiana with peeling skin and a dark mind, but as he drove down 65, something shifted in his chest when he saw the first stretch of corn stubble. Then a turkey vulture standing in a field like a little bald man in a shabby coat. A candy shell of ice on the telephone wires. Closer to town he saw Truck Farts and Hopkins' Chevrolet and he felt something like comfort. Rolling through downtown, Pete nodded at people through his truck window like they were old friends and he realized that's just what they were. By the time he passed the wooden Episcopal church that looked like an ark run aground in a soybean field, he found himself looking forward to laughing about his trip over Wild Turkey Manhattans with Pastor Jim, spinning his sadness into a funny story. In short, Pete was no longer pretending about this place. Morocco was home.

But he still wasn't sure if he was ready for love, or even companionship. Or maybe he'd already missed his window of readiness. Maybe that's why he felt queasy as he clicked through screen after screen of girls promising to keep a clean house, be a good cook, bear many children. He wished one of them would say something spiky. *I promise to call you the worst names in my own language.* Something Ana would say.

While he waited for a page of bios to load, he opened a new tab and ran a simple search on her case. This wasn't breaching any firewalls, technically. It wasn't like he was looking at case files; he would just browse some articles in the Baltimore papers, the same as any interested citizen.

Veedy's arrest popped up first. Daniel "Velcro Dan" Teller, charged with human trafficking. Trial in late May. If convicted, faces up to life in prison.

A few more articles about the arrest, then the trail vanished. Nothing else about Veedy or Ben DeAngelo, and Pete didn't know what else to search. After tapping his fingers lightly against the keys, he typed in "Daniel Webster Boxelder."

Not much came up. Apparently, Boxelder was pretty good at keeping himself out of the public eye. Here was a bland quote on the impending retirement of Sherwood. A stub of an article about Boxelder's nomination to direct the Program. The stub ended with a mention of his confirmation hearing, scheduled for June. Right after Veedy's trial.

Huh.

Following the trail a bit further, Pete found that the Senate Committee on the Judiciary was chaired by Senator Robert Mulcahey, D-Maryland.

Maryland. Home of the Tippy. Home of Veedy's warehouse. Home of the senator who would oversee Boxelder's confirmation hearing. Lot of stuff lining up. Was it actually suspicious, though, or was it a handful of minor coincidences that only a nutbar like Govert would spin into a conspiracy of—

"Pardon my intrusion."

Pete clicked spastically, managing to minimize the window, only to discover a rogue pop-up ad featuring a woman making sexy eyes over a steaming casserole, as though offering to spoon-feed the viewer in bed. He Xed that ad, but another one popped up—and then another and another. The faster he closed them, the more they plastered across the screen. Why wasn't the actual internet this fast? At last he bumped the monitor's power button with his elbow as he turned to Wanda and did his best to sound casual. "Just fine, thank you."

He held his smile, hoping she would nod and move on. How much had she seen? Enough, apparently, because she was pulling up a chair.

"Look," Pete started. "I—"

Wanda held up her hand. She was older than Pete, but not by much. She'd put on a little weight since he'd last seen her, as though her body was an air bag slowly deploying to cushion the blow of middle age, but she was still a handsome woman. Dark hair sweeping her glasses, ankles crossed under her windowpane skirt, excellent posture, the picture of poise. When she leaned toward him, though, Pete saw that her foundation was caked on to mask old acne scars. "I already know," she said.

His smile slipped. "Know what?"

She sighed. "Ever since Govert downloaded pictures of two...very friendly ladies along with about five different viruses, it's been library policy to monitor our patrons' internet usage."

His neck crawled with heat. He waited for her to call him a perv, or to ask about his interest in Baltimore crime—oh shit, he had searched for Ben DeAngelo and WITSEC. Oh, *shit*. The dots practically connected themselves. He'd told Ana to keep her head down, and here he was, out in *public*, for God's sake, outing his witnesses—

"I'm sorry," Wanda continued, "that you feel you have to hide, but I understand. I can only imagine what Beth might say if she came back here."

"Beth?"

"And I can only imagine what it's like to be a man searching for a wife in this town."

Oh, thought Pete with massive relief. *That* search. Okay, this was embarrassing, just what he'd hoped to avoid by going into the stacks, but the damage was limited to his dignity. Ana was safe. *Ben* was safe, he corrected himself. The witness was the priority.

"Sorry about the pop-ups," he said. "I didn't know..." He waved his hand at the blank screen, wondering if the little boxes were still reproducing in the dark like mushrooms. "I'll shut it down."

"You misapprehend me." She reached into the pocket of her cardigan and drew out a key. "Use my office. It's private. If anyone asks, I'll tell them you're working on a genealogy project."

Pete blinked at the key. It had been a while since he'd been so glad to be wrong. "Thank you," he said when he found his voice.

"Good hunting," she said, and they gave each other a curt nod, the bow of the Midwest.

Chapter 21
Second Coming

From the parked car, the yard looked like it was underwater. The fat moon laid a watery light on the grass, mottled blue and silver. The shipwreck of the fallen bough. The shot-up armoire, a rotting chest without treasure. Ana sat in the passenger's seat in a long down parka. The coat had shown up in the mail last week—an anonymous gift—and she'd meant to chuck it just like she chucked Droop's pity groceries, but she made the mistake of trying it on. She ended up sleeping in the coat that night. It had been a long time since something had felt so nice. Now, from inside the fur-trimmed hood, she sang, "Fifteen men on the dead man's chest."

In the driver's seat, her father sang back softly. "Yo-ho-ho, and a bottle of rum."

Most of their communication was in song now. She couldn't tell how much he understood, but at least he got the lyrics right.

Ana sang, "Smoke and the devil had done for the rest…"

Her father tightened his brow like he was trying to tune in her signal but couldn't find it. Could he tell she'd messed up the song? That she was high? High as the moon? You'd have to be oblivious to miss that red-eyed fact, but then, he *was* brain damaged. Still, the therapist claimed her father could understand gestures and situations, so maybe he knew but didn't care. Least of his worries. Bigger fish in the barrel. Was that the saying? Ana's brain was feeling a little damaged itself.

"Don't mind if I do," she said accidentally out loud, fishing another joint out of her shirt pocket.

Her father's face clouded. "Star shit," he said firmly, but Ana paid him no mind. She lit the joint and smoke slid down her throat like a blade.

"I don't remember the future," she croaked, then blew the smoke onto the flipdown shade, feeling like baby Godzilla. "That particular TV is dead, man."

This was the single advantage of her father's aphasia: she could say whatever she wanted. It was no small relief to let go of the twin burdens of restraint and making sense. Their conversations had started a couple of weeks earlier, shortly after the Old Liars shut her down. At first she worried her father might find it cruel, like a taunt. *Can't understand me? Too bad. Here's some more shit you won't understand.*

But wouldn't it be worse to say nothing? To freeze him out? And if Ana was being honest, she'd have to admit she was talking to him for her own sake, too. Mostly for her own sake, actually, because who else did she have? Her mother wouldn't take her calls off switchboard anymore, and when they talked over the switchboard, they couldn't say anything that mattered. As for Logan, he was *persona non grata. Non grata* to the *n*th degree.

Which left Ana alone with the questions that hung over her like meat hooks, snagging her a hundred times a day. When she ran to work in her parka: should we go home or stay here? When she called home at lunch and her father didn't answer: is he okay? Am I stupid for leaving him by himself? When the school announced the deadline to sign up for the spring SAT: should I even bother taking it, since it looks like I'm going to be stuck playing nurse to my dad for the foreseeable?

In the car, her father held out his hand. Ana stared at his palm for a long, stoned moment before she realized he wanted her to pass the joint. She hesitated—How would it affect his medications? Shouldn't he set a better example for her to ignore?—but she passed it over. She wasn't in a position to reprimand anybody.

The joint went back and forth like a shaky firefly, the car getting creamy, the underwater world trembling and gleaming, star shit everywhere.

Earlier that day her English class was discussing a bullshit condensed version of *The Odyssey*, and before Ana remembered that she didn't talk in this school, she found herself volunteering that Odysseus must have had mixed feelings about coming home. "What do you mean?" the teacher asked.

"This is a guy who can seduce goddesses and slay monsters," said Ana. "If he really wanted to get home, it wouldn't have taken his ass ten years."

"Well," Mr. Kenley reminded her, "there was that little matter of interference from the gods."

Titters in the classroom. Anger like a geyser in Ana's chest. "There were no gods," she said. "Poseidon and Athena were just excuses he gave his wife so she wouldn't know he'd spent the last decade treading wine-dark water, making up his mind about whether to come back to the farm."

The class was silent, Kenley included. Ana bent over her notebook and etched savage pyramids onto the page, tracing them over and over until they burned through the paper.

After school she stopped by the Kitchen to buy weed from Karen. Smoked one pinner with her by the dumpster, and another one on the dark walk to the farmhouse. Now, she was in the rustbucket Fairlane and her father was in the driver's seat and someone was saying, "They put a spell on the queen so every time you ask her a question she turns into a baby." It might have been the radio or it might have come from Ana, she wasn't sure. Then she found herself pulling keys from her pocket, slipping them into the ignition and—a minor miracle—the car started on the first turn.

She gestured widely to the windshield, as if to say, *All roads are open.*

If he drove them to Baltimore, fine. If he turned off the car and headed back inside the farmhouse, also fine. If he tore down the road and headed west until the Fairlane ran out of gas, Ana would not voice a single word of complaint.

Her father stared into the seascape, looking troubled.

"Please," she said. "I can't make this call. You gotta decide."

He laid his forehead on the wheel.

Ana's high turned leaden. She felt tired, tired unto death. She had thought—oh, this sounded stupid when she admitted it to herself—that at her lowest moment, in her hour of need, when all would be lost if she didn't get just a touch of help, that's when her father would understand her. That's when he would slingshot around the dark side of the moon and start back toward himself.

Droop was right: she watched too many movies.

"Fuck me," she croaked, reaching for her door handle.

He pulled the gearshift into drive. The car leapt into the wine-dark lawn, jackhammering across frozen earth, the engine clawing through its gears. When he switched on the headlights, the oak tree jumped in front of them and Ana thought with curious detachment that crashing was a choice she had not considered—but her father turned the wheel and carved a wide speedboat arc around the tree, the engine yowling as they wound around and around the oak, the farmhouse sliding across Ana's window repeatedly until she felt nauseous and wondered why she had thought it was a good idea to hand the keys to a brain-damaged man.

Though in a way it felt good to let someone else make terrible decisions for once.

As the car turned in a widening gyre, something in the engine knocked and knocked like it wanted out. With a chirp, the tires caught on the road and they were flying along flat country highways with no names, taking corners hard enough to make Ana wash up against her door. Warning lights flickered across the dash like heat lightning. Outside, it was dark and there were no landmarks, only land—corn waste and rocky fields and scrub meadows hunchbacked by frost—so it was hard to tell where they were headed, and easy to mistake speed for progress. When she noticed that the low glow of downtown Morocco was fixed in her father's window, though, she realized they were still going in loops.

Ha.

She touched his arm. "I shouldn't have gotten you worked up," she said. "It's okay. We can go back to the farmhouse."

Instead, he cut the wheel toward town. Smoke pearled up from under the hood, wisping over the windshield. They clattered down Main, past Govert slumped over the wheel of his John Deere outside the White Owl, past the reach of the street lamps, and the engine gave one more loud knock and went silent. They coasted to a stop in front of the Video Emporium.

The CLOSED sign was up. The glass box of light was empty, save for a boy at the counter, snapping and unsnapping little boxes.

"Dad," Ana started.

He tipped his head toward the store without looking at her.

Would she ever stop underestimating him? Somehow, despite the fact that his brain made a hash of her words, he understood what was going on. Which was more than anyone could say for her.

She kissed her father on the temple. Then she opened her door and stepped out without another word, because just then she didn't have any, and he didn't need any.

When she knocked on the door of the Emporium, Logan flinched and dropped the box in his hands. As he came toward the door to let her in, Ana looked over her shoulder. Her father was walking down the street, away from this wreckage, leaving the two of them alone, together.

◆   ◆   ◆

Logan opened the door and Ana brushed past him. When she heard it shut behind her, she wheeled around. "Why did you lie to me?"

His face twitched. "I'm well, thank you for asking. And how are you this fine evening?"

"Logan, why did you pretend to be gay?"

"For the record," he said slowly, "other people called me gay. You called me gay. I never said I was."

"*For the record*," she said, "you never corrected me. Why? Was it your über-pathetic way of getting the new girl to let down her guard so you could mount her?"

His face reddened except for two nubs of white where his eyebrows pressed together. "No."

"So what is your *deal*? Do you actually like girls, or am I so butch I remind you of a dude?"

Logan looked up at the hanging fluorescents, struggle all over his face. He was about to answer when someone spoke behind Ana.

"We're closed."

Jared. She recognized his voice, but when she turned around, she was a little surprised by his appearance. Something about him was different. His hair? His *hair*. Still curly like Logan's, but shorter and tipped with garish highlights.

"You," said Jared, and the strangest feeling came over Ana. She almost didn't recognize it, it had been so long since she'd felt calm. All the shit spinning around her heart like a dirt devil—all of it slowed. Quieted. Nothing had happened yet, but already she sensed how this encounter was going to play out. No: more than sensed. She knew. She could see it.

Jared dropped a box of microwave popcorn on the counter. "I'm only going to ask you one time to get your skank-ass out—"

"Or what?" Ana stepped closer. Her voice was light, almost breathless. "You gonna put your hands on me? You gonna choke me like you do to your brother?"

Jared looked over her shoulder at Logan. "Shouldn't be telling stories, bro."

Ana took another step. Jared was still looking past her, so he never saw her reach inside her parka.

"You're getting your hag to fight your battles for you now?" he said. "Real cool. Real manly."

Ana grabbed his belt buckle. "What do you know about manly, Highlights?"

Jared sneered at her, but his expression went loose when he saw the gun in her palm. He tried to shrink away, but she held onto his belt buckle, keeping him close enough that the security cameras couldn't see the gun. A part of her—the deepest, ugliest, most powerful part—prayed for him to do something stupid. Push her. Reach for her throat.

"What are you doing?" cried Logan. Jared craned his head back like he was trying to peel himself away, but she wouldn't let go.

"You want me to leave, I'll leave," she whispered into his neck. He smelled like gooseberries, sharp and sour. The yellow tips of his hair trembled. "But if you lay a hand on your brother again, I'll be back. He won't even have to tell me. I'll just know, and I'll come back."

She let go of his buckle and he stumbled backward. Turning, Ana slipped the gun into the back of her jeans. "Let's go," she said to Logan.

He gripped the counter, looking shaken.

"Let's *go*," she said again, grabbing his arm. They were halfway out the door before Jared found his voice. "They're real," he said.

Ana looked back to see him pointing at his hair, which looked like a clump of dying grass. He said, "I went skiing and the sun—"

The door shut behind them with a jingle. Ana was done with lies and masquerades. It was time to give the truth a whirl. "Come on," she said, towing Logan to his car. "I've got something to tell you."

From the written statement of D.W. Boxelder:

It's the rare witness who doesn't confide in somebody. Usually that confession destroys the relationship. Either the listener gets scared you might hurt him (you gangster!) or that he might get caught in the wash of violence if your former associates find you (those gangsters!).

Even if the listener gets over his initial fear, he tends to feel betrayed that you've lied to him for so long, and that, Madame, is a death sentence for any relationship.

So I wasn't worried when Ana had Logan park in a field under a windbreak elm so she could tell him the truth about what brought her to Morocco. Her confession must have sounded lurid and pulpy to her own ears—Mobsters! A bomb! A hit man!—but by the end she didn't sound self-conscious at all, only relieved. (What did I say about the urge to confess? Truth is like a bad amoeba in your gut. That shit wants *out*.)

Logan did not share her relief. By the end of her confession, his face was waxy with sweat. His hand was on the door handle, though whether it was to steady himself, or he was getting ready to bolt/vomit, Ana couldn't tell.

"I can't lie," said Logan. "I am freaking out right now. To the extent that it makes me ask myself, 'Have I ever truly freaked before?' And the answer, it occurs to me now, is no. Not like this."

Silence from Ana. She must have been wondering if she'd made a terrible mistake.

Logan turned to her. "What if they find you? What if I'm there when they do, and I get caught in the crossfire—"

"Don't be dramatic. There's not going to be any crossfire."

"Because they'll snipe you from a rooftop, right? *Death from above.*"

"No death, Logan. Not from anywhere."

"We'll just be walking along and then—*pfft*—you'll fall to the ground, blood pouring out of a little hole in your head and I'll be like, *Ana? Ana!* Then the sniper will talk into his sleeve, like, SHE'S GOT SOME GUY WITH HER, and the mastermind will come back at him with, NO LOOSE ENDS, CARLOS, and Carlos will be like, AFFIRMATIVE. Meanwhile, there I am—" Logan began acting out the scene, holding out his arms in an invisible hug. "—kneeling on the sidewalk, cradling you and wailing to the stars—ANA, NOOOOOOOO—as a tiny laser dot appears on my chest and traces its shaky way up to my forehead before: *Pfft.* Fade to black, man. Fade. To. Black."

Logan fell back against the headrest, exhausted by the pitch for his own death.

Madame, allow me to pause here, in this last moment before this case went off the rails. Allow me to chart out the intended trajectory of my plan in the same way Logan narrated his execution.

Just then, Logan was a hot mess. Seconds away, it seemed, from saying *I'm sorry, Ana, but I can't be around you anymore*—and that would have been it. Game over. The final thread in Ana's frayed rope, snapped.

From there, everything would have fallen into place. Ana, isolated, would have stopped bucking, and focused on caring for her father. With a little luck (and of course the motivation of staying in the Program), Ben would have remembered how to speak in time to testify, and the trial would have moved forward. Following a sure conviction, the government could have seized Veedy's assets, including his property. Cue the demolition crews to turn that whole blighted block into a baby canyon. Cue the confirmation of Daniel Webster Boxelder as the next director of the Program.

What an elegant chain of events.

But as you know, Madame Inspector, that's not exactly how it played out. If it had, I wouldn't be telling you this story, would I?

So how did my beautiful design get fucked up? Who tramped through my garden? Who blazed a new path that led us all to this investigation?

A sexually confused dork from the sticks.

Logan unbuckled his seat belt. Ana thought he might run from the car, but he turned to her with open arms.

She drew back.

"Just a hug," he said. "Nothing weird."

Ana didn't lean in, but she didn't push him away, either. A brief clinch, she told herself. A couple of brisk pats, then a clean break—but he turned out to be as fleshy and warm as a grandmother. He was a squeezer and rocker, not a patter, and she found herself holding onto him.

"I don't like girls," he said, "but I like you." He sighed, and a hum resonated through Ana's chest. "I still do, but I won't be a creep about it."

Closing her eyes, Ana rocked with him. When was the last time she'd held somebody?

The day she cradled her broken father by the roots of the oak tree.

Logan gave a sad laugh.

"What is it?" she said.

"I'm just thinking of all those hours I was going *blah blah blah* about movies, while you must have been scared to death that someone would find out who you were. I can't even imagine…"

Just then, I was at a loss, too. How could Logan pivot so quickly from envisioning his own death to expressing sympathy for this little siren? If you can't bank on self-interest, Madame, what can you count on?

I see now what I failed to see then. If anyone in Morocco knew what it was like to live in fear, to harbor secrets, to know the pain and danger of being outed, it was our mutual friend here.

"I'm sorry," he murmured. Ana felt something crack inside her chest and then her face was wet and she was gulping and Logan kept swaying, absorbing it all.

So Logan was the last thread, all right. A thread that, when tugged, unraveled the shimmering, nearly flawless garment of my making.

Chapter 22
Men of Lawlessness

In the valley where Zeeshan was born is a snowmelt lake. The dark water is renowned for healing—local legend says it can ease pain in the joints—but it almost killed Zeeshan when he was a boy.

Like many of his neighbors, Zee was a shepherd, and he brought his sheep to the lake to drink. If the sun was hot and the day was dusty, the shepherds would take off their dhoti kurta and slip into the water.

The water was bracing even in July, so most boys would jump out after a minute or two, rubbing their arms and cursing through chattering teeth—but not Zeeshan. He swam across the lake in long, smooth strokes, pretending the cold didn't bother him. By the time he reached the far shore, his fingers and toes would feel numb, and the cold would be crawling toward his heart, but instead of climbing onto the bank, he would turn and stroke back to his clothes, his sheep, his shivering friends who thought he was crazy.

One day, in the middle of the lake, something latched onto his toe.

Zeeshan tried to kick it away, but it held fast. Trying not to panic, he pulled his foot up to the surface, but all he saw were his own toes, now as twisted and gnarled as the fingers of Gautum, the old man in the village so crippled by arthritis that his grandson hauled him to the lake every morning in a wheelbarrow. Zee tried to swim back to shore where his friends were smoking cigarettes, but the harder he churned, the faster he sank. A ghost was twisting his toes, tying his calves into hard knots.

Zeeshan slapped the surface of the water. "Hatoo!"

His friends looked up, then at each other. Zee was in the middle of the lake, farther than any of them had gone under normal circumstances. Now it looked like something was attacking him, and none of them were eager to swim out there.

Zee slapped the water again, and the ghost climbed up his thighs, grabbing at his stomach with long claws. He heard himself whine like a dog just before lake water leaked into his mouth. When a wave washed over him, his hair slicked over his eyes, and he couldn't lift his arms to push it away. Zee tipped back his head, let out a cry, and stopped churning.

The ghost stopped climbing.

Lying still with his head tilted back, he saw a slice of sky through his hair and heard the muddled shouts of his friends. They weren't coming to help him, he knew. Whatever happened next was between him and the ghost. And if he slipped under the water, he may not come back up.

He fluttered his hands. Small, small, like a mahseer waving its fins. Small, so he wouldn't wake the ghost, still locked onto his legs, but no longer climbing.

Through the split in his hair, Zeeshan watched the clouds and did not panic when the occasional wave lapped over his face. His heart was slow as sleep, his blood thick as slush. Clouds scrolled across the sky, but he couldn't tell if they were moving or if he was, and he didn't dare roll over to look at the shore. The ghost was sleeping and he kept fluttering until a staff touched his shoulder, and then his friends were hauling him out of the lake.

In the end, he lost the toes on his right foot. "Frostbite," said the doctor who visited the village a week later, but Zeeshan knew this was where the ghost had taken hold first and stayed the longest. The ghost took his toes and left him with a wooden block in his shoe, but it also gave Zeeshan a blessing. The boy knew how to slow his mind, fill his veins with snow. In situations that would make anyone else panic, Zeeshan slowed down, waited for a solution to float up, then executed it—no matter how hard, no matter how long it took. The day he almost died was the day he became inexorable.

Which is why he had such a hard time understanding Americans: they never thought anything through. Snap decisions, shortcuts, grabbing short-term gains without a thought for long-term consequences—they're *children*. Like the way Ben turned on Veedy, making that decision in a single panicked night in the ER.

Or like Kate, who, after all of Zee's slow, patient persuasion, had suddenly decided to freeze him out.

He'd wanted to work with Kate, but from the beginning he knew she might spook. So when they'd returned to her house after visiting the warehouse, he waited for her to go to the bathroom. Then he scrolled through the numbers on her caller ID, and there it was: a series of long-distance calls to and from the same number.

In his pocket now was a scrap of paper. On that scrap was a phone number with a 219 area code.

The trial was less than two months away. Time and options were running out. This was the moment an American would have panicked, but Zee pulled the scrap from his pocket, smoothed it over his gabardine thigh, and slowed his heart.

Until the only solution presented itself.

When the moment comes, Veedy had said, *you will do what is necessary to save the operation.*

Yes, he would. Could it still be done without killing anyone?

He hoped so. But that hope was small now, smaller than the need to fix this problem.

Zee put the paper back in his pocket. Then he packed a bag to begin fluttering his way toward Indiana.

From the written statement of D.W. Boxelder:

This is the difficult part, Madame.

I'm tempted to leave it out—I could, you know, and no one would be the wiser—but I made certain promises. The whole story, etcetera.

The other night, I couldn't sleep, so I turned on the radio and heard a woman talking about how sharks were disappearing from the oceans. Good, I thought, because who likes sharks? But the woman said no, not good, because sharks are the scavengers of the sea. They pick off the weak, the sick. They keep the ocean clean and healthy. Losing sharks, she said, would be like losing your garbage service.

When I was in seminary, I used to wonder why God suffered the devil. (Stay with me, Madame. I'm building to a point, I swear.) If God truly had divine foreknowledge, why didn't He stop the devil before he caused trouble? If He knew how everything was going to play out, why create the devil in the first place?

Because the world needs a devil, Madame. Without a devil to fear, the world would be even worse than it is. The threat of hell is the only thing that keeps the world from becoming hell. Once I figured that out in seminary, I knew I couldn't hold that knowledge back any more than parishioners could bear to hear it, so I dropped out.

I trust that you can bear the truth, Madame Inspector, so here it is: I watched Zeeshan pack. I knew where he was going, and I did nothing to stop him.

My big job is to manage the whole Program. Keep the system healthy. My small job at that time was to bring the Easterday case to successful completion. It just so happened that Zee's trip would serve both ends.

If Zee picked off Ben, any prosecutor with a functioning frontal lobe could convince a jury that Veedy had ordered the hit. Down goes Veedy. Down go the rest of the dominoes, and I'm left with a cautionary tale to keep the next generation of witnesses and their families in line. *See why we have firewalls? See what happens when you don't play by the rules?*

What I did, I did for the good of the Program. The greater good of all our witnesses, present and future. This was foremost in my mind as I watched Zeeshan strap on his ankle holster.

Ana should have been safe. Zee had no reason to hurt her. My plan was to reunite her with her mother afterward, but as you know, that didn't exactly work out, either.

If I made a mistake here, it was trusting my foresight too much. But what else did I have to go on? At that point, what else could I do?

With apologies, Madame, I'm going to stop here for the night. I'm tired, and I have paperwork to fill out for a new witness before I can rest. The job marches on, investigation or no. I know you're impatient for the rest of the story, but you'll have to wait until you find my next letter.

Waiting isn't easy, I know. I'm reminded of the early believers, always pestering the apostle Paul about when Jesus would come back. My favorite answer from Paul isn't the old chestnut quoted by every hack who ever filled a pulpit: *The day of the Lord will come like a thief in the night.* What a dodge. For my money, I'll take the more specific prophecy he gave to the church at Thessalonica: *That day will not come until the rebellion occurs, and the man of lawlessness is revealed, the man doomed to destruction.*

The man of lawlessness. I always liked the sound of that. In any story, you need that man. Without a catalyst, you don't get combustion. Without Judas or the serpent or Zeeshan, you don't have a story. No destruction, no resurrection.

In the end, this story—like every story in the Program—is about resurrection.

PART 3

GHOST EXCHANGES

Chapter 23
Come in from the Cold

Tuesday afternoon, graylit sky. Ana was supposed to be in school, but she and Logan were maneuvering a small cart down the cramped aisles of the IGA, picking out peanut butter, ramen, dented cans of soup, rolling past the produce section, which was little more than a few bushels of apples and onions. Add that to the list of weird shit about Morocco. Outside, it's plant city: corn, soybeans, tomatoes, asparagus, blueberry. Inside the grocery store, it's all canned goods and meat. So much meat. The shop might have been small, but the entire back half was a meat counter. Slabs of chicken, cuts of beef, long trays of pork. No fish, but five different kinds of ham. The store smelled like a freshly-opened pack of slim jims.

Once, back in the fall, Ana had picked a half-dozen ears of corn from a field on her way home. Even though she boiled them over twenty minutes, she nearly chipped a tooth when she bit into the first ear. It was like gravel on a stick. Rock-kabob. When she mentioned this to Logan under the flag of *You people can't even grow corn right*, he appraised her for a long moment. "I've never met anyone who tried to eat field corn after it dried," he marveled. "I never thought I would."

Around here, vegetables were for animals. Animals were for people. You knew your place on the food chain and you stuck to it.

If you could afford your place, that is. The Easterdays couldn't, not even with Ana's wages supplementing the tiny stipend provided by the

Program. She took one look at the price pins in the meat, stuck another complimentary pretzel log in her mouth, and rolled on. "Help me find the cheapest veggies," she told Logan.

"Popcorn's a vegetable. I'll run by the Emporium later, get you some."

Ignoring him, Ana squatted before a low shelf of canned vegetables. Logan bent over her, curls tumbling over his eyes. "You know what this whole thing is like?" he whispered. "*Three Days of the Condor.*"

Since her confession a week earlier, they'd talked about her situation more or less constantly. At first it was a relief: finally, she could tell someone the shitty truth! But after a few days she got tired of talking about it—they kept butting up against the same questions and couldn't figure out a way around them, so what was the use?—but like any new convert, Logan had zeal coming out his eyeballs.

"It's not like *Three Days of the Condor*," she said, running her finger over the price tags on top of the cans. "It's not like a movie at all."

"Robert Redford wanted answers, too, but he couldn't find any until he figured out who to trust. That's the place to start. Who do you trust?"

She gave a light snort. "No one."

He grimaced and Ana realized he had hoped she would name him. God, why did she have to be this way? If she bothered to take the career aptitude test the guidance counselor was pushing at her, it would probably come up *Harpy*. "Logan," she started, but he wasn't listening. He tossed two cans of mixed vegetables into the cart. "Two for a dollar," he said. "And this way you don't have to make a choice."

By the time they left the store, the weather was turning. Sleet fell alongside flurries, the mixed vegetable of weather. The road was a hard-pack of ice, studded with salt and grit, dirty as the devil's tongue. Wind ran across the stubblefields to shoulder the car. Earlier, she had tried to get Logan to stay at the farmhouse with her father while she shopped (mostly to buy herself a moment of peace), but Logan had taken one look at the sky and insisted on driving her. She'd been annoyed, but now she was glad she wasn't walking back to the farmhouse with wet paper bags falling apart in her hands and sleet pouring down her neck. She was about to thank

Logan—her mouth was shaping itself around the awkward words—when he pointed through the windshield. "Expecting somebody?"

The farmhouse was ahead on the right. Close enough to see a man on the porch, but not close enough to see who it was. "Slow down," said Ana. "Drive past if I say so."

"He's facing the road."

"So?"

"So he's not looking for your dad. He's waiting for you."

The roof of the porch hid the man's face until they were nearly even with the driveway. Then he leaned against the rail, and she saw it was Droop. Strangely, she didn't feel relieved. Not entirely. Something about him looked different. The stubble on his cheeks was the color of gunmetal; a hank of hair stuck up on the crown of his head like a single fat feather.

"Keep going?" said Logan.

Ana was tempted to say yes. Droop wore a sour expression; whatever he had to tell her wouldn't be pleasant. But if she avoided him now, he would just keep coming around, so she groaned and told Logan to pull in.

"How about you put away the groceries, give us a minute to talk?" Ana said when Logan put the Escort in park.

Logan didn't joke or protest. He got out and carried the groceries up to the house. If anything passed between him and Droop on the porch, Ana didn't catch it. She looked out her window at the fallow field beyond their overgrown yard. Snowflakes stuck to the glass.

The driver's door crumped open and Droop slid inside.

"What happened now," Ana said flatly.

"I helped you."

She looked at him. "So my dad is not—he's fine?"

"He's fine. You're fine, too. Or at least you will be."

Ana narrowed her eyes. "What did you do?"

"I looked into your case." He drummed his fingers on the wheel, frowning. "But you're not going to like what I found."

◆　　◆　　◆

Pete had not intended to do any investigating on Ana's behalf. After the close call at the library, he had sworn off any further snooping. But then Pastor Jim showed up on his doorstep with a bottle of Basil Hayden's. After a couple of toddies, Jim volunteered that he wasn't entirely comfortable with the way Ana was being railroaded by the other Liars. Pete allowed that although Ana was a complete pain in the ass, her suspicions about her father's case might not be entirely insane. Around the time they ran out of honey and substituted maple syrup ("Eureka," said Pete), Pastor Jim said it was a shame that no one could look into Ana's questions about the legitimacy of the case, as a few answers might settle her hash more effectively than browbeating her.

"I see what you're doing here," said Pete.

"I'm having a drink with my friend." Pastor Jim swirled his mug. A wisp of steam rose to his face. "It's probably impossible for you to find out anything at your pay grade, anyway."

Pete laughed softly. "Asshole."

He should not take this bait. He knew that.

The next afternoon he turned up at Pastor Jim's house, saying his phone line was down, which was not true, but sounded less crazy than saying his boss might have tapped his phone. Would Jim mind if he made some private calls from the parsonage?

He spent hours on the phone, starting with old colleagues in Chicago and working his way outward until he found himself talking to an informant who knew a few Kashmiri girls that Zeeshan had brought over.

Why did he make these calls? Maybe he did want to help Ana, and he thought Pastor Jim was right about the way to do that. Maybe his curiosity had been awakened by what he'd learned at the library, and his punishment hadn't entirely snuffed those flames.

Maybe he thought he could find something that would hurt Boxelder. But he didn't.

In the car, Pete turned to Ana. "The case isn't bullshit. Veedy really is running a prostitution pipeline."

"He's not. Sure, he's bringing in people illegally, but it's to work."

"That's what these girls thought, too."

According to Pete's informant, the girls showed up in town expecting to work in a restaurant or nail salon, only to get turned out on the corner of West Madison and Kostner. To make sure they didn't leave, the pimps held onto their documents—both their old real ones and their new forged ones—and gave the girls only enough money for the day. As a carrot at the end of the stick, some pimps told the girls they could buy out their bondage, earn their freedom, but since they charged the girls for everything—room, board, clothing, even booking fees—the debt turned out to be a slippery hill they could never climb.

Other pimps favored the stick. *If you try to escape and fail,* they told their girls, *I will kill you. But if you succeed? I will kill two of the other girls.*

Ana put her forehead against the window.

"I'm sorry," said Pete. "I know you were hoping for a different story, but the case is legit. These people are dangerous." He drummed his fingers on the wheel again. "Will you leave it alone now?"

Ana didn't answer. The window was getting steamy from her breath. *Frogged up,* she used to say when she was little. Her father had loved that saying. It made him think of a car full of frogs, swamping it up with their croaking. Over the years he took to saying the phrase without appearing to realize it. *My sunglasses are frogged up.* How long since she'd heard him say that?

Long time. That part of her father, that part of their lives—it was gone and there was no way of getting it back, no way of going home, that's what Droop was trying to tell her.

The shittiest thing about Droop's story? He was right: she should leave it alone. Zeeshan was lying about the operation. Which meant it wasn't safe to come home.

"Such an idiot," she muttered.

"Who?"

"All of us. Mostly me."

"Nah," he said. "If anything, you're too smart for your own good. Which is why you'll ace the SAT."

"Not taking it." She sniffed hard. "Also, you can't ace it. It's not—oh, never mind."

That's when Droop told her about a second favor. To help her move on, he'd signed her up for the test, paid the fee, no need to thank him. She didn't. In fact, she told him it was probably a waste of time. If her father didn't get better, no way could she go off to college and leave him alone. "Especially if he can't testify and you fuckers cut him loose," she said.

"Look at it this way," said Droop, steering the conversation away from that black hole. "Taking the SAT doesn't mean you have to go to college. It just...opens up the possibility. That's all I'm asking here. Leave open the possibility that your dad will get better, and you'll get to go to college. All right?"

That's where it would start: as a possibility. But it would only be a matter of time before Droop started pushing her to go to college, and it would be just like last fall, when her father was trying to get her to leave this town to save herself.

She dropped her forehead against the window. The thought of reliving that fight exhausted her.

"All right?" Droop said again, and she nodded wearily. Anything to be done with this conversation.

"I'll pick you up at six on Saturday morning," he said. "Be ready."

He was talking about being ready to roll out of the house, but she got the sense he was talking about something bigger, too. Something about allowing an ending, and a hard new beginning.

She nodded again without looking over, and Droop got out of the car, leaving her there, alone in the passenger's seat.

Chapter 24
Professional Courtesy

As usual, Zeeshan picked up the new ya:tri at the Mohawk reservation on the US/Canada border, and drove them down to Baltimore in the cargo van. After parking in the underground level of the warehouse, he told his passengers to remain still and calm, their next driver would be here soon.

Per routine, Zeeshan walked out to the road, put the van keys in the mailbox and raised the plastic flag. But then, instead of leaving the premises as he was supposed to do, he walked back to the van to wait for the next driver, who would not be expecting him.

Why haven't they arrested you? Kate had asked.

He told her he didn't know, and that was the truth. But he had a theory. When he was a boy, men in tan coats came through his village in search of markhor, a wild goat with corkscrew horns. The men carried guns, but they shot tranquilizer darts, not bullets. They only wanted to attach radio collars to a few markhor, they said, so they could track their migration.

Zeeshan believed these men, which made his friend Sameer scoff. "Sure, they won't kill the first one," he said. "They'll strap on a collar just like they said—so they can follow it back to the herd and kill a dozen at once."

Maybe the Feds were watching him, tracking him somehow. Hoping he'd screw up, or lead them to something that would crack the case wide open. What Zee needed was to get out of their view.

He was going to Indiana; that was decided. But he wasn't going to drive, pulling a tail of Federals the whole way. He'd go through the operation, because it had a long track record of traveling under the radar.

As an added benefit, he'd get to see the entire operation for the first time. Up to this point, he'd only experienced his leg of the trip before passing the ya:tri off to the next driver. After this ordeal was over, after Ben was no longer a problem, he could go to village leaders in Jammu and Kashmir and say, *I have gone where your sons and daughters will go.*

Veedy wouldn't be happy with him for breaking through his firewalls in the operation, but Zee wasn't worried about that. If this trip failed, Veedy would be in jail for the rest of his life. If it was successful, Veedy's ass would be saved along with the operation. He'd either be gone or grateful. Either way, Zeeshan would be untouchable.

In the van, Zeeshan watched a single dust mote travel through the cabin like an astronaut on a space walk, eventually crashing into the dashboard, a graveyard of dust. He took off his watch so he would stop checking it, but at least two hours passed before the corrugated steel wall across the warehouse pulled back, and a man stepped out of the freight elevator.

Zee made a hushing noise, but the ya:tri all seemed to be asleep, or in some jet lag-induced state of suspended animation. Or maybe it was just now sinking in that they might never see their families again.

Zee opened the van door and the man ducked behind a pillar, cursing softly. No panic, no shouting, and when the man peered around the pillar, he brought up a revolver with two hands. Police or military training, most likely. Thank God. Less likely to panic and start spraying bullets around the warehouse.

"On the ground," called the man with a light Paki accent. Punjabi, if Zee had to guess. "Get down and put your hands behind your head."

Stirring in the back of the van. "It's all right," Zee called to the ya:tri before getting down on the gritty floor and lacing his fingers behind his neck. The man walked toward him, slowly at first, then quickly on the last few steps. He wore Adidas trainers and a track suit, though the man looked too fat to be a runner. Pressing the muzzle to Zee's neck, the man ran a hand down his sides, over his ankles, up his thighs.

"I left my gun in the van," Zee said.

"That was dumb."

"If I shot you, I wouldn't know where to go next."

The man squatted down to look Zee in the eye, but didn't take the gun off his neck. "You're the first guy? The one who brought them here?"

Zee unlaced his fingers enough to nod.

"Huh." The man sounded impressed. "You're even dumber than I thought."

◆　　◆　　◆

The man let Zeeshan sit up, but situated him behind a pillar so the passengers wouldn't overhear their conversation, and so they wouldn't have to watch him shoot Zee, if it came to that. "Though I hope it doesn't," said the man. "Leave now, and I'll forget to tell Veedy you fucked up. But if you're still here in one minute, I will have to kill you."

"A generous offer."

The man shrugged. "Professional courtesy."

His name was Ali. He had a puffy, fast-fed look. His goatee and gold necklaces were attempts to frame lines that were no longer there: *this is a chin. This is where neck becomes shoulder.*

Still, Zee could tell the man was serious, as was his warning. He took a breath, slowed his heart. "You like this job, Ali? Are you pretty comfortable?"

"More comfortable than you're going to be in forty-five seconds." Ali talked like an American, but his voice still carried the lilt of the subcontinent.

"What did you do before this? For a job, I mean."

Ali looked disappointed. "Tell me you're taking this situation seriously."

"I am."

"Because you need to take this seriously. I don't bluff."

"I believe you."

"You're making a mistake if you think you can talk your way out of this."

"Indulge me," said Zeeshan. "Think of it as a condemned man's last request. Before you came on board with Veedy, what did you do?"

Ali blew a puff of air, equal parts disbelief and admiration. "Just before? I drove a cab."

"Tough job," said Zee. "Long hours, rude customers, never knowing if you're going to get a fare…"

The side door of the van slid open with a heavy clunk. A girl with tangled hair hung out the door, looking around. "Hey!" she shouted. "What's going on?"

It threw Zeeshan off. Just slightly, but enough so that when he looked back at Ali, he was surprised to see the man tapping his watch with the barrel of the gun. "Last chance to take my offer, friend."

Zee closed his eyes briefly. Then he let his question roll out like a marble across the floor. "When Veedy goes to prison and all of this falls apart, will you go back to driving a cab?"

Something changed in Ali's face, or maybe just behind his face, and Zee could tell he was no longer counting seconds, but wasn't ready to admit it yet.

"I'm not asking you to change plans," said Zee. "Same route, same process. Just take me with you."

"Why?"

Better that you don't know, Zeeshan wanted to say, but that would not cut ice right now. He had to give this man something. "I'm going to fix things so the operation continues running smoothly, which will benefit all of us."

Ali seemed unconvinced. From the van, the girl shouted again. "Where did you go? Hey, don't leave us here!"

"Come back next week," Ali said to Zeeshan. "Let me clear it with Veedy first."

"He doesn't want to know. That way, no matter what happens with this trip, he can't be accused of orchestrating it."

"We've faced problems before," said Ali. "We always stay the course, and they always go away."

Zee got to his feet and brushed off his pants. Looking Ali in the eye, he said, "Who do you think makes the problems go away?"

Chapter 25
The Standardized Flipout

Checking in for the SAT was like entering a refugee camp. After waiting in a long line of the downtrodden, Ana handed her registration papers to a pinch-faced woman at a bowed table. As the woman scrutinized her student ID with the kind of intensity usually reserved for checkpoints along a contested border, sweat prickled Ana's hairline. Was something wrong with her ID? Did some tiny flaw reveal that she was fake? She glanced back at Droop, but he had already settled into a seat in the lobby and was paying more attention to his newspaper and cup of coffee than to her. When they'd pulled up to the school, she said it was cool to just drop her off, but he insisted on sticking around to make sure she went through with the test.

"There's an old saying," he told her as he parked the Bronco. "Trust in Allah, but tie up your camel."

"I'm not a camel."

"You ain't Allah, either."

The pinch-faced woman handed the card back to Ana with a scowl. *You win this round*, her look said as she waved Ana into a holding pen constructed of scarred folding tables.

Because the registration sheet had said to CHECK IN AT LEAST ONE HOUR PROIR (sic) TO TEST TIME LATECOMERS WILL NOT BE ADMITTED NOR REIMBURSED, the holding pen was already packed with drowsy teens. Ana made her way to a spot by the portcullis that separated the foyer from the cafeteria.

She slid down the tile wall to sit on the tile floor. This school was like a drunk tank built for five hundred. She touched her forehead and her hand came away slick with sweat. Was she getting sick? No way Droop would buy that. He'd call bullshit from ten paces. Whatever was happening to her, she'd have to muscle through it.

She stood, but her legs were shaky and she grabbed the portcullis to steady herself, which of course made a huge rattling noise. A few kids looked over, but no one said anything. She wobbled to the bathroom, sat on the toilet in the handicapped stall and put her head between her knees, but no, that wasn't going to do the trick, so she kept sinking and sinking until she ended up on the floor with her shoulders pressed to the cold tile. Her head weighed eight hundred pounds. Sweat pooled in her belly button, which didn't make sense because now she was cold. She was a sliver of ice sliding around a hot pan.

Someone came in. Two someones. She saw the jellies on their feet, heard them say, "What's wrong with *her*?" in shitty little voices, like Ana was doing this to get attention. She was relieved when they left without further fuckery—but a minute later the door opened again and she saw penniless loafers and fat calves inside modest hose.

Don't let it be the check-in lady, Ana prayed to the ceiling.

The check-in lady squatted down in her skirt to peer at Ana under the stall door. "Young miss, are you all right?"

Ana tried to nod, but instead her teeth chattered. Someone had rewired her brain. Was this how her father felt all the time?

The lady cocked her head. Her gray cap of hair did not move. "Do you want me to call your parents?"

Ana tried to laugh, but she gave a shivery moan and to her horror she felt tears run down her temples. Oh, great. Now her hair would be wet and festooned with grit from the floor. If she did manage to walk out of here, it would look like she swabbed the tiles with her head.

"Okay," said the lady, though the situation was the opposite of okay. "How about you let me in and I'll see if I can . . . I'll just see what I can do."

When Ana didn't respond, the lady rattled the door until Ana sat up and unlatched it. Midwesterners could be ruthlessly kind. The lady wiped at Ana's forehead and neck with a wet square of paper towel. "Little case of the nerves?" she guessed. "I see it all the time. This test, it does feel like a lot of pressure, doesn't it?"

Ana nodded, wiping her eyes.

The lady cocked her head again. There was something bird-like about her, a robin listening for worms. "You know," she said, "if you don't do as well as you hope, you can always re-take the test. Or start at community college." She smiled and patted Ana's back lightly. Ana felt bad for thinking of her as Frau Gestapo earlier.

"Remember," said the lady, helping Ana to her feet. "This isn't the only time or the only way. There's more than one path to a good future."

Ana smiled thinly, and managed to turn to the toilet before throwing up.

Chapter 26
Charm/Offensive

Ali might not make idle threats, but he didn't have any qualms about idle promises. The moment he climbed into the van, Ali started a patter of reassuring phrases in Kashmiri. *The hard part is over,* he called over his shoulder. *Your new life is just around the corner.* Zee wondered if this had been his shtick as a cab driver, spewing positive bullshit.

Ali kept it up—*Soon you will be in your new home, eating as much as you please!*—until it seemed like he might be reassuring himself as much as them, easing his own mind about bringing Zeeshan along. *You will not regret this, to be sure!*

To get Ali to stop, Zeeshan asked him where he learned to speak Kashmiri. "I picked up the basics from refugees around Karachi," Ali said, "then polished it in the army. They sent me into the mountains as part of a charm offensive. My job was to talk to village leaders and convince them it was a bad idea to deal with India."

"How did that go?"

Ali flashed a grin. Apparently his soothing patter had worked on himself. "They didn't need much convincing. Your people aren't interested in dealing with anybody." He called over his shoulder again. *Your employers await you with open arms. The weather is always pleasant in your new town.*

Zee looked out his window so Ali wouldn't see his irritation. After this mess was over, he would talk to Veedy about cutting Ali out, sending him back to the metered world to peddle his happy horseshit to distracted businessmen and drunk tourists. Replace him with someone who lied only when they needed to lie. Someone who didn't say "your people." For now, though, Zee kept his mouth shut, because the ya:tri were quiet, and there was no sense in upsetting them by getting into a squabble with Ali.

On Haines Street, Ali maneuvered the van into a parking spot. Zee was surprised to see a bus station. "Greyhound?"

"Low security," said Ali, extolling Greyhound's number one virtue. "Best way to travel if your documents aren't entirely in order."

The thing was, their documents were in order. The ink on the forgeries was dry before the van ever left the Mohawk reservation. It's just that the papers were sent directly to their employers, who held them as a kind of bond until the teens fulfilled the terms of their agreement. But maybe it didn't have to be that way, Zee thought. Maybe they could hand out the documents the moment the ya:tri landed in Canada. They could cross the border as citizens and fly to their new homes. Everything legal(ish), everything (seemingly) above board. And this way, they would no longer need someone like Ali.

In the parked van, the girl with tangled hair and a scrawny boy crept toward the front, holding hands. "To Chicago," Ali said slowly and loudly. "Understand? Tell the ticket lady you want Chicago."

The boy tried to say *Chicago*. He sounded like a vacuum cleaner sucking up a bolt. The girl pushed her hair back from her face and said, "I got it."

Zee unbuckled his seat belt. Ali put a hand across his chest. "Where do you think you're going?" he said.

Zee looked down at the man's hand. It occurred to him how satisfying it would feel to break Ali's wrist, to hear the carpal bones snapping like suspension cables on a bridge. Then he could break the man's jaw, so the surgeon would have to wire it shut.

Instead, he removed Ali's hand with exaggerated politeness. Just because his old urges were still there didn't mean he had to give into them. "I'm headed through Chicago, too," he said.

"Not with them, you're not. If you all walk in there together, it'll draw too much attention."

"Let me worry about that."

Ali shook his head. "Buckle in. I'm taking you to a different station."

And make him lose the trail of the operation? No way. "I'm going with them," said Zee through his teeth.

"No more than two at a time in a station. That's the rule. Veedy made that crystal clear."

Shifting and murmuring in the back of the van. *Welcome to your freedom*, Ali barked over his shoulder. *The streets of your town are clean enough to eat off!*

Zee's own suspension cables were stretching and whining. If Ali's lies were isolated to this trip, they would have been somewhat easy to ignore— but this was just the tip of the bullshit iceberg. His lies went back at least as far as that charm offensive. Zee wished he could have been there to fall crying from the sky like a shrike, a hara wataj, the little executioner. He would have cut out Ali's tongue, sent his shifty ass running back to Karachi.

"Stop lying," said Zee through his teeth.

"The less you freak them out, the less I'll have to lie."

Zee struggled to keep his cables from snapping. Maybe Ali was right; maybe walking into that bus station with these two would be an unnecessary risk. The operation needed stability, and Zeeshan's presence was already throwing off its balance. The more he stressed the system, the more likely he was to break it instead of save it.

His primary goal was to get to Indiana. Could he get there by starting at a different bus station? He could. And if he lost the trail of the operation, so be it. He could always conduct his audit later, after this ordeal was over.

Zee sat back.

"That's better," said Ali, removing his hand. "When I drop you off, you can express your gratitude in the form of cash."

Not long ago, Zee would have expressed his gratitude in the form of zip ties and kitchen shears. But Zee wasn't that man anymore. With a little luck and cooperation from Ben, he wouldn't have to be that man at the end of this trip, either. This could be a charm offensive. His goals were modest: he didn't need to bring Ben back into the fold; he just needed to convince him it was a bad idea to deal with the government. As long as he didn't testify, there would be no threat from Zeeshan. Ben could be out from under Veedy's thumb, free and clear.

But if Ben wouldn't listen to reason, Zee would be the hara wataj one last time. But only once. One job isn't a relapse; just a revisit.

The girl with tangled hair was still hovering behind them. Ali touched her shoulder with surprising tenderness. "A man will meet you in the Chicago station. Don't worry about finding him; he'll find you. He'll drive you to your new home in Dubuque. Beautiful town. Always sunny. Any questions?"

The girl shook her head and took the boy's hand. Other hands reached up to touch them as they opened the sliding door. Cold air poured in, and the two teenagers stepped into the darkness together, looking like skydivers leaving a plane without their chutes.

Chapter 27
Do Not Go On

The pinch-faced lady tried to send Ana home, but Ana pleaded to stay, saying the nausea and nerves were gone—all better now!—and she couldn't afford to lose the registration fee, and going to college was so, so important to her. The truth was that she didn't want Droop to haul her to another testing center on another Saturday morning. She was here; let's do this fucking thing.

Once she was in the testing room, though, she couldn't concentrate. She'd start bubbling in dots, then catch herself doodling in the margins. Stars, hats. It wasn't until she sketched an alligator that she realized she was drawing the same pictures her father made for the therapist. When she'd fished his sketches out of the trash, she thought they were visual gibberish, but now she saw what they really were: images from his old life. She could picture his old closet, the crisp line of hats on the top shelf, the soft pile of knit shirts with alligator logos.

It does feel like a lot of pressure, doesn't it? the pinch-faced lady had said. It sure does, lady. Pressure had crumpled her family like a tin can at the bottom of the ocean. Pressure had treed her father. And even now that he was back in the house and she knew they could never go home, the pressure was still there, because the trial was looming, where he would either testify or be kicked out of the Program. And then? Would there be any let-up? No. Even in the best case scenario—he testifies, he puts Veedy away—Zeeshan would still be out there, haunting him if not hunting him.

Ana stopped filling in a circle. Somehow she had never realized that before. There would never be an end—not for her father, and not for her, either—as long as blowing their cover was only a word away. As long as they were alive, there was no end. Only pressure.

STOP, said the bottom of a page. THIS IS THE END OF THE SECTION. CLOSE YOUR BOOKLET AND PUT DOWN YOUR PENCIL. DO NOT GO ON.

She stopped. She closed her booklet. She put down her pencil.

With that kind of pressure, her father would never get better. Not entirely. Which meant she could never leave him, whether he was in or out of the Program.

If you don't know the answer, counseled the test-prep books, *see what answers you can eliminate.*

Droop was wrong: going off to college was not a possibility. That had been ruled out the moment her father fell from the tree; she just hadn't realized it. Apparently Droop—that dopey, hope-sick man—hadn't realized it, either, or he wouldn't have wasted his money on this test.

She was stuck here. That was the only answer left.

Or was it?

Ana shoved her chair back. The proctor, a balding man in owlish glasses, lowered his newspaper and blinked at her in surprise. "It's not time for a break," he whisper-shouted.

Ana walked to the door, feeling all the eyes in the room on her. *This isn't the only way,* the pinch-faced lady had said. *There's more than one path.*

"Your test," said the proctor. "It'll be invalidated!"

Like that was the worst thing that could happen to her. Which was frankly hilarious, but not as hilarious as the proctor's bewildered look when she gave him a wild smile. Then she was out in the empty hallway, her shoes chirping on the gleaming linoleum. She winged her sweaty pencil into a dark classroom. She didn't feel sick or hot or cold anymore; she felt clean, burned clean. She'd found a different answer, though it wasn't one of the standardized choices.

When she reached Droop, she pulled down his newspaper. "One of them can testify," she said.

He looked around the foyer, but there was no one around. No parents, no pinch-faced lady. Just the empty registration table, paper signs waving in an indoor breeze. Still, he leaned in close before speaking in a low, tight voice. "We had an agreement."

"Those passengers—the ones Zeeshan brought over—they know the trafficking operation from the inside. Any one of them would make a better witness, and my dad would be out of the mix." She almost laughed, it was such an elegant solution, so *obvious* once she said it out loud, but somehow Droop failed to see its perfection.

He closed his eyes. His face was all jumpy. "Here is what is going to happen," he said deliberately, each word a burning coal of anger. "You are going to turn around. You will walk your self-destructive ass back to that classroom and—"

"Pete." She grabbed his shoulders. "Pete, please. Help me."

A hard tremor ran through him. The newspaper crinkled in his hands. "That," he said, "is exactly what I'm trying to do."

She stepped back, looking at him like she'd never seen him before in her life.

"Ana," he said. When she headed for the door to the parking lot, he said, "Come on, now. Don't—"

He didn't get a chance to finish that line, because the door was closing and she was already gone. Ana was running.

Chapter 28

Nothing Goes Smoothly on a Greyhound

Zeeshan's bus was ready for departure on time, loaded with bags and riders, only to idle for forty-five minutes before the driver showed up. In Pennsylvania the bus ran smack into a blizzard, near white-out conditions that forced other cars to the side of the road while the Greyhound slid past like the Titanic through a fog bank. Though the holiday season was over, the bus driver whistled "We Wish You a Merry Christmas" through his teeth, the melody floating like a descant over the husky cries of a baby in the row behind Zee.

None of the other passengers seemed to notice the noise, much less struggle with the urge to kick out a window and hurl themselves, screaming, into a snowy ditch. Most of them looked merely tired, long-suffering but patient, as though this minor hell had been promised in the small print on their tickets. The baby's mother, gazing out the window with a soft smile that suggested the gauzy grip of barbiturates, seemed to have mastered the art of ignoring discomfort.

The bus caught fire outside of Elkhart. One minute they were cruising along at a smooth fifty-five, and the next minute they entered a cloud of smoke. The driver pulled off the road, threw it in park and hollered, "Everybody out!" in the same way someone else might yell, *Quittin' time*!

The driver was the first one out the door, leaving everyone else to follow or choke to death inside the bus, to each his own. Zeeshan turned to assist the baby's mother, but she was already bustling up the aisle and the reinforced corner of her diaper bag clipped him in the eye socket.

By the time Zee got off the bus, his fellow passengers were sitting on top of their suitcases a mere twenty feet away, holding out their palms as though the smoking wreck was a bonfire. A young man with a narrow face and a braided goatee pulled a bottle of Hot Damn! schnapps out of his backpack and offered it around. Zee demurred, but the goatish man said, "You better warm up your insides, bro, because your outsides are gonna freeze before another bus gets here," so Zee took the bottle. It was like drinking embalming fluid through a cinnamon stick. His head, already soupy from twenty hours of travel punctuated by a stiff pop from a diaper bag, got even soupier, though not in the worst way.

"Is this normal?" Zee asked, gesturing at the bus with the bottle he seemed to be holding for the second or fifth time. A pillar of smoke rose up to space like something from the bible.

"This is Greyhound, bro," said Goat Man, who began twiddling his thumbs in the air and making video game noises with his mouth. *BLEE BLEE BLEEDOO-BLEEDOO!*

Zeeshan was a grown man. He was familiar with the language, the culture. He had not recently left his family, his country, and spent days huddled in the back of a windowless van before setting out for parts unknown. So if he felt like he was sinking in despair, what must it be like for the ya:tri? What must they think of America when they find themselves stuck between a flaming bus and a Goat Man who sounded like an arcade?

Still. Transitions were tough. Every exodus has to pass through the desert before reaching the land of milk and Hot Damn!

But not every traveler makes it through the desert. After hours of huddling on the side of the road, absorbing slaps of wind from passing cars, putting on every article of clothing from his bag in a futile attempt to keep warm, and passing around the apparently bottomless bottle of schnapps, Zeeshan began to wonder if this little tribe had been forsaken. The bus was still smoldering, but the driver had gone back to his seat, eaten an entire box of Kit-Kats and then sprawled across the wheel, asleep. Possibly dead. No one had bothered to check.

Zee had the nagging sense he should do something—flag down a car, organize a scout party to strike out for the nearest exit, light the suitcases on fire for warmth—but the snow and liquor conspired to make him slower than slow. Sluggish. The ghost from the lake was wrapped all the way around him. Zee was going down in cold water, and this time nothing was stopping him.

No one dies like this here, he told himself. America won't let it happen.

His phantom toes throbbed, freezing all over again.

As the sun deflated on the horizon, Goat Man stood unsteadily and with an exaggerated underhand swing, lofted the empty bottle high in the air. It spun gracefully through the snow falling out of the dirty sky. *PEW PEW PEW*, he shrieked, finger-gunning the bottle until it detonated against the windshield of the bus. The driver jerked, snorted, and without opening his eyes, reached over and shut the door.

I don't *think* America will let us die like this, Zee thought.

By the time another bus arrived, it was the frozen heart of night. The new driver was surly, like he suspected the passengers had set the fire on purpose to spend more time in this scenic hellscape, but he did pass out vouchers for a free night at the Motel 6 in Elkhart. Weary, drunk, and so cold he could no longer feel his good foot, Zee tripped on the first step into the bus, landing on the same eye that was bruised from the diaper bag. The driver bent down and said, "You're holding up the line."

At the motel, Zee ordered Chinese takeout and turned on the shower to let it warm up. When he sat down to untie his shoes, he fell into a sleep as deep and dark as the bottom of a snowmelt lake, and not even the delivery guy's pounding on the door could wake him.

Chapter 29

Ghosts in the Maze

Four-thirty in the afternoon, and the sun had set. Shorn fields crowded the interstate. The occasional oak rose out of flatness like a frozen mushroom cloud. On the southbound side of the divided highway, a few drivers were heading away from Chicagoland, but hardly anyone was heading north on a Saturday afternoon, so Ana let the Escort drift over the lane marker.

She was playing a game with herself, pretending the car was Pac Man eating up the dashes, on the run from ghosts. *WAKA WAKA WAKA.* It helped maintain her line and nerve. She hadn't gotten behind the wheel since her aborted attempt at Driver's Ed, but like any kid, she'd logged hundreds of hours behind a joystick. If she could pretend it was a game, she'd get a handle on this driving thing in no time. Logan drove, for Christ's sake. How hard could it be?

Don't ask. Don't think. Only munch. *WAKA WAKA.*

Besides, it's not like she had any other choice. Her father couldn't help with this mission, and Pete wouldn't help. She'd pinned her last hope on Pastor Jim. He wasn't down with the Liars' crackdown on her, she could tell, so she went straight from the testing center to the parsonage. She asked him for a ride to Chicago, but he refused. "You have your answers," he said. "Now you have to live with them."

"Spare me the shitty sermon," she said. He offered her a cup of tea, which was obviously a trap. He wanted to keep her here, just like everyone else, from Boxelder to Droop to the Liars. They were ghosts in the maze, hemming her in.

Thank God for Logan. Thank God one person in this town knew how to say yes. All it took was a single call for him to ditch work and come to the farmhouse to keep an eye on her father. Leaving her father alone for a school day was one thing, but this trip might be overnight, might be a couple of overnights, actually, and he really shouldn't be alone that long.

When Logan asked how she planned to find one of the former passengers in a city of three million, Ana admitted she didn't know, but she had to try. "Ana, seriously," said Logan. "What are the odds?"

"Better than if I look around here."

She was her father's child, bullrushing a problem, using desperation as high-octane fuel. Logan frowned. His car keys were in his hand, but now he seemed to have second thoughts.

"I'll ask around," said Ana. "You know I'm not shy. Is that enough of a plan for you?"

"Ask *around*? Well, that's a great way to put yourself in danger, but I fail to see how—"

She grabbed the keys from his hand. If she allowed herself to think about odds, risks, consequences, she wouldn't go. And if she didn't go, she'd have to stay and face the alternative—this maze, forever—and that was the one thing she couldn't do.

"Hey," said Logan when she reached the door. She half-turned, expecting him to demand his keys back, but he only said, "Good luck," and raised his arm in a dorky salute.

Ana stopped herself from rolling her eyes. She returned the salute. It was the least she could do. Logan was the best goddamn friend she'd ever had.

◆   ◆   ◆

For about fifteen unimpeded miles Ana was free to gobble up dashes in the road, but when she passed Demotte, a truck came flying down the ramp behind her. At first she pretended it was part of the game—*Oh no, a ghost!*—and goosed the accelerator to pull away. The truck caught up fast, though, so she backed off the gas and pulled over to the right lane, gripping the wheel at ten and two to keep it straight.

The truck pulled up behind her. Headlights poured into the cabin. "Go around, dickhead," she muttered, but the truck stayed on her ass, even when she took a hand off the wheel to wave him around. The whole highway was open, and this guy was trying to inspect her tailpipe.

She slowed down, but when the truck still didn't swing out and pass her, a bad feeling came over her.

The truck flashed its brights.

Ana slid her hand under the blanket on the passenger seat until she touched the pocket gun. It didn't subtract her fear like normal, but she closed her hand around the sticky grip anyway and floored the gas pedal. She started to pull away, but now the truck swung out into the left lane and reeled her in, creeping up in her side mirror.

Don't make a ruckus, they had said. *Keep your head down. Don't call attention to yourself.*

Those fuckers, they might have been right. Maybe the Liars weren't the ghosts after all; maybe they were the maze itself, keeping her hidden. This truck, the one appearing in her window—this was the ghost.

Ana looked over to see the truck's window sliding down. Strangely, she felt calm, detached. It was here; it was happening. No longer would she have to worry about finding a witness, or her father's recovery, or college. All her questions about the case shook out of her heart like so many tangled fish hooks. Her future was short, her hopes were small.

She hoped it wouldn't hurt too bad.

She hoped her father wouldn't find out about her death before he met his own.

There was only one thing left to do, one final gesture. Ana cranked down her window. The frozen air made her feel violently alive. She switched the gun to her left hand and pointed it at the truck. She might die, but she would get off one or two shots of her own first. Glancing at the road ahead, she saw that her car was steady between the lane lines. Would you look at that? She was a good driver, after all.

Looking back at the truck, she expected to see a gun pointing back at her, but what she actually saw was a finger. Jabbing at the side of the road. Attached to a windblown Droop, looking offended by the pocket gun aimed at him as he shouted *Pull over, pull over!*

Chapter 30
Cock's Crow

Zeeshan arrived at the bus station in Chicago a full day behind schedule. The ya:tri should have been states ahead of him, but there, huddled against the wall, was the scrawny boy and the girl with tangled hair. He wasn't surprised. *This is Greyhound, bro.*

The surprise came when the girl walked over to let him know it wasn't Greyhound's fault. They'd gotten to the station on time. Which meant they'd been waiting here nearly thirty hours. Where was the person who was supposed to pick them up?

Her face was slack and gray. She smelled like a man. In crossing the station, she'd caught the attention of the security guard leaning against the wall, who probably thought she was homeless. Which, it occurred to Zeeshan, wasn't entirely off base.

"The driver will be here soon," said Zee. The words were out of his mouth before he realized he sounded like Ali.

"We're hungry," she said. "Do you have money?"

In the corner was a vending machine. As luck would have it, the machine was next to a NO PANHANDLING sign so ancient and battered it looked like a grimy shield. When the girl held out her hand to Zeeshan, the guard lifted his chin in what passed for high alert in a bus station.

Zee hesitated. He wanted to help them, he really did, but he couldn't attract attention from law enforcement. If he jammed up the operation over a pack of animal crackers, he would never forgive himself.

He was trying to figure out a workaround when the boy came across the station, holding out his hand. "Please," he slurred. English fit his mouth like a bad pair of dentures.

The guard shoved off the wall with a sigh.

"No, thank you," Zee said firmly enough that the guard wouldn't think he required any assistance, then he walked away from the ya:tri, over to the scuffed pews at the far end of the station. Sitting down, he was dismayed to find the girl standing where he'd left her, glaring at him in fierce disbelief. She looked like she was about to make a scene, but at last she took the boy by the arm and hauled him back to the corner by the trash cans. The guard leaned back against the wall with a clear look of relief.

You don't understand, Zee wanted to tell the girl and boy and the guard and Ben and Kate and the Feds and the world. *I am doing what is necessary. I am making things better. In the long run.*

Sometimes, though, the long run was hard to see. But a hungry girl glaring at him over her knees? That was easy to see. She was only a few yards away, just as miserable and alone as Zee.

◆   ◆   ◆

Hours passed. Or maybe minutes, it was hard to tell. Bus travel shares more than a few symptoms with carbon monoxide poisoning. Zee stared blankly at a free tabloid. Across the station, the boy and girl sat cross-legged on the floor, occasionally casting him dark looks in case he'd forgotten they were pissed. The guard leaned against the vending machine, possibly asleep on his feet.

Then the door opened and a woman walked into the station with a cold wind at her heels like a pack of low dogs. She was tall, with wheatish skin. Older than the boy and girl, but not yet, if Zee had to guess, in her thirties. She was frowning, but that might have been due to the cold outside, or because she was embarrassed to be so late.

"Vuni ma shong," she said to the boy and girl. *Don't sleep yet.* An odd welcome, but at least it was in their mother tongue. This woman was probably a former passenger who could reassure them with the example of her new life. *It worked for me*, she could tell them, *so I came back to help you.*

This could be the model for the whole operation, thought Zee. All Kashmiri. One wave of immigrants helping the next.

The tangle-haired girl asked a question, but the woman made a sharp sound—*zzzt*—and hauled her roughly to her feet. Well, that was a little brusque, but she probably had a good reason. He would give her the benefit of the doubt.

The guard wouldn't, though. He pushed away from the vending machine and stepped toward them. The woman turned to the guard. "Patience," she said. "Branko will call you."

The guard nodded. The woman towed the boy and girl into the cold.

The whole encounter couldn't have taken more than a minute. As soon as the woman left, the rest of the travelers sank back into their stupor, but Zee folded his tabloid and walked to the grimy windows. Outside on West Harrison, a station wagon was double-parked. The woman bent at the waist and said something to the boy and girl. Her face was tight, and the two ducked their heads and hurried into the back seat.

Why was she angry? Why was she so late? And who the hell was Branko?

Stepping back from the window, Zee revised his assessment of the operation. They would have to clear the deck, he'd tell Veedy. Ali, this woman, the rest of the operators: gone. Start over with a new crew, a new culture. Firewalls between every layer of the operation were fine in theory, but a little oversight would go a long way, and Zee would be happy to provide it.

He buttoned his sport coat. Plucked a bit of fuzz from his sleeve. Change was in order. Starting now.

He walked over to the security guard, who straightened and touched the butt of his Taser. "Pardon me," said Zee. "Can you tell me how to get to the Amtrak station?"

Chapter 31
Offerings

After fielding a call from a worried Pastor Jim, Pete had a choice to make. Actually, he had three choices.

He could let Ana go up to Chicago on her own, probably get her dumb ass killed.

He could haul her back to the farmhouse.

Or he could escort her up to Chicago in a safe and controlled manner, if she swore to God and every last angel that she would not attempt such a trip again.

Hearing this last option, Ana raised an eyebrow. Pete didn't blame her for being skeptical; he could hardly believe himself. After all, he'd already caught a suspension for merely giving her Boxelder's number. What would happen if Box found out Pete was offering to chaperone this fishing expedition? What would happen if Ana took him up on this offer and—God forbid—the trip went sideways?

But what else could he do? If he dragged her home, she would just attempt another trip as soon as his back was turned. That much was certain. So you might say he was making this offer for her safety. You might also say—if you really wanted to be honest—that he was sick to death of Boxelder. If Pete was forced to choose sides, he wouldn't choose the guy who was threatening to abandon a disabled witness. He would choose the Easterdays. Did Ana understand that?

The Bronco faced north, two wheels in the scrubby grass. Ana stared bleakly ahead. She hadn't said a word since getting in the truck. Whether she was considering his offer or ignoring him, Pete didn't know. "Whatever way we go," he said, holding out his hand, "you'll need to give up the gun."

Wind moaned across the fields. A semi blew past them, and the Bronco rocked on its struts. She didn't look at him.

Pete pulled back his hand, feeling foolish. This situation wasn't covered in the handbook. That's what his wife used to say when their daughter would eat a handful of grass, or push apple seeds into her ear canal, or do any of the other million crazy things kids do for no good reason. "They didn't warn us about this in the handbook," she'd say with more weariness than humor. They were happy then, even if they didn't know it most of the time. They thought they were tired and poor and cranky and working harder and enjoying themselves less than everyone around them. Now he knows he'll never be that happy again.

"I had a daughter," Pete heard himself say.

Nothing from Ana.

"She'd be about your age now." He cleared his throat and squinted out the windshield. "You make me think of her, you know. Wonder how she would have turned out."

"I'm sorry."

"It's better than forgetting her."

Oncoming headlights bleared the windshield. Pete covered his mouth and looked out the window. What a head case he'd turned out to be. What a sack of regret. What a foolish, foolish—

He felt something touch his knee.

The gun. Ana was still holding it, but she had set it on his leg. The barrel was pointed away from him, which was fortunate because the safety was off.

"You can take me up there," she muttered. Her eyes slid away, as though she was embarrassed. "I appreciate it."

Pete put his hand on top of her hand. Before taking the gun, before stowing it in the glove box and driving on to Chicago, leaving Logan's car on the side of the interstate, he let his hand rest there a minute. He let them both rest.

Chapter 32
Double Exposure

Logan and Ben were watching *Tron*. Actually Ben was watching *Tron*. Logan, who had seen the movie forty-nine times, was thinking about attempting a conversation with Mr. Easterday. It was the polite thing to do, plus he was curious about the man, and, okay, Logan felt a strong urge to let him know that he, Logan, knew who Mr. Easterday really was, and it was okay! Logan was cool, Logan could be trusted, and if Mr. Easterday had anything he wanted to get off his chest, any secrets or confessions or whatever, Logan had all night to listen and decode.

Question: how do you have a conversation with a guy whose mind is like a food processor, except instead of food it chopped words and julienned sentences?

Corollary question: why does a food processor cut up food, but a word processor makes words? One destroys, the other builds. *Totally illogical, Captain.*

Yes, Spock, but also mysterious and beautiful. Our mother tongue is a fickle mistress.

Captain, your metaphors make no sense, but your sideburns make me feel a confused urge to stroke your face.

Stroke away, Spock. As long as I can return the favor vis-à-vis my tongue and your—

Logan pinched his own bicep hard enough to raise an angry welt. He was done with that gay stuff, in case his brain didn't know. No more *Trekki-erotica*. He could be a regular guy. With boners for girls. His little incident with Ana, bad as it was, had proven that much.

When he saw Mr. Easterday looking at him, Logan stopped pinching his arm and lifted his can of ginger ale. "Nazdarovya, comrade."

Mr. Easterday warily lifted his own can in a mini-salute.

Nazdarovya. My God. Dude can't even understand English so you throw a little Russian at him? Idiot. Dope. Faggot. Dicklicker. Sometimes Logan wished he could kick himself in the balls.

Everyone makes mistakes, Captain.

Not everyone has a crew depending on them, Spock. When I screw up, men die. Can't you understand that, you heartless Vulcan? Men die!

No one has died here, Captain. And have you considered the possibility that our host is not being entirely honest with us?

What are you saying, Spock? You think he's faking?

Mr. Easterday took a sip of his ginger ale. Logan gave him a sidelong glance until his eyeballs ached. Could he be faking? No. Maybe? No. See: Occam's razor. The likeliest explanation was that Mr. E was simply gone, gone around the bend like Colonel Kurtz in *Apocalypse Now.*

Hypothesis: maybe Kurtz had brain damage, too. That would explain his crazy-ass poetry.

That was one excellent movie, *Apocalypse Now.* Logan had seen it nearly a million times, but the ultimate time was at the IMAX theater in Indianapolis. When he found out they were screening it on a Tuesday afternoon, he ditched school, raced down 65, and paid an outrageous twelve dollars for a ticket. A handful of viewers were scattered throughout the theater, stoners and layabouts, but even they sat in pairs, and as Logan settled into his seat in the dead middle of the auditorium, he felt a little weird about being alone. Correction: more than a little. He felt untouchable, repellant, like a freaking pariah: all the SAT synonyms bum-rushed his brain to flagellate him.

Who cares? he told his brain. *It's not like I'll ever see any of these losers again.* For a moment that notion actually made him feel lonelier, but then the screen dawned—there's no other word for the way the filmlight broke upon the void of the screen—with the opening shot of a ceiling fan and the sound of a Huey's blades going ZHWHOP ZHWHOP ZHWHOP all slow, and Logan's bad feelings blew off like a light fog. Every worry and memory and niggling thought blew off, too, until he felt naked and clean before the screen. Logan's goose bumps were sharp as pins. His loneliness was beautiful and sacred. He gripped the armrests, closed his eyes, opened his throat to the screen and made a garbled noise of ecstasy, which, thank God, was drowned out by the roar of the world-eating THX speakers.

It was his ultimate memory.

Sounds kind of gay.

Not at all, Captain. It's love, that most illogical notion, though not of the sexual variety.

Deep-throating a movie screen. Sure, Spock. Not sexual at all.

Logan had two dreams for his life. One was to be a bum in California, where you could sleep outside in total comfort year-round and pick fruit right off public trees and panhandle enough to buy a single movie ticket, then spend all day sneaking from screen to screen, watching everything.

His other dream was to fall into a movie.

Like in *Tron,* where the guy enters the video game and becomes awesome. Becomes a hero, actually.

It had felt like that could happen at the IMAX. Like all he had to do was let go of his armrests, and he would have fallen into the screen, which would have turned out to be like the surface of a pond, and at his splash the stoners in the audience would have gone *Whoaaaaaaa* at the sight of Logan on the PT boat with Martin Sheen and a skinny Laurence Fishburne, steaming up the Da Nang to find Kurtz reciting his crazy lines. Which actually weren't so crazy, if you knew how to listen to them.

Huh.

Logan turned to Mr. Easterday. "So," he ventured. "You like the movie?"

With a sigh, Mr. Easterday settled deeper in his armchair. "Slime."

Logan hesitated, then pressed on. "I know about...your situation."

He waited to see if recognition bloomed on the man's face. It did not. Proceed with caution. "I want you to know that I stand with you. I'm a friend." Logan put a hand on his own chest. "Logan, friend." He drew a heart around his heart. "Friend."

Mr. Easterday picked up the remote and turned up the volume.

Logan said, "I dry-humped your daughter."

Mr. Easterday glanced over, and Logan's heart went into warp speed. He was about to shout out that he was just kidding, gotcha, you should see your face right now, when Mr. Easterday grunted, "Shadely. Your show plays bone."

Can you decode that transmission, Spock?

Negative, Captain. It appears our host has scrambled the signal.

So he's not faking.

My earlier deduction may have been off the mark.

I'll give you a chance to make it up to me. Meet me in my quarters in—

Logan shut his eyes to flush his mind. Then he leaned toward Mr. Easterday and let out something he had barely admitted to himself, much less to anyone in real life. "I keep having this dream where Ana's trapped in a tower and I come through the window as rain. She puts out a bucket, and when there's enough of me in the bucket—*poof*—I turn into a man."

Logan's heart was still racing, but no longer from fear. What was this feeling, what would you call it? It must be the thrill that exhibitionists get from exposing themselves, trotting out their ugliness, knowing the other person just has to take it. Logan had been on the receiving end of ugliness his whole life; why couldn't he be on this end for once? Besides, it was okay! Mr. Easterday didn't understand what he was saying. In fact, he wasn't even really paying attention. He was looking somewhere over Logan's head.

"I used to think something was wrong with me," Logan went on. "In the sexual department. I thought—okay, I'll just say it. I thought I was, you know, *gay*. But now—"

The armchair squeaked as Mr. Easterday raised his hands. Logan stopped talking. What could this mean? I surrender? I give up this pretense of not understanding? Then Logan noticed that Mr. Easterday was looking beyond him.

Logan turned. By the door was a slim man in a wrinkled suit. In his hand was a gun.

Logan's mouth went dry. His hands curled into claws. His spine tried to fold in half. He didn't want to die. This wouldn't have been a revelation to anyone else, but it was to Logan. A hell of a way to find out.

To find out.

Oh, *fuck*: the slim man must have heard everything Logan said to Mr. Easterday. Everything Logan had kept secret for so long. This shouldn't have mattered—Logan knew this was the smallest and stupidest of his concerns at the moment—but this made everything so much worse.

When the man limped closer to the television, Logan saw that he was light brown, like foreigner brown, and he felt an odd hope. Maybe the man didn't speak English? Maybe Logan's secrets were safe? But then the man said to him, "I'm sorry you're here," and Logan blurted, "I'm sorry, *I'm* sorry," and then he stopped talking because his throat was full of bile.

Exposing yourself might look the same as being exposed, but it's not. Not the same at all.

Chapter 33
Little Faith

Pete stopped in Gary to make a call. Another stop in Calumet Heights for another, longer call. Back in the truck, he told Ana he'd arranged to see one of the girls, and left it at that. She left it at that, too, until he tried to drop her off at a Taco Bell on Pulaski, telling her to wait there "for her safety" until his meeting with the girl was over, at which point Ana refused to get out of the truck. Pete started to argue, but gave up quickly. Time was short, and he must have guessed that she'd win this argument anyway. "Fine," he said, pulling back into traffic. "But you'll have to hide. If the pimp sees you, he'll either get suspicious or want to charge extra."

Pimp. The word sent bad electricity through her system. To avoid it, she latched onto *charge extra.* For the rest of the ride to the skeevy motel in West Garfield Park, she rode Pete's ass about being cheap. She didn't let up, even as they poked around the motel room, looking for a place for her to hide. "When you go to the drive-in, I bet you make your date climb in the trunk, don't you?"

He lifted the bed skirt. "I don't know if you've noticed," he said, "but I don't have the busiest social calendar."

Ana brushed her fingers across the wire hangers in the closet, making them jingle. "Maybe your love life would improve if you loosened the death-grip on your nickels, Scrooge McDuck."

"You're probably right," he said, opening the doors to the TV cabinet. "I'm sure it has nothing to do with the fact that all my waking hours are taken up by witnesses trying to get themselves killed."

He carried himself differently up here, she noticed. Sure and fast and testy. This should have stopped Ana from needling him, but she couldn't help it. This was how her nerves worked themselves out. "Your lifestyle might have something to do with it," she allowed. "But if you pin it all on that, you're bullshitting yourself."

A muscle flickered in his jaw. He stuck his arms into the cabinet, bear-hugged the television, and with a deep grunt, wrenched it free. Whoa. That TV was not small, but Pete lugged it out the door, wires trailing after him. Maybe he wasn't the bumbling Pooh bear she'd always taken him for. Maybe he was a different kind of bear, and maybe she should stop poking him with a stick.

When he came back into the room, his face was dusky and slick with sweat.

"Look, man," said Ana. "I'm sorry. That was a cheap shot. I—"

"Get in," he said, tipping his head toward the empty TV cabinet.

"Pete, that's tiny. I appreciate you thinking I'm petite and all, but—"

"They'll be here any minute."

"I'll hide in the shower. I won't make a peep until the guy is gone, I promise."

He gave her a look so dark her heart shrank. "Get your ass in the cabinet."

She got her ass in the cabinet. It was a tight fit, but she squeezed in there, chin between her knees, toes bent against the wall. When he closed the doors, all she could see was a thin band of light. Closing her eyes, she tried to ignore the pain that was like a pilot light in the base of her spine.

They'll be here any minute, Pete had said, but the minutes stretched on. A siren rose and died away in the distance. The pilot light in her back ignited into a sheet of fire.

By the time Ana heard a muted knock on the motel door, she couldn't feel her arms where they wrapped around her knees. She heard Pete say, "I hope you brought company."

"Hands up for a pat," said a man in a thick voice. Czech? Greek? Ana couldn't place the accent, but English was sour in this man's mouth. The band of light flickered as the man passed the cabinet. A moment later she heard a metallic shriek as he tore aside the shower curtain. Score one for Pete. Ana closed her eyes, praying the doors of the cabinet wouldn't fly open—but Pete had been right about that, too. The man ended his search after jingling around the closet, apparently satisfied that the room harbored no other johns or surveillance equipment.

"Okay, buddy," said the man. "I bring her up. Twenty minutes starts now."

"Now? She isn't here yet."

"You want, we can stand here and argue. Is your time."

Pete mumbled something and the motel door closed. A moment later, Pete opened the cabinet doors. "Doing all right in there?"

"Not really," she croaked, shielding her eyes from the light. "Now that he's gone, can I—"

Footsteps clanged on the steel walkway outside the room. "Hang tight," said Pete, closing the cabinet.

Ana tried to lean back, but she was already as far back as she could go. She tried not to think of coffins. She tried not to think of the armoire her father had shot a few months ago. The bullet hole in the side. Tipped over, with one door open, as though letting out a spirit.

The motel door opened—"Eighteen minutes," said the man—and then closed again. A moment passed before Pete said, "You speak English?"

The girl. She was here. This was happening. Ana strained to hear her answer, but either her voice was soft or she only nodded because the next thing Ana heard was Pete's voice again. "Would you like to get out of here? Away from that man? I might be able to help you."

"We should stay in the motel," the girl said firmly. Clearly this was not the first time she'd been propositioned by a would-be rescuer. Her English was good. The Chicago heaviness of her consonants was leavened by a slight lilt. "I've got other appointments."

"What if you didn't have to go to those appointments? What if you could—whoa, hold up. Put your shirt back on."

"Jesus," groaned Ana. She elbowed open the cabinet, tried to step out with her numb legs, and fell like a stone.

The girl turned, and Pete clamped a hand over her mouth before she could make a sound. She spiked her heel into his foot, but he didn't let go. When she went for his other foot, he swept her legs and she went down hard. The impact must have knocked the wind out of her because she was quiet long enough for Pete to pull a small roll of duct tape from the pocket of his jacket, tear off a strip with his teeth and slick it across her mouth, all while telling her to relax, hold still, he didn't want to get her hair caught in the tape.

Her hair. It was the wrong thing to notice at such a time, but Ana couldn't help it. It was thick and dark and, like, luxuriant. That was the word they'd use if this girl was in a shampoo commercial, lifting her hair and letting it fall again like expensive fabric. Ana had always assumed hair like that was a trick of the camera, but here it was in real life, on this girl in a bra and a tape gag.

After Pete finished taping her wrists together, he shook his head at Ana. "I should have left you at the Taco Bell."

The little awe she'd felt for Pete earlier was gone now. "She thought you were trying to take her out for coffee, bonehead."

"I just needed a minute. You should really work on your patience, you know that?"

"You should learn how to talk to girls."

"You should get tested for ADD."

They glared at each other for a moment before turning to the girl, who wasn't thrashing or moaning. Pete had propped her up against the bed, and she watched them with a look of patient suffering, as if this kind of thing (or worse) happened to her all the time. She looked older than Ana, but not by much.

"Take off the tape," said Ana.

"Are you kidding me?" said Pete. "One scream, and her big friend comes through the door with the safety off."

"He's not her friend. She knows that." Ana squatted on her heels to look this girl in the eye. "She's not going to scream."

"You don't know that."

But she did. Call it a premonition or high social intelligence or whatever you want. The knowledge felt solid and real, less a thought than an observation, something she was merely pointing out to Pete. She was already reaching for the tape on the girl's mouth when he caught her wrist. "Give me a second," he said. "I'll think of a different play."

"There isn't time," Ana said. "Take off the tape."

Pete glanced at the door, then back at the girl, looking unsure for the first time since they'd gotten to the motel. He seemed to be asking himself, *How the hell did I end up here?* With a sigh, he reached into his back pocket, drew out a pocket knife, and cut the tape on the girl's wrists and ankles.

The girl pulled the tape from her mouth, wincing when a few strands of hair caught. She didn't scream for the man, but she didn't seem grateful, either. Without a word, she pulled a crushed soft pack of cigarettes from her pocket along with a lighter. She lit the cigarette, then rested her elbows on her spread knees, the cigarette dangling from her fingers, a weary look on her heart-shaped face. She turned up her palms. *Well? Let's have it.*

Pete made the same gesture at Ana, which struck her as more snotty than generous.

"Okay," said Ana. She rubbed her hands together briskly. Her show now. She just had to figure out how to run it. "Okay. So. I know you're being forced to … do what you do. I know this wasn't the deal you signed up for."

The girl blew a jet of smoke at Ana. "You don't know anything."

Pete lifted the edge of the curtain to peer outside.

"I know you're from Kashmir," Ana said.

"And you"—she pointed her cigarette at Ana—"are from America. So what?"

Ana felt like she was sinking. The solid feeling she'd had when she told Pete to take off the tape was getting swampy.

"Six minutes," said Pete.

Fuck. She needed more time. She needed options. If only this were a multiple choice test. She could weigh each answer, think it through, find the most sensible solution provided by the well-meaning folks of the College Board. But even the Board would have a hard time coming up with a plausible solution for this little story problem.

Though plausible didn't necessarily mean truthful.

Ana took a deep breath, stepped into the unknown, and found the solid footing of a lie. "I know," she said, "the man who sold you out. I know where you were supposed to go. And I can get you there."

The cigarette stopped halfway to the girl's mouth. Her eyes narrowed. "Who *are* you?"

"Shit," said Pete. He let the curtain drop. "He's back."

"But it's not time," said Ana. Even as the words came out of her mouth, she heard how stupid and childish they sounded. *It's not fair!*

The girl stood, grabbed Pete's belt, and with an expert jerk of one hand, unbuckled it. "What are you doing?" said Pete, grabbing at his pants.

"Branko always comes back early for a shakedown," the girl said. "Get naked and pay him."

Branko pounded on the door. Pete dug out his wallet, opened it, and showed it to Ana. Empty.

"Oh, you *tight*wad," she said.

"You don't have money?" said the girl. For a second she seemed disappointed, then she took a thoughtful drag off the cigarette and slipped on the mask of patient suffering again. "Too bad."

The pounding made the door jump and shiver.

Pete slid a side chair over to the door, wedging the back under the handle. Then he went to the phone, moving as quickly as when they first came into the room. "Yes," he said into the receiver. "I would like to report a robbery in progress at the Revis Motel on West Washington. A man is breaking into a room on the second floor. Yes, *right now*. That's what in progress means."

Branko kicked the door hard enough to shake powder from the ceiling. "Open!" he yelled. Pete retrieved his .45 from the nightstand.

Ana turned to the girl. "Call him off," she said. "Tell him you need the whole time. Tell him—tell him he can take your cut."

The girl picked a tobacco flake off her tongue. She shook her hair away from her face. "Who are you?" she said again.

The door shuddered. Wood splintered. Pete thumbed down the safety on his .45.

"We are the ones who were supposed to pick you up when you got here," said Ana.

Something crumbled behind the girl's mask, a landslide of relief and recrimination, though the only outward sign was a slight tremor of her eyelids.

Another kick, and the deadbolt tore through the frame. The chair fell to the ground and the door opened an inch; the only thing keeping it from swinging all the way open was a slender golden chain. Pete raised his gun. His eyes were wide and he was breathing heavily through his nose, but his hands were steady.

The girl stubbed out her cigarette and went to the door. "Stop," she said into the narrow gap. Her voice was quiet, but urgent. "The man, he—I thought he just passed out, but now I think—" She glanced behind her, in the direction of the bed. "Branko, I think he's dead."

"Let me in, Radha."

"What if the police think I killed him? Should we call the police so they don't think I have anything to hide?"

"Don't touch the phone. Don't touch *any*thing. Get Kleenex. Use it to unlatch the chain."

She slipped behind the door, looked at Pete and Ana, and put her finger to her lips. A moment later, she stepped back to the gap. "There is no Kleenex," she said. "Would toilet paper be okay?"

Branko kicked the door again in frustration. "Listen to me—"

But then he stopped, and they all heard the siren. It was growing louder. "Radha, what did you do?"

Pete pulled Radha back from the door. "They'll be here in less than a minute, Branko. I'd run if I were you." Pete turned to Ana and spoke softly. "When I say move, we move. Got it?"

Ana nodded. Heartbeat in her fingertips, heartbeat in her eyes.

Pete looked at Radha. "You're with us, right? Tell me, after all that—"

Radha nodded. She didn't look scared, but she wasn't patiently suffering anymore. Little muscles shifted in her face, a different expression every second, her mind flipping through its channels. The siren grew louder and Branko kicked the door half-heartedly and the golden chain danced and they heard the heavy sound of his boots clunking away on the steel walkway. A second siren joined the first. In the parking lot, a car coughed to life.

"Now," said Pete, and he rose and Ana rose with him, watching the gun in his hand. If she could just hold it, maybe her heart would stop trying to exit through her mouth. Maybe her legs wouldn't feel like they might go crazy on the walkway and carry her skittering over the railing, hitch-kicking all the way down to the parking lot. As they passed each stairwell, she expected Branko to step out of a doorway and shoot them where they stood, let their lives drain out through steel rebar. And if Branko didn't get them, a search light from a cop car would surely pin them to this stucco wall that was so dirty it looked toasted. But somehow they made it to the truck and the dome light shined on the sweat all over Pete's face.

"Get down," said Pete. "Branko might still be around."

Ana let him know that she was good and tired of being bossed around and crammed into tight spaces, but she told him this while huddling down on the bench seat with this girl who smelled like lilac, a grandmotherly perfume. Pulling out of the motel lot, Pete glanced at the rear view. Headlights washed his face. "There he is," he said.

Radha didn't say anything, but a shudder rolled through her body.

For the first time Ana felt a prick of guilt. What would happen if her dumbass idea *did* work out? How could Ana leave Morocco with a clear conscience, knowing this girl would have to serve out their sentence? That was some *Tale of Two Cities* shit right there. It was a far, far crappier thing that she was doing, than she had ever done.

Or was it? After all, what was Radha leaving behind? This girl wouldn't want to go back to either of her old lives, would she? In a sense, Ana had been telling the truth when she said she would deliver on all the old promises: a new life, a chance to be who she wanted to be, a chance to become. Isn't that what people meant when they talked about the American Dream?

So why did Ana feel so rotten? Carsickness, maybe. Pete made turn after turn, rarely stopping. The truck sped up to merge with interstate traffic, then slowed for an exit ramp, only to repeat the process a minute later. Ana closed her eyes to quell the sickness, but Radha was soft and the truck was warm and the adrenaline of the escape bled away, and soon enough Ana was slipping in and out of sleep, like a needle sewing thread. Is this how her father felt, coming in and out of awareness? Or was he always under the cloth now, bumping against it but unable to pierce through?

Sometime later, the truck swerved off another exit, and Pete uttered a quiet *ha*. "You can sit up now," he said, but nobody moved. Radha seemed to be asleep. Ana didn't want to sit up. Didn't want to open her eyes. Didn't want to reckon with what they had done, and whatever would come next. She felt awful, but also—for the first time in so long she couldn't remember the last time—safe. Taken care of.

She patted Pete's knee, then nestled against her substitute, the girl she was saving and sacrificing all at once, and let herself fall asleep.

Chapter 34
Snicker-Snack

Around the time that Zeeshan zip-tied Ben's wrists to the arms of a kitchen chair and took a seat across from him, Ben realized the situation was worse than he'd thought. Zeeshan wasn't here to kill him; he wanted to talk.

Which was bad juice for Ben. Total garbledysnock. Like sweeping the radio tuner across the mile. Zeeshan was trying to explain something— Ben could tell as much from the stretch of the sentences, the hand that was scooping an invisible bowl and offering the contents to him, the nodding eye, the query face—but the huger Ben listened, the worse it slot. Once in a while a word slipped through his mental grinder—trust, Feds, Kate—but everything else got smurred or skorped.

Now Zeeshan was asking him a question and it was just...total mangle. Nary survivors. When Zee paused for a reply, Ben filled the gap with a question of his own. "Did you kill the boy?" he said.

Since Zee had taken Logan to a back bedroom, Ben hadn't heard a sow from the kid, which wasn't like that jabanape atoll.

Zeeshan gave him an odd look, wonder and disgust twirled together, so Ben tried again. "Did you—" he meant to start, but heard himself say, "Dishes."

He tried again, but this time it came out *Dogshit.* He tried to make a helpless gesture, but (ironically) this was hard to do with his wrists and ankles zip-tied to a chair. Don't get frustrated, he told himself, remembering what the pathologist had told him. Stay calm, and the words have a better chance of making it through. Stay cool, and—

Zeeshan pulled a folding knife from his pocket and set it on the table. Oh, slit.

Looking into his eyes, Zee said, "Willy sampan supercilious?"

Ben shook his head shitely, burly skivvering it. Meaning: *Meaning?*

Zee unlocked the blade. Turned it to sharp over Ben's pinky.

Zee's face had please all over it. He didn't want to do this and Ben didn't want him to do it, but when is that ever enough in this world? Ben skivvered again—*I can't, I don't*—and the blade snacked so fast. The overhead light shot out spiky bolts, a burning mace of light. Pain fucked his arm.

Zee zipped a tie to the stump of his pinky, slowing the blood to a drip. He took the finger to the freezer and dropped it in the ice tray. Ben was swimmy, shimmy.

"Le disarm giddle dubat," Zee said, turning back around. Or maybe, "Shantiff cremble terramung." Doesn't matter what he said. All that mattered was that he kneeled before Ben and laid the knife flatwise against his ringer fing. Ben may not have been able to communicate, but he saw with resolute clavicle that Zee was going to shoe that ginger, and dungeon flex sum, and the sex, until there came a point when Zeeshan put an end to thim, to Allah hiss.

Ben closed his eyes and struggled to slow his wind. Whatever Zeeshan wanted, Ben couldn't help him. Couldn't help himself, either, or Logan. The only person he could possibly help now was Anza. And the only way to help her was to get Zeeshan out of the house before she got back home.

The only way to help his daughter was to die quickly.

He opened his eyes. Zeeshan was waiting for him to speak.

Words were tar. Even nonsense. Especially nonsense.

Ben cleared his throat. When Zee leaned in to listen, Ben spit in his face.

Tender blade went snoke. Ben shoat so wide it spilt his lips, but he didn't mate a song. Just hopen, hopen, hopen, like he was feeding all the silence in the world.

Chapter 35
Visitors

Pete, in a truck filled with the sleeping breath of women.

He had intended to wake them as soon as he reached the farmhouse, but once he put the truck in park and looked over at Radha leaning against his shoulder, with Ana propped against her, like a loose shelf of books, he decided to let them rest a while longer.

There was a night years ago, driving home after fireworks at the high school football field, the air sweet with bug spray, when his wife and daughter fell asleep in the car. He parked in his driveway, listened to the murmur of talk radio and the distant pops of Black Cats and Whistling Witches, and breathed in his family.

A long time ago. A different life.

He looked over at Ana. She was out. Mouth open, eyelids blue. If she woke up and caught him watching, she'd call him a perv. Weirdo. Predator.

But he wasn't being pervy. If the rest of her plan worked—if Radha agreed to testify, if Ana and her father left the Program—he'd never see her again. Who could blame him for not wanting to rush her out of the truck?

Still. It would creep her out if she knew he was watching her sleep. So he would stop. Soon.

He used to watch his daughter sleep. Late at night, after double-checking the locks in the house, his last task was to uncover his daughter. She couldn't fall asleep unless the comforter was over her head and pillows were piled on top like a puffy cairn, even in the summer. By the time he unstacked the pillows and peeled back the comforter, he'd find her soaked in sweat but deep in sleep. He'd pull wet strands of hair away from her face, flap the comforter a few times to let out billows of heat, and if she was really sweaty, he'd sit her up to pull off her wet pajama top. She might grind her molars to express her irritation at being tussled, but her eyes would stay shut.

Sometimes, before he left, he put his ear against her mouth to hear her breathe. Shallow breath, tiny bursts. Amazing how little air it takes to run a body.

At the hospital, her bed had been made all wrong. The sheet corners were aggressively tucked in, the blankets folded down curtly across her chest. She lay on her back, stiff as a doll, an unwaking doll on a dollhouse cot.

The hospital was a ceaseless place. Pete was never fully asleep or awake. Nights in her room, he slouched in a vinyl chair with his feet up on another vinyl chair and covered himself with a scratchy blanket, but he only floated on the dead sea of sleep. His wife told him to go home. To shower, eat, rest. "You'll feel better," she said, but he didn't want to feel better.

Late one night, when his wife took her own advice and went home to sleep, Pete tore out the hospital corners on his daughter's sheets so she wouldn't feel trapped. He pulled the covers up over her face, tossed the scratchy blanket over the top. Then he checked the hallway to make sure the night nurse wasn't around. There would be no easy way to explain why he was heaping pillows over his comatose daughter's face.

After what seemed like a long time, he began his ritual of unstacking, peeling back, folding down.

Why did he do this? What was he hoping for? Pete couldn't have said. All he knew for sure was that when he lifted the last sheet and there was no wave of heat, no sheen of sweat, no grinding of molars, he felt let down by the universe. There was no going back, he knew then, except in memory.

Or maybe you can't go back at all. Maybe the past has to come to you, like now, in a truck that smelled like women.

If his wife were here, she might have stroked the back of his head and given him the little smile that meant she didn't buy his idea, but she was glad he'd had it. Or that's what she would have done before they lost their daughter, anyway. Afterwards, she would have said, *Does it matter, Crews? Does it really matter?*

Maybe it doesn't, Leah. But maybe it does. If you're the traveler, you can leave. But if you're visited by ghosts of the past, it's not your game. You have to wait until the ghosts finish their business. Or until something scares them off, like a light flickering to life somewhere deep in the farmhouse, making the living room curtains glow.

The ghosts vanished and Pete took a deep breath and the truck was just a truck, and these girls were not his girls.

A shadow crossed the curtain. Ben, probably. Getting more active, must be feeling better. Ana would be pleased. As pleased as that girl could be, anyway.

Across the bench seat, her lips were parted like she was about to sing. Carefully, so as not to wake her, he pulled a strand of fine brown hair away from her mouth.

Five more minutes. Maybe ten.

◆   ◆   ◆

In the end, Ana woke on her own. Stretching, she pushed her knuckles into the sagging cloth at the top of the cab and made a stuttering noise through her teeth. She squinted at the farmhouse. "How long have we been sitting here?"

"Just pulled up," said Pete.

Ana looked down at Radha, who was still asleep. "How old do you think she is?"

"Hard to tell with all that makeup."

"But if you had to guess."

"Twenty-two, twenty-four. Somewhere in there."

"Jesus." Ana shook her head. "What if I ruined her life?"

"You didn't ruin her life," he said. "I don't think you ruined her life."

"I lied to her."

"Not a total lie."

"Half-truths are worse. Now when she finds out the whole truth, she's not going to trust it."

"I'll handle that part," he said, absently touching Radha's hair.

"I mean it," said Ana. "The shit is really gonna hit the fan."

Pete couldn't help but grin. "Not for nothing," he said, "but who do you think flung that shit?"

Ana tipped her head from side to side, as close to a *mea culpa* as she was going to get, and he told her again not to worry, he'd figure it out in the morning. She got out of the truck and closed the door quietly behind her. Pete didn't exactly decide to get out of the truck, too, but that's what he found himself doing. After easing Radha down on the seat, he stepped out to the yard.

Ana gave him a look. *What are you doing?*

He didn't know. He had no idea anymore. Gesturing at the farmhouse, he said, "Want me to walk you up there?"

He stiffened as he said it, knowing she would come back with something like *Good idea, I might get lost,* or worse, *I'm not giving you a good night kiss, Droop.*

Instead she took two steps toward him and wrapped her arms around his neck, which surprised him so much he didn't even hug her back at first, just stood there with his arms out. She rested her head against his shoulder and sighed the way a kid does when you carry her, half-asleep, from the car to her bed. "I'll be okay," she said, and all he could do was nod curtly and pat her back because his throat was flooded.

By the time he was reasonably certain he could speak again, she was already staggering toward the farmhouse. Pete leaned against the hood of the truck, wanting to call out to her, but, unable to think of anything to say, kept his mouth shut and let her go.

Chapter 36
Visions

Ana was tired, tired. The curtain was coming down on her consciousness. Here were the black gathering edges. Here the rustle, here the fall. Her brain was responding only to the most basic commands: find a flat place, fall down, curl up to sleep. Even that seemed like a lot of steps.

Once inside, she leaned against the wall and slid down the hallway. The kitchen light was on, but she didn't even peek in there in case her father was reprising his old days of sleepless patrolling. God, wouldn't that be a kick in the teeth if he recovered enough to get back to a state of armed paranoia?

Fuck it: whatever he was doing in there, she'd deal with it in the morning. Or the afternoon. Whenever she woke up.

In her bedroom, she pulled her shirt over her head and threw it into the closet, only to discover that she was hallucinating. How else to explain the vision of Logan huddling in her closet with a strap across his mouth? Weird. Super vivid. Maybe she was still asleep in the truck. Or maybe this was a waking dream, the kind that usually involved peyote.

"Hun," said Logan through the strap. His eyes were wet and crusty. "Hun ah-ay. Hun. Ah. *Ay*."

Ana leaned closer, swaying. He seemed real. How on earth had he gotten stuck in her closet, though? She was reaching for the strap across his mouth when she heard a man's voice behind her.

"Turn around."

All at once the soft-boiled scene hardened into reality, and she understood what dream-Logan had been trying to tell her. *Run. Run away.*

She should have been a better listener. The whole past year, really, she should have listened.

By the time she turned around, she knew what she would see: her father's prophesy, come to pass.

"Into the kitchen," said Zeeshan from the doorway, a gun aimed at her chest.

Ana found herself raising her hands, though he hadn't asked her to do that. Weariness was no longer a problem. The shadows burned with dark fire. "Can I put on a shirt at least?"

"From the top of the pile."

Ana picked up a shirt without looking away from Zeeshan, and pulled it over her head. Holding his eyes, she tucked in the front, then the sides, her hands spading around to the back where she found . . . nothing.

For weeks she had carried the pocket gun, and now that she finally needed it, where was it? Entombed in Pete's glove compartment. Goddamn you, Droop.

"Ready?" said Zeeshan, stepping into the hall.

She wasn't, but it didn't matter. If she'd learned anything in the past year, it was that *Ready?* wasn't a question at all. It was a mask, a code. *Brace yourself,* Zeeshan might as well have said. *This is going to happen now.*

◆   ◆   ◆

It's hard to say why Pete didn't drive away once Ana got in the house. Maybe it was the fact that a single light deep in the house stayed on, but no other lights came on. Or maybe because Logan didn't come out to ask for a ride home.

Of course, all of this could be easily explained—they could be hanging out in the kitchen, or Logan could be staying the night because his car was stranded on the interstate—so maybe the real reason Pete stuck around was because years of frozen parenting instincts had thawed all at once, flooding him with overprotective urges.

Overprotective: the word soured his mouth. And that was a gentle term compared to what Ana would say if he came up there to check on her.

His job was done; he should leave. That's what a sensible person would do. Then again, tonight he had risked his life and career to kidnap a prostitute, so why start acting sensibly now?

He would just check on her. Say sorry to bother, make a joke at his own overdrawn expense, then go home. It would take two minutes, and he'd be able to sleep.

He looked at the truck. Radha was still asleep on her side, hair spilling out across the bench seat. She'd be fine by herself for two minutes.

◆   ◆   ◆

Too much noise in the kitchen. Ben was silent, his head lolling on his chest, but Ana wouldn't stop mewling and trying to chew through her gag, until at last Zeeshan had to put his hands over his ears. Listened to the hush of his breath. Focused on a single blood spot on the linoleum. Tried to quiet his mind.

For a moment there, he had lost himself. For a moment, things had gotten out of hand.

He had tried to be reasonable, hadn't he? He'd told Ben about the ya:tri, just as he'd told Kate. He proposed a way to end this trouble without any more pain for anyone—he'd even offered to let Ben come home, for God's sake—but when Ben stonewalled him, Zee fell back on his old ways. Just a little. Not all the way. Not yet.

Then came Ben's daughter with her story about aphasia, but at first Zee didn't believe her. It sounded like something out of Mother Goose: *my father fell out of a tree and scrambled up all his words.*

That's when Zee lost himself.

Now there were four fingers in the icebox. Now the floor was tarry with blood. Now Ana's explanation seemed to be the only puzzle piece to fit the jagged hole of Ben's silence.

Still. The fact that Ben couldn't speak right now didn't give Zee much reassurance. His speech might come back. Or he might peck out his testimony on a keyboard with his remaining fingers. Or maybe the A.D.A. would hold up a doll and ask Ben to point out where the bad man had cut him—the point was that Zee didn't know what could happen, and for the sake of the operation, he could not leave matters uncertain.

Across the room, Ana rocked in her chair, trying to tip it over, though he had her wedged into a corner. Zee watched her blankly for a moment, then closed his eyes, looked into the deep lake of his mind, and waited for a solution to float up.

There was nothing.

Nothing but the old way.

If there was no testimony, there would be no case. No case, no problem. Killing everyone in this house was the elegant solution.

He kept his eyes closed. Waited for another answer.

He was no longer the man who did those things. And even when he had been that man, he'd never killed a child. That was a line. Ana and the boy in the closet, they were children, even if they didn't know it.

Zee remembered his righteous disgust for Ali's golden lies. He remembered the way he'd felt in Chicago when the woman barked at the boy and girl after stranding them in the station overnight. What were those offenses compared to murdering a brain-damaged man and a couple of children?

But what else could he do? So many ya:tri, present and future, depended on him. Their lives, the lives of their children. Think of all the lives he could save tonight.

If he did it, it wouldn't turn him into the man he used to be; no, he'd be something new and terrible.

But if he didn't do it, he'd be the man who killed the operation.

I know how important the operation is to you, Veedy had said. *Which is how I know, when the moment comes, you will do what is necessary to save it.*

He walked over to Ana. "I won't make you watch," he said, tipping back the chair to tow her out of the room.

She thrashed and bucked, and Ben shouted *Shana! Shana!*—and then a high, tiny whine cut through the noise. A squeak. From a hinge in need of oil.

Zee let go of the chair. Ben shut up. They all looked across the kitchen, where the door to the basement was swinging open.

◆　　◆　　◆

When Pete had walked up to the porch, he struck a bargain with himself. He wouldn't actually knock on the door; he'd just take a quick look through the front window, and as long as nothing was amiss, he'd call it good and get on out of there. The gap in the curtains was tiny and the ambient light in the house was low, but he could just make out a tweedy couch, a swaybacked easy chair, a soda can tipped over on the floor… but no Ana, no Ben, no Logan.

No problem, he told himself. They must have forgotten to turn off the kitchen light before going to sleep, that was all.

To his surprise, Pete felt a touch of disappointment. Apparently he'd imagined himself as the hero of the story, the woodsman to her Red Riding Hood, the *deus* in her *machina*, when in reality he was closer to a Peeping Tom.

Well, he thought. That's that. He turned around to head back to the truck, and that's when he heard the scream. Short and muffled, but undeniable.

He tried the front door, but it was locked. He backed up to the edge of the porch, but before he could step forward to kick in the door, he saw the storm cellar.

Getting in the basement was the easy part. The storm cellar doors were unlocked, maybe from the days when Ben would sneak down from the tree and greet Pete at the front door. Climbing up the ancient staircase to the kitchen without giving himself away had been harder, but if he spread out his weight by crawling, the wood complained less. At the top of the stairs, he paused to listen, but the voices were too muddy to make out. Praying he was overreacting, that they would all laugh about this in a week, he gave the door a gentle push and listened to it shudder inward.

The hinge sang. The voices stopped. Pete drew his gun, and waited.

For what? To be ready? He'd never be ready. Ready isn't a far shore, like he'd always thought. Ready is a horizon you never reach.

Pete rose and stepped into the light.

Chapter 37
Revelation

Everything moved at underwater speed. The front legs of Ana's chair touched down on the linoleum. Pete followed his gun through the doorway. A long dark feather bloomed from the muzzle of Zeeshan's revolver. Across the kitchen, a cupboard grew a terrible mouth and Pete fell behind the island. Yelling, they were all yelling, but Ana couldn't make out a single word. The gunshot had flipped her eardrum inside out, and mostly she heard her own breathing, surprisingly deep and even. Then a hot metal finger touched her temple and everyone stopped shouting.

A haze clung to the lights. The air smelled like the Fourth of July. Her right ear was totally offline, but her left ear had recovered enough to hear Zee tell Pete to slide his gun across the floor if he wanted the girl to live.

"Don't be stupid," Ana shouted. Meaning: get out now, while you can still save yourself. Meaning: she wasn't coming out of this alive, no matter what Pete did with his gun, that much was clear. *Stop. This is the end of the section. Do not go on.*

She hoped Pete would understand this, even if her father didn't. In his chair, he strained against the zip-ties hard enough to cut red into his wrists. She wished he would stop. She wished she could go over to him, shush him, ease his mind. He used to do that for her, and she missed that. She missed *him*. How he used to be, how he would be now if their lives hadn't jumped the track.

In some parallel universe, they were on a campus visit right now, and she was making fun of him for wearing Italian loafers while other parents strolled in Reeboks. Or maybe they were at the Tippy. It was a slow night, so he came over to the hostess stand where she was doing Trig homework under the brass lamp. Jingling change in his pockets, he asked her what she was reading in English class, then told her for the eighty millionth time that his favorite book was *The Baltimore Colts Story.* Of course, it was the only book he'd ever finished.

Ha ha, she said.

Ha ha, he echoed, then kissed the side of her head, smelling her hair as he did so, which she had always thought she hated, but now she didn't think she did. It was just embarrassing because it was tender.

Do you need anything? he asked before walking away.

If they were at the Tippy now, she would grab his hand so he wouldn't leave. It would be too tender, but who cared. It was the answer to his question.

Pete's gun skidded across the kitchen floor, pinging off a table leg and coming to rest near Ana's foot.

Her heart deflated. She remembered her Uncle Rooster's terrible joke about the guy who lost a couple of quarters in the outhouse, then threw in his wallet after it. Someone should tell that joke at Pete's funeral.

Pete held up his hands behind the kitchen island. "Unarmed," he announced. It still sounded like Ana was listening through a wall, but she could make out his words. He said, "Don't shoot."

Zeeshan didn't answer.

Pete stood slowly, pausing when he could see over the island, and when he wasn't shot, he stood all the way up.

"Lift your shirt," said Zee. "Turn all the way around."

Pete complied, revealing a doughy stomach, but no secondary weapon. "Your pant legs," said Zee, and Pete stuck out each leg to show dark socks and ghostly calves, but nothing else.

"You shouldn't have come in here," said Zeeshan, sounding exasperated. "Foolish."

Pete took a cautious step away from the island. "I just want to talk," he said. "I trust you won't shoot an unarmed man."

"*Foolish*," said Zee. With his free hand, he pushed away Ana's face and told her not to look.

Another creak came from the stairway to the basement.

Zeeshan's hand fell from Ana's face.

Ana craned to see. My God, was that Radha stepping into the kitchen with a gun, the pocket gun?

"Oh, for Christ's sake," said Pete. "Why didn't you stay in the truck?"

"I wasn't about to let you out of my sight," she said to Pete while keeping her eyes on Zeeshan. "I don't trust any of you people."

"Put down the gun," said Zee.

"It *is* you," she said. "I thought I recognized your voice."

Zee pressed the muzzle against Ana's temple, hard enough to bend her neck. "Put down your gun," he said, "or I will kill her."

Radha took a step forward, scuffing through fallen plaster. She kept the gun leveled at him. "Do you remember me?"

"I am not your enemy," Zee said. "I'm here to help you."

"I've heard that before." She took another step. "Do you know what your help has gotten me so far?"

Zee's gun slid back to Ana's ruined ear, but he didn't answer. Across the kitchen, Ben stopped straining at his ties.

"It's a real question," she said. "I want to know what you knew. When you sent me to Chicago, what did you think was waiting for me?"

"A new life." His voice was dry, barely more than a breath. "A job."

Her shoes crunched on broken glass. "What kind of job?"

"Restaurant. Or a dry cleaner. Maybe housekeeping."

Radha stopped in front of him. She could have reached out and touched Ana's cheek, she was that close. One word, one puff of breath, like blowing out a candle. "No."

His gun slid down Ana's neck. "All of you?"

She nodded.

The gun trembled against Ana's collarbone. Zeeshan made a noise in his throat. Then he set the gun down with a soft *clack* on the table, and all at once everyone was moving again. Everyone who wasn't strapped down, anyway. Zee slumped to the floor. Pete came over to zip-tie his wrists and ankles. Radha cut Ben loose with the bloody knife. Then she started toward Ana, but Ben caught her arm. He held out his hand, his undamaged hand, for the knife.

They all watched him move across the kitchen to his daughter. Kneeling before her chair, he murmured something. Ana didn't think she heard him right, so she asked him to say it again, and again, and they both wept.

Ana, he said. *My Ana.*

Chapter 38
Gathering of Liars

The important thing, Ana told herself as she scrubbed the blood-tarred lino-leum and listened to the Old Liars jaw and kibitz, was not to rush these guys. Not to snap at them. Not to tell them, for instance, to get down to business, decide what you're going to do and get to it, *chop chop, motherfuckers.*

She took a deep breath. They were doing her a favor, she reminded herself. And unlike her, these ex-criminals had experience with this kind of mess. That's why she'd called them. Now she should really stay out of the way and let them do... whatever they were going to do to make this all go away. Which apparently started with a buttload of grousing. But hey, that was probably an important part of their process, right? At the very least, it was who they were, so she would have to live with it.

But, Jesus, did they have to do so much of it?

Forty minutes. That's how long they'd been standing around making zero discernable progress. Forty minutes of *Should have known.* Should have known Ana wasn't going to listen. Should have known she would act out, screw up, rain fallout over all their houses. Should have known this girl was a fly strip for trouble.

The question before them now was: what to do with this fly?

Zeeshan sat quietly in the corner, wrists zipped to ankles, head resting against the wall. He looked blankly at Radha, who was asleep with her head on the table.

All the other problems in the kitchen were small by comparison. Sure, it would take a little time and bleach and carpentry to put everything right, but a cabinet wasn't exactly Humpty-Dumpty, it could be fixed. Ben wasn't in great shape, but he would live. Big Mike had taken him and the ice tray of fingers to the emergency room with a cover story about some late night woodworking.

But Zeeshan—what to do with this guy? It was like disposing of a leaking barrel of nuclear waste: stash it wherever you want, it'll poison you eventually.

Little Mike cleared his throat. "I'll take him," he said. The corners of his mouth were doing a funny jerking thing, and he wiped them with his hand, as though smoothing wrinkles out of a tablecloth. "I'll take him to Truck Farts. Line a trunk with Visqueen, pour in some lime—"

"Whoa," said Pete, coming in from the living room with a ratty afghan to drape over Radha. "You can't talk about killing someone in front of a marshal, Mike. You just can't."

"You got a better idea?"

"How about not killing him?"

"Please," said Little Mike. "You knew the way this had to go when you called us."

"No," said Pete. "No one's killing anyone here."

Little Mike looked more weary than angry. "If you wanted him taken alive, you would have called in the Marshals Service. But you didn't, did you? Because if they found out what happened here, your career would be over. You called us in to cover this up, so kindly move aside and let us save your ass."

"*My* ass?" Pete's face went splotchy. "You think I'm worried about *my* ass?"

Silence in the room. Ana stopped scrubbing.

"Think it through," Pete said. "If the marshals rolled up to this scene, they would consider the whole town compromised. By noon, every one of you sad bastards would be in the back of a van, clutching a garbage bag full of your earthly possessions. If I called down the marshals, you'd all get relocated, only this time, you wouldn't be together." Pete sat down, shaking his head. "As for my ass," he said, "it's done as soon as we get this mess cleaned up."

Ana sat back on her heels. "You're quitting?"

He nodded. Ana dropped her brush, feeling sick. Too late, she understood what the Liars had tried to tell her in the walk-in freezer: this is not just about you. This is not even about your family. Everything you do affects us, and you are a part of us.

"Let's all just take a breath here," said Little Mike. "Maybe there's another way out of this, and Pete, maybe you'll feel differently after it shakes out, so—"

He stopped when he saw Ana pick up the blood-crusted knife from the counter. "Hey," he said, but she held out the blade. *Back off.* "This is my mess," she said. She tried to sound fierce, but it came out as a whine. God, she was tired. Tired and sick and sorry. All she wanted was to shut her eyes on this business, and these guys would let her do it, too, but she couldn't allow that. Just as she couldn't allow Little Mike or anyone else to relapse for her sake. The damage had spread far enough, and it was time to bring it to a stop. Or at least to redirect it away from these people who loved her more than she deserved. "It's on me," she said, turning the knife toward Zeeshan.

"Don't be stupid," said Vernon.

Ignoring him, she knelt before Zeeshan. "Why'd you put down your gun?"

His lips parted, but he didn't say anything. He looked as tired as she felt. After a moment he shook his head.

"All that shit you told my mother—about saving these people, giving them new lives—you believed it, didn't you? Veedy let you believe it. That's how he used you." Zeeshan looked at her blankly. "I was a fool."

"You're in good company."

With a clean snap, she cut through one zip tie, and then the other.

"I said *don't* be stupid," said Vernon, though he sounded half-impressed, if only by the magnitude of her stupidity.

"Ana," warned Little Mike, "If you let him go, he will be back here in no time to finish the job."

"The job has changed." She searched Zee's eyes. "Hasn't it?"

He glanced at Radha before nodding.

"New plan," said Ana to everyone. "My dad and I will drop out of the Program. With no witness, the government will have to drop its case against Veedy." She turned back to Zee. "And when Veedy comes home, where will you be?"

"Waiting for him," said Zee.

Silence in the room, everyone considering. Little Mike was the first to speak. "That is a terrible plan."

For once, all the Liars agreed. There were no good solutions here, but this one might be the worst, certainly the riskiest, possibly the stupidest—

"Listen," said Ana in a voice that surprised her. The whine was gone. All the anger and impatience, too, replaced by a calm note that sounded familiar. It was the sound of someone who knew how to fix things. The way her father used to sound at the scene of her mishaps. And look: they were all listening, even Pete. She kept talking so she wouldn't lose that sound. "No one here has less reason to trust this guy than I do. No one has more to lose. Which makes it my call."

She looked around, expecting protest, but there was none. From the Liars. A freaking miracle. "My call," she said to Little Mike directly, "and I'm asking you to drop Zeeshan off at the bus station."

The faucet dripped in the kitchen sink. Govert twined his fingers in his beard. At last Mike put up his hands. "Okay," he said. "Okay." He turned to Zeeshan. "On your feet, fucknuts."

Ana said, "Mike, if you're lying to me—"

"No lie," he said. "You have my word."

He had a few words for Zeeshan, too, as it turned out. He lectured Zee all the way out of the farmhouse about how Ana was, to his mind, making a deeply unwise and Pollyannaish decision, but everyone in this house would make sure she wouldn't regret it. Morocco was a small place with a lot of eyes, and now that those eyes knew what to watch for, Zeeshan could not sneak into town. "We know you now," he said at the door in a light tone, the way he might invite a customer to take a spin in a new Monte Carlo. "If you come back, you will never leave."

A moment later, Pastor Jim had to leave for Bible study. Vernon said something about his morning constitutional. Pete draped his coat over Radha and led her to the door. Ana could see these two gravitating toward one another—Radha bumping against him, Pete holding her elbow—but she couldn't tell if it was attraction or exhaustion. "Where are you taking her?" said Ana.

"Home," he said. "My home. She can stay with me while she figures out what she wants to do."

Ana started to protest, but Radha interrupted her. "This one is my call," she said.

Ana shut up. Of course it was. Pete opened the front door. "You want some breakfast?" he asked Radha. "I know a place."

When the door closed, Ana sat down on the couch and all the weariness in the world caught up to her. But she couldn't rest, not yet. Govert was in the kitchen with a mop, alone with the mess. "Gove," she started.

He waved her off. "Go lay down."

"I can't let you do it alone," she said mechanically, because that's what you did around here, you fended off favors and compliments. Midwesterners—and that's what she was now—were grace-resistant.

But they were also pushy with the grace they offered. "Go to sleep," he said. "It's fine. I always wanted to be on this side of a cover up."

She was so grateful she could have kissed his sloppy beard if she'd had the energy to cross the kitchen, but she did not, so she gave him a wave of gratitude before listing down the hallway. Was it possible that only a few hours had passed since they were on the run from a pimp named Branko? Was this still the same night she'd driven a car for the first time, and almost shot Pete on the highway?

She was so tired she didn't startle when she opened her closet door and saw Logan again. He blinked in the light. His long lashes were caked with salt. She unknotted the gag and touched the deep red marks at the corners of his mouth. "I'm sorry," he rasped, but she hushed him. God help her, she couldn't say or hear another word right now, she really couldn't.

She couldn't help him up, either, so she sank into the shoe-smelling grunge of the closet with him. Across the room, the sun lipped over her windowsill. In town, she knew, a few Liars gathered at the long table, bitching merrily about potholes, Karen's coffee, the price of hot dogs—call it foreknowledge or imagination, precognition or bullshit, the term doesn't matter, she could see this scene like a movie, she could hear the way they were burying the events of the night under their jokes and complaints. From the kitchen came the music of a spatula ringing against a grill, the hiss of hash browns hitting the hot iron. Right about now the back door was opening, letting in the smell of dumpster and freeze-dried morning air and a whiff of sinsemilla. Here came Karen, stepping through the door, adjusting her wig, grabbing an apron from the hook. "Looks like we lost another waitress, Lu."

Luis smiled at the griddle. "You must of took off your wig and scared her with your baby head."

"Actually," said Karen, looping the apron strings around her stomach to tie a lopsided bow, "she told me your hot cross buns were making her crazy with unreputed love. She couldn't stand to be so near to you, and yet so far."

"Unrequited," he corrected her.

Karen frowned. "What did I say about speaking Spanish in here?"

"Speak American."

"Speak American is right." As she passed Luis to go to the tables, she slapped his ass. "*Ándale* with the hash browns, heartbreaker."

With her flat Indiana accent, the word came out *un-delay*. Which, you know what? Makes sense. Meaning can be born in mistakes. The word danced in Ana's mind—*un-delay, un-delay*—as the sun rose in her bare window. It would have been easy enough to snag the closet door with her toe and pull it shut so they could sleep in the dark. She could summon enough energy for that. But instead she tucked her face into Logan's warm shoulder and went to sleep in the light of the world.

From the written statement of D.W. Boxelder:

Afterword

The day Veedy was released, I patched into the prison's security system, and there he was on my screen: This man who specialized in the import/export of lives, this great and powerful Oz whose real wizardry was partitioning and parceling out knowledge. A little thinner than he was going into prison, but with the same long, swinging arms and a rolling walk. He tipped a pretend hat to the guard at the gate. No audio on the feed, but it wasn't hard to guess what passed between them. *Keep moving, asshole,* the guard might have said, because it looked like Veedy grinned at him and said, *Don't worry. I will.*

Not for long, friend.

Two days later, the police found his body in his office at the top of the warehouse. What they couldn't find, however, was his head. This set a pattern for the rest of the investigation, which was characterized by missing links in the chain of evidence, blanks that couldn't be filled, pieces that didn't quite fit together. Truth be told, no one worked real hard to solve these puzzles. Certainly no one connected the dots between this crime and a similar murder in Chicago a few days later, the decapitation of one Branko Kovačević. In Baltimore, detectives half-heartedly canvassed the area around the warehouse, which by that time was a ghost town. Most of the other buildings had already been knocked down. The few people in the area thanked the detectives for delivering the good news of Veedy's death in person.

Because he had a motive, Ben was briefly a Person of Interest, but one look told the detectives he wasn't capable of this job. A surgeon had reattached Ben's fingers, but as soon as he regained his speech, he went to Johns Hopkins and told an orthopedist to take them back off. The doctor protested—of course the hand wouldn't ever be the same, but with time and therapy, some feeling would return, along with rudimentary coordination—but Ben insisted on a clean cut at the wrist. They offered him a cosmetic hand, but he declined. No more faking. He was who he was. A hook was more functional than a mannequin hand, anyway.

With no leads and little pressure from the captain or the press to find this scumbag's killer, the detectives dropped the case not long after clearing Ben. What else could they do? It's not like they knew about Ana's decision to cut Zeeshan loose and aim him at Veedy.

At this point, Madame Inspector, you might be wondering why I withheld evidence that pertained to a murder investigation, but I'll ask you to remember a couple of things. First, knowing something isn't the same as possessing evidence. Secondly, I wasn't completely sure at the time that Zeeshan was the killer. It didn't fit his m.o. Whenever he did a job, the mark disappeared. Zee had his own relocation protocol. The mere fact that the cops had found (most of) Veedy made me wonder if someone else had gotten to the old boy first, but eventually I understood: Zeeshan left the body behind as evidence. Not for the cops; for Ana. So she would know his word was good.

By the time I figured that out, Zee was back in Kashmir. Never mind the fact that the region does not have an extradition treaty with the U.S.; the marshal does not exist who could bring him out of those mountains.

Though I would have gladly sent Droop on that cherry of a mission to punish his wayward ass, but he'd followed through on his threat to quit. Gave up his badge for the glamorous life of a non-traditional student. Now he drives to West Lafayette five days a week to work on his M.S.W.

As for Radha, she took over the morning shift at Karen's, and the last I checked she was still living with Droop, though the nature of their relationship remains unclear. A part of me is tempted to pry, but my time is running short, and besides, if anyone deserves some privacy, it's Radha.

Anyway, back to Zeeshan: Don't give up heart, Madame. The Feds may get another shot at him yet. If I know Zee—and at this point I feel like I do—he's working his contacts, setting up a new operation. The day is not far off when the shepherd will return with a new van full of ya:tri.

But for now he's in the wind, and the murder investigation is cold. Veedy's property was purchased from his estate, and my confirmation hearing was a breeze.

Don't fret if you can't connect the dots, Madame. Ana couldn't, either, though she came pretty close on the day of Veedy's trial. Of course the actual trial had been canceled, but I had a promise to keep. When she'd called me from that freezing gas station in DeMotte, I told her I would see her on this day. I didn't know if she would remember, but I always keep my word.

◆   ◆   ◆

Picture a warm day in early May, a park across from the courthouse. I sat on a picnic table in the shade of a broad pin oak, watching prom couples take pictures under the pink petals of crab apple trees. The air smelled like fabric softener. I told myself I should get out of the office more often.

I kept an eye on the courthouse steps, but there was no sign of Ana. In my pocket was a little box, one I had gone through a lot of trouble to obtain, so I did hope she would show. A breeze carried the salty smell of hot dogs, and when I turned to look for the cart, I saw her. About fifty yards away, sitting on the backrest of a green bench. Her hair was longer than it had been in Morocco, but it was still dark and lank. She rested her elbows on her knees, watching the people eddy in front of the courthouse. Observing from a distance. Watching for me. My heart swelled with something like pride.

I slipped down from the table and looped around the park, intending to appear by her shoulder, but physical stealth has never been my strong suit. At my approach, she stepped off the bench.

"Mr. Boxelder," she said over her shoulder. "Let's walk."

◆   ◆   ◆

On the sidewalk she put me on her left side, because she still had trouble hearing out of her right ear. Her legs were long and she was wearing jeans and a T-shirt, and she walked fast. I am neither tall nor all that young, and the day had felt a lot more pleasant when I was contemplating a hot dog in the shade than when I found myself hustling under the full sun in a dark suit.

I asked about her re-acclimation to Baltimore, not because I didn't know (please: I had done my homework), but to see if talking would slow her down. Also to see if she would lie to me. It didn't, and she didn't.

The Tippy was boarded up, she told me. Though her father was getting better, he was still adapting to the hook and needed help with the house and sundry activities, which made it hard for Ana to have a job, or a life. She went to see her mother at Gram's house a couple times a week, and that was about the extent of her social life.

We crossed the street on a yellow, which necessitated jogging. Already my oxfords were blistering my heels. Goddammit, I thought. This is why I stay in the office.

"It's not my old life," she protested over her shoulder, though I hadn't suggested it was. "It's another relocation."

I touched the box in my pocket. Was now the right time to give it to her? It would give us an excuse to stop walking. Before I could pull it out, Ana hailed a cab.

"Where are we going?" I said.

"You don't know?"

She smiled. A taunt. I'd seen that look on my monitors, but in person it was more unsettling. Like coming across an amused moray eel.

"I like that," she said, "you not knowing. Let's keep it that way a little longer."

◆ ◆ ◆

We didn't keep it that way for long. As soon as I saw the dead smokestacks of the repurposed power plant on Pratt, I knew where we were going. The cab let us out on a narrow, crumbling sidewalk. A high chain fence surrounded the crater that used to be Veedy's warehouse.

"Ah," I said. "You want answers."

"What a mind-reader."

The fence was covered with green sheeting, and on the official sign that read COMING SOON THE NEW HOME OF THE BALTIMORE RAVENS, people had scrawled their own messages, including *Welcome home* and *You'll always be the Colts to me* and *You still suk*. Before Ana could press me, I dug out the box and handed it to her. "A little something for your troubles," I said.

She gave me a dubious look, but snapped it open. Reflected light played across her face. She didn't say a word. Maybe I should have given her some time to process, but I've never been able to hang onto presents or good news, and this purple heart was both in one package. "Your father earned it in Vietnam," I said.

"He wasn't in Vietnam."

"According to the official records," I said, "he was."

I paused to let it sink in, this favor I had done for them. "His service entitles him to military health care for life"—and here I leaned in to deliver the best part, at least for Ana—"which has a nice provision for home health care."

She gave me a sharp look. I understood. Nothing stings so much as help from your enemy. Having to say thank you can feel like knuckling under.

"Incidentally," I added, "his medal makes you eligible for a host of scholarships."

I'd thought about taking the extra step and lining up a few grants for her, but she only would have resented me more. Better, I'd decided, to lob her a softball and let her knock it out of the park.

She snapped the box shut. "You're not buying me off. I still want answers."

Unbelievable. If Ana was drowning, you could throw her a life preserver, and she would complain that it bumped her head. I didn't need to hear a thank you, but would it have killed her to acknowledge this authentic medal that was about to change her life?

"You know," I said, "there's more to life than answers."

"Easy to say when you're not the one with questions."

Something pulsed in my forehead, and I lost my patience. "No, see, that whole pattern is a problem. Question, answer, question, answer—it's ruining your generation. Whatever happened to living with mystery? Getting comfortable with the unknown?"

Ana snorted lightly, dismissively.

At the time it made me bridle, but now I think she was right to scoff. If I was so comfortable with mystery, why did I wire her house? Attempt to predict Zeeshan's actions? Play omniscient?

The truth, I see now, is that I wasn't comfortable with mystery. What I liked was being the mystery.

She turned to the construction site. "The government wanted this property. Veedy was in the way. Now he's gone, and here comes a football stadium." She looked over at me. "And you've just been confirmed as the new Director."

"*Post hoc ergo propter hoc*," I said. "Just because one thing follows another doesn't mean that one caused the other." I shrugged. "It's a logical fallacy. You'll learn about it in college."

I waited for her to call me a condescending asshole, but she only gave me another moray smile. Where was my angry girl? The spit, the spite, the spiky threats? This new *tranquillo* act was unsettling, mainly because I couldn't see where it was coming from. Did she know something I didn't know?

"I was thinking of a different Latin phrase," she said. "The way I see it, someone wanted to build a stadium. You removed the roadblock, and now you're getting your reward. Sounds like *quid pro quo*, doesn't it?"

"Interesting theory," I allowed. "Got any actual evidence?"

Inside the construction pit, a lone machine started up, whining and smashing, whining and smashing, probably trying to crack the granite under the rocky soil. Ana hooked her fingers in the chain link and swayed back. For a moment, she looked like a kid again. "You're right," she said. "It's just a theory. Guesswork, mostly." She stopped swaying and looked at me. "But Pete thinks it's enough to start an investigation."

I had to clear my throat before I could answer. "What do you mean?"

"I sent a letter to Madalyn Karr. Maybe you've heard of her? She's the Inspector General in the Department of Justice. And just in case that letter happened to get lost, I sent a copy to all seventeen field offices."

Outflanked. Now I knew how Kate's father must have felt when Ben outplayed him at his own game and stole his daughter. I had to grab the fence to steady myself as Ana told me how helpful Pete had been. "He said it didn't take much to whip up an investigation in Washington, and this should—"

"Take the medal," I said.

"You're not hearing me. The letters have already gone out. I can't take them back. And even if I could, I wouldn't."

"I know." That's what had poleaxed me: The sudden knowledge that I was finished, even as I stood there. Already I could see the days I would spend writing this confession, the spectacle of my inevitable hearing, the headlines, the humiliation, the end, my end.

I held out the box again, feeling like Logan on her doorstep with the pathetic offering of a burrito. "Just take it," I said. "Please."

She looked at me, trying to figure out my angle, not understanding that my angles no longer pointed at her. That's when I told her she would get what she wanted. If she would accept this small reparation, I would give her a full explanation in the fullness of time. "I keep my promises," I reminded her. Then I set the box down on the sidewalk and walked away without looking back.

Until later, that is. The parking garage across the street had a security camera. A quick scan revealed that she had walked away, too (damn your pride, Ana) but thirty seconds later she was back in the shot, picking up the box and looking around before tucking it in her pocket (bless your brains).

About that medal: Okay, fine, Ben wasn't technically in the military. But he came under fire. He was wounded in the service of a larger cause. So what if he didn't understand that cause? Did every doughboy grasp the geopolitical nuances of the struggle with the Axis? Did Truman give soldiers a pop quiz before pinning some bright hardware to their chests? He did not. If such a test was not applied to them, then neither should it be applied to Ben. He may not have earned that purple heart by the letter of the law, but he earned it in spirit. Not in fact, but in truth.

What I'm saying, Madame, is that you should let him hang onto that medal and its trailing benefits. Don't unweave that loom; don't punish him and Ana for my infelicities.

That's it, my last plea. Now it's time for me to keep the rest of my promises, Madame Inspector. Once I finish this statement, three copies will go out by courier: One to you, one to Ana, and one to Senator Mulcahey.

◆   ◆   ◆

To understand the final piece of this puzzle, you have to go back to a cold spring night in 1984. Picture a line of Mayflower vans outside a football complex. At two in the morning, the Baltimore Colts fled the city that had been threatening to take the team away from its owner. A few days later, the team reappeared in a Midwestern town with a new identity: The Indianapolis Colts.

But this story isn't about becoming; it's about what was left behind. Baltimore reacted like a spurned lover, with bitterness, threats, brooding. The town never really got over the break-up.

Skip ahead a decade. Enter Senator Mulcahey, D-Maryland, chairman of the Senate Judiciary Committee. Mulcahey headed up a group that quietly approached Art Modell, owner of the Cleveland Browns. Modell was fighting with Cleveland over remodeling the stadium. Modell wasn't happy, and the group offered him an alternative: What if you moved the Browns to Baltimore?

The political calculation was as simple as it was elegant. Bringing a team back to Baltimore would make Mulcahey a senator for life. Bread + circus=re-election, *ad infinitum.*

Deals were made in secret and details were hammered out quickly until it came to the stadium. The team could play for a season or two in the old Memorial Stadium, everyone agreed, but a new home would have to be built.

The problem wasn't selecting a site. The group had already picked out the ideal location—not in one of the *frou-frou* suburbs, but near Camden Yards and the Inner Harbor, all the better to revitalize the heart of the city— and they picked up the property for a song.

Except for the warehouse.

The whole process ground to a halt. No warehouse, no stadium site. No site, no team. Modell wasn't about to trade one uncertain stadium situation for another.

It was the fall of 1994 when Mulcahey first called me to his office. The room was surprisingly small, or maybe he was surprisingly large, filling it up with his craggy face and pipe smoke. His teeth and shirt were the same shade of ecru. He had the weary but indomitable manner you see in statesmen and old newspaper editors who live at their desks. *We both know I'm going to get my way,* his look seemed to say. *Are you really going to put me through my paces?*

"I hear Sherwood is retiring," he said around his pipe as I squeezed into a child-sized chair across from his desk. "And you're next in line."

"That's right."

Smoke furled around him. His office smelled like a burning apple orchard. "Nomination," he said, "is the easy part. Once you get to the confirmation hearings, all bets are off." He'd been chairing these hearings for nearly a decade, he told me, and he'd seen just how unpredictable they could be. You never knew what could happen! He'd like to see me make it through my hearings cleanly, though. He'd like to do what he could to make my path straight and smooth. Oh, and as long as I was in his office, there was one other small matter he wanted to talk to me about.

Here it is, Ana: The *quo* hooked to the *quid.* He wanted me to figure out how to take down Veedy so the warehouse could fall. The good people of Baltimore would get their stadium, and I would be confirmed as the next director.

I said no.

Politely, even delicately, without any outrage or threats of exposure, but in no uncertain terms. I didn't want to make an enemy of this man, but I wasn't going to be his puppet, either.

"No?" he said.

I'd like to help, I told him. I wish I could do something, but the Program was in the business of protecting witnesses, not actively going after gangsters.

He raised a thatchy eyebrow. "You're part of the Department of Justice, aren't you?"

"Not the part you need."

"You're the part I have."

I smiled as politely as I could manage. "With respect, Senator, you don't have me."

I wished him a good day and left his office, believing it was over. Clearly, Mulcahey was overplaying his hand. What could he do, really, to derail my confirmation hearing? At that point, I had nothing big to hide, no bloody bones in my closet.

I didn't even make it back to my office before he put a secret hold on my nomination, delaying my confirmation hearing indefinitely.

◆   ◆   ◆

It took me a week to rationalize a different answer to his request. Sure, my methods for taking down Veedy would verge on the extralegal, but the end result would be good. Good for Baltimore, good for me, bad for the human trafficker. All the good guys win.

For the record, I thought Ben would be safe in Morocco. I thought—Oh, this sounds painfully naive now, so very *Quiet American*—I was doing him a favor. I was getting him out from under Veedy's thumb, giving him a chance to go legit. And Ana—yes, Ana, you were in my plans from the beginning—would have grown up far away from the influence of gangsters.

A fresh start. New opportunities. Like Sherwood, I believed in these things, as much as I believed in my own foresight.

Turns out I'm as nearsighted as anyone else.

Of all the awful things to realize about yourself, this might be the worst. But don't take my word for it, Madame; you'll experience it yourself soon enough.

Time to wrap up. Please accept this document as my official resignation letter. (My apologies for not mentioning that in the first installment, but would you have read this far if I had? For reasons that will soon become infuriatingly clear, I needed you to be preoccupied with a little light reading this weekend.)

Look at it this way: You're getting the same result you would have gotten had I consented to sit through your circus of a hearing. I wasn't going to come out of that chamber with a job, so why bother going into it? No one in this town ever steps back to look at the greater good; we focus on the small snags in a beautiful tapestry. For each flaw, we demand a head.

As a parting gift, let me offer up three heads. The first, as you might guess, belongs to Mulcahey. The banker's boxes in your office are not just filled with junk; they also contain audio files of every conversation I had with the man. Congratulations, Madame: You went fishing for a marlin and hooked a fucking narwhal.

The second head is mine. Go ahead and take it, I won't be needing it anymore. Like any informant with half a brain, I'll be following up my testimony with a disappearing act.

(One final confession: I'm afraid I've abused my office privileges. Over the past week, I've made a new character for myself. Go ahead and put out an APB, pin up my old picture in every post office, raise a posse if you must, only don't get your hopes up. By the time you read this, I'm approximately a light year away from D.C., and already I look like a different man. I act like a different man. Because I am a different man, and this time I'm not going to be in charge of anything. I'm going back to being a second-guesser, like I used to be. Like you, Madame.)

About the last head on my platter: I'm afraid it's your own, Madame Inspector. Remember what I said about this town's focus on small flaws? Even if you manage to hook and land Mulcahey, some other fisher of men will reel you in for your own hearing. *How could you have let Boxelder slip away?* your inquisitor will want to know. *Has there ever been a greater flight risk? How could you have failed to foresee and forestall this eventuality?*

You may want to start thinking about your next career, Madame. Political lives may be shorter than ever, but there are always lobbying gigs and think tanks and speaking tours.

I told you this was a story about resurrection; it's hardly my fault if you didn't realize you were one of the characters. It might not be the worst thing to ever happen to you, though. Someday, you might look back on this time and thank me. Resurrection certainly worked out for the apostle Paul. In his first act, he was known as Saul of Tarsus, hunter of Christians. But after getting struck by lightning on the road to Emmaus, he flipped sides, changed his name, and became the prime witness of this fledgling religion. But his real genius? The reason we all remember Paul instead of the countless other evangelists wearing out their sandal-leather along the coast of the Dead Sea? He set his thoughts down in ink. He committed himself to paper and posterity.

Letters are fine, but a book is better. I think I'll write one, call it a novel.

Ana, Godspeed. I look forward to seeing who you become. I won't have any special equipment or security clearance, but time and technology is only making it easier for all of us to peer into each other's lives. We're all in the business of surveillance now. Omniscience is the new literacy.

God bless America, the land of second acts. Good night, and good luck to us all.

Acknowledgments, or:
Four Short Essays of Creation

Years ago, Debra Spark mentioned that she had once interviewed the founder of WITSEC for a piece she was going to write about how he was the ultimate author: He created characters who went on to live in the real world. In the end, she abandoned the piece, but those tapes—which no one else has ever heard—were still in her attic.

I wanted those tapes. I dogged her about them, but she turned me down, and eventually I had to write this book to work out my wondering.

I think she knew exactly what she was doing.

Along the way, I wrote something like fourteen drafts. In the early stages, some very good writers and readers helped me with the story: Andrew Scott, Victoria Barrett, and Sarah Layden. Later on, Erin Harris of Folio Lit, worked with me on developmental editing. In the next-to-last draft, my wife showed me exactly what was still wrong with the book and then kept me from hurling my laptop into a ditch. Diane Goettel and Angela Leroux-Lindsey of Black Lawrence Press went over every line with a jeweler's loupe. Writing is a social activity, and books are collaborations. I forget that sometimes.

Getting a book into the world is also a collaboration. Victoria Barrett (Sugarcube Writing, Editing, and Design) and Julia Borcherts (Kaye Publicity) helped this book find its way into your hands. Andrea Boucher made it look so good you'll want to keep it on top of the stack on your nightstand. Thanks, too, to Dan Barden and Mindy Dunn for hosting the launch party.

A book is an electrical circuit between a writer and a reader. Without a reader, the circuit is left open; no electricity flows. Thank you for completing this circuit.